HARBINGER

PROJECT FALLEN ANGEL
BOOK 2

ANNA NOEL

"YOU'RE THE KEY TO EVERYTHING. THE END OF IT ALL."

HARBINGER

PROJECT FALLEN ANGEL

BOOK TWO

ANNA NOEL

Project Fallen Angel: Harbinger

Copyright © 2023 Anna Noel.

For more information about the author and her books, visit her website— https://annanoelbooks.com/

Book design: Anna Noel

Formatter: Anna Noel

Editor: Alaina Morris

Proofreader: Amber Letto

First Edition: October 23rd, 2023

www.annanoelbooks.com

❀ Created with Vellum

AUTHOR'S NOTE

This book is a little emotional for me.

I started writing this book when I was in middle school. I was a girl with a keyboard, a wild imagination, and a fierce love for the Fast and Furious movies.

The original book was directly inspired by the Car Scramble scene in Fast and Furious 2. It started out about a group of misfit criminals who stole cars and lived in an abandoned warehouse, and twin sisters who were raised very differently.

Although the story changed so many times over the years, there were two constants. Sydney and Jerry. Two of my most beloved characters. Their names never changed. Their appearance never did, either.

As this story grew up with me, Sydney and Jerry did too.

Reprisal came about because I was too nervous to make this book my debut. I was too nervous, and needed to have something else under my belt before it.

But now it's to you, in your hands.

I hope you love and care for these characters as much as I have.

TRIGGER WARNINGS:

    Child abuse/ SA (mentioned, alluded to, none on page)

    Graphic violence

    Panic attacks

    Suicidal ideation (mentioned)

    Death of parents (off page)

THINGS TO KNOW ABOUT HARBINGER:

    -Forced marriage of convenience

    -Espionage

    -Enemies to lovers

    -Found family

    -Morally grey MMC

    -Stuck together

    -Praise/ degradation

    -Tension/Steam

PLAYLIST

"Aimed to Kill" by Jade LeMac
"Panic Room" by Au/Ra
"Angry Too" by Lola Blanc
"Start a War" by Klergy, Valerie Broussard
"Female Robbery" by The Neighbourhood
"Control" by Halsey
"cult leader" by KiNG MALA
"killer queen" by Mad Tsai
"god sent me as karma" by emlyn
"Do It Like A Girl" by Morgan St. Jean
"Devil I Know" by Allie X
"I am not a woman, I'm a god" by Halsey
"SINS" by Red Leather
"Serial Killer" by Moncrieff, JUDGE
"Devil Is A Woman" by Cloudy June
"Bury Me" by Friday Pilots Club
"martyr" by KiNG MALA
"COFFIN" by PLVTINUM

To those who love Fast and Furious, spy movies, and Taylor Swift as much as I do.
But most importantly, to the girl who wrote a version of this book for the first time at 13. You didn't think you'd end up publishing it, did you?
Keep dreaming.

"Women, they have minds, and they have souls, as well as just hearts. And they've got ambition, and they've got talent, as well as just beauty. I'm so sick of people saying that love is all a woman is fit for."

Louisa May Alcott

ONE

SYDNEY

ONE OF THE only things I remember from my childhood is my father murdering a man in cold blood right in front of my eyes. I knew at that moment that I needed to get out.

I was seven.

If I close my eyes and think hard enough, I can still smell the smoke from his cigar mixed with a metallic tinge as blood seeped from the bullet hole. The only thing he did was cast an evil downward glance the man's way, his face twisting in disgust as he placed his gun back down on his desk.

He sat there then, looking from me to my mother. She was furious at first. Her words lashed out at him like fire. But when he looked me in the eyes and told me that one day I'd have to do the same, her voice quieted.

It was understood that this was necessary. Something needed to desensitize me.

It never did.

It didn't take me long to realize my parents weren't good people. Pain and suffering followed them. Followed me. I spent most of my teen years away, and eventually, they stopped calling. Stopped expecting anything of me.

Eventually, I escaped.

So when I got the call on Wednesday that they had died in a tragic accident, I didn't feel much at all. I still don't, despite the fake tears running down my face and the perturbation in my heart as old family acquaintances approach me, asking me how I've been.

I've been good. I've been doing fine on my own. I never missed them. Maybe the world will be better now that they're gone. Do you know what they've done? Do you know how many innocent people they've slaughtered without a care in the world?

I want to scream. To run away from here. To go back home, curl up under my covers, and only emerge when this is over.

"Are you okay?" Adam asks, his hand on my upper back. His presence always soothed me, making me feel a little less alone.

I nod, running my fingers through my hair, desperately wanting to put it up after an older woman I didn't recognize told me I look so much like my mother. We always had the same flaming red hair and the same green eyes.

She meant it as a compliment. It was sincere. Friendly and warm. But to me, it felt like a slap in the face. Words meant to cut deep. I smiled at her anyway, despite feeling the words hit me like a gut punch, and told her thank you.

"We're definitely going out after this," he mumbles, looking around at the hundreds of people who showed up to celebrate my parents' lives. I wonder how many of them are secretly glad they're dead, too. I wonder if any of them feel the same way I do.

"I'm going to need a drink for sure," I say, picking up my bag. I look around the room at all the faces that showed up, and unease rips through me, settling on my shoulders like the weight of all the lives they took have transferred to me. Squeezing my eyes shut, I count to three.

One… two… three.

When I open them, nothing changes. I groan, annoyed.

Then I close my eyes again, hoping, praying that surely this time it'll work.

This time, I focus on what I can smell.

Cheap perfume, death, and, underneath it all, iron.

I need to stop thinking, I think to myself. But in reality, I think I just need to find a better fucking therapist.

"I need a second; I'll be in the bathroom," I tell Adam, not bothering to wait for his response. I move through the room, attempting to avoid all the eyes watching me go. I keep my head down, not bothering to be polite when hands reach at me. Grab me. I keep going.

How do I talk to these people when their condolences all sound like admissions of guilt?

The voices grow louder, pulling me in every direction, and I squeeze my eyes shut, wishing they would just stop.

And when I open them, everything stops.

A large man stands in the corner in a black suit, his black hair messy and his eyes dark. His tan skin glows under the dull fluorescent lights. And he's looking right at me.

My breath catches, and I look for Adam, finding him talking to a group of girls across the room. I'm not sure who they are or why they're here, but it's not unusual for Adam to find girls to talk to wherever he goes.

Trust him to find a gaggle of them to flirt with at a funeral.

Looking back to the corner, I find it empty. No man in sight.

You've been tired. He probably wasn't even there. Just keep going, the voice inside of my head says.

As I turn the corner into the hallway, I ricochet off a broad, sturdy chest. For a split second, I wonder if it was the man from before. But this one is different.

"Oh, I'm sorry," a deep voice apologizes as large, powerful hands steady me. I flinch as he makes contact, much like when any stranger touches me.

I give a meek smile as I brush myself off. "It's fine," I start as I finally meet his eyes... and stop.

This man is the definition of tall, dark, and handsome.

He smiles, but it doesn't quite reach his beautiful brown eyes. His maroon suit fits him perfectly in every place it matters, his dark skin glowing in the warm hallway light.

There's a moment of silence before he extends his hand, reaching for mine to shake. "Jeremy," he introduces himself as his hand envelopes mine.

I shakily return the smile, a little suspicious. "Sydney," I tell him, not breaking eye contact for even a second. I don't know who this man is or why he's here, but I know the kind of people my parents had in their circle. No one here is innocent, not even me.

Dropping my hand, Jeremy places his in the pockets of his maroon slacks, looking around the room. "Nice night, eh?"

My eyebrows shoot up. "If you mean a nice night for my parents' funeral, then yeah, I guess."

His full lips twist in a smirk as he meets my eyes once more. Fucker.

"Now, if you excuse me, I was just on my way to the bathroom." I attempt to push around him, but he steps into my path again, blocking me.

I feel a pit of rage rise up my chest, and I shoot him a scowl, about to tell him off.

"Get a drink with me later." It isn't a question; it's a demand. His hand grabs my arm, and I eye it before my gaze makes its way to his face.

"I don't think so."

"I want to apologize for my comment about tonight. Please. We can just go next door."

I think about it for a second. I have backup here. Adam has been my trusty sidekick for what feels like ages. One text to him, I'm out. Besides, who would turn down a free drink?

Certainly not me. Certainly not tonight.

I smile, tossing my hair behind my back before looking up at him with my most angelic smile. "Sure, handsome. That sounds great."

If there's one thing I learned from my parents, it's how to get what I want while fucking someone over.

"I don't know, I just think that whales are really cool," I say, taking another sip of my bourbon.

"They're interesting," Jeremy smiles, looking at me over the rim of his glass.

I wonder if he's falling for it yet.

It starts with asking for the manliest drink you can think of. You take a sip, wincing even if it goes down smooth, and shoot him the most deer-in-the-headlights look possible. Most men can't resist the doe eyes, especially paired with feigned ignorance.

Let him tell you about the much better, top-shelf bourbon he has at home, and tell him that he should absolutely let you try it as you toss your hair back, shooting him the most dazzling smile you can possibly muster. Make sure to crinkle your nose, complimenting how intelligent they sound. Tell them their job sounds *so interesting* and you'd love to hear more about it.

Tell them you love Taylor Swift, and they'll think you're a lovesick puppy just looking for someone to give them attention. None of them know that you need a god damn dictionary to decipher half of her songs. They'd rather think of themselves as more intelligent than her.

Smarter than you.

Slowly start talking about more random things. Start with something somewhat related to the conversation and shift slightly to something completely different. The more bizarre, the better.

Added plus if you can slip a line or two about your daddy issues.

Not only will men buy you drink after drink thinking they're getting lucky, but they'll show you who they really are. If you're comfortable going home with them, then do it. We're all humans with specific needs. Certain desires. If you feel safe with a man dumb enough to fall for your act, you'll likely control the whole fucking night, and he won't even know it. Do what you have to do. But if they show themselves to be a creep, shoot your best friend a text, or in my case, a look across the room, and they'll bail you out.

"So what about you?" I ask him.

"There's not much interesting about me," he starts, looking me up and down again.

I'm not a stupid girl, but that's precisely what I'm hoping he thinks. He's trying to get me drunk, and I want to know why. He's not flirting with me, which makes me think it's not because he wants me to come home with him.

A familiar feeling has been creeping up on me all night. I may be in danger right now, but part of me is too curious to care.

Part of me is too *reckless*. I want to be in danger. The thought of it sends a shiver down my spine and a tickle up my neck.

I can feel Adam's eyes on me across the room as his woman of the night presses her ass into him, grinding to the beat of the music thundering around us.

The second this turns weirder than it already is, I'm out.

Jeremy licks his lips, his head tilting to the side curiously as he examines me. I tip my cup slightly, sloshing the amber liquid, almost spilling it. But not quite. That's the finale.

He bites his lip. "Do you know what happened to your parents?" Jeremy asks, putting his glass down.

"I don't." *They were killed in a fire. Burnt to a crisp. Barely recognizable.*

"I only met them a few times, but they seemed like good people."

I scoff on the inside.

"They were great people. I'm sad I didn't see them before they were cremated." *Their bodies were scorched. There was nothing to see.*

I didn't believe they were dead at first. I thought for sure they were off hiding somewhere. It was something they would do—fake their deaths—but thankfully, it was really them. They were really gone, and the world is better for it.

I promptly had them cremated without a second thought to seeing them beforehand.

"I'm sure," he tilts his head again, reading me.

I'm in danger, is all I can think.

I look down at my lap, my face twisting in fake agony as I wring my hands together, sighing.

"I really appreciate you taking me out," I tell him, my eyes brimming with real tears. A party trick I learned. Hopping off of the barstool, I teeter in my heels. I launch forward a bit, putting on my best drunk girl act and splashing my drink all over my front. "Oh my God, I can't believe it. Fuck. I'm so sorry; I have to go clean this up quickly. I'll be right back, handsome."

He nods, smiling a little as I turn my back to him, heading toward the back of the club.

Adam's eyes watch me as I go, knowing not to step in unless I signal for him to.

The club is packed tonight, the lights down low, the music thrumming through the floor. I've been here a couple of times with Adam, each leaving with someone else. It's a nice place. Generally safe, I haven't had many poor experiences here. Now, the old stoner bar down the street—that's an entirely different story.

I count my footsteps as I walk toward the back, trying to force myself not to look back. I don't want to see if Jeremy is still watching me. I don't want to know if he's following me. I want to get to the bathroom, collect my thoughts, text Adam, and get out of here.

The second I round the corner, I feel a hand on my arm, dragging me to the corner.

"What the f—"

The hand covers my mouth, the scent of whiskey and bergamot suddenly surrounding me like a cloud, and I go to bite it. "Sydney, you need to listen to me," a masculine voice says, and I stop, turning slightly to see if I can get a better look at him.

They spin me, and I come face to face with the man from before. The man from the funeral home. The one in the corner. The hall is dark, but his eyes are darker, holding an urgency in them that confuses me.

"Who the fuck are you?"

"I think you should've grilled your little friend out there a little harder before you got too deep," he says instead of answering my question, spinning me and shoving me along the wall, coming to a large back door.

"What's happening?"

"He's FBI, Princess."

My eyes go round, looking behind us. "What do you mean?"

"The guy was about to take you into custody. They think you have information about your parents."

My heart starts beating a mile a minute, my stomach dropping. "I don't. I haven't talked to them in years." I tell him, trying to calm the building anxiety in my chest.

He tosses the door open, leading me outside into the dimly lit side street.

Letting go of me, his head swivels from side to side, and I

take him in, trying not to focus too hard on how handsome he is.

Because he is. Handsome, that is. His broad shoulders are something I'd gape at in any other social setting. His suit fits perfectly, his thighs stretching the material in a way that would be the absolute death of me if we met at a party.

And when his deep brown eyes meet mine, I melt.

"Who are you?" I ask again, massaging my wrist nervously.

"Ronan. I'm getting you out of here."

TWO

SYDNEY

"I NEED YOU TO START TALKING," I tell him as a plate of fries is set in front of me. They're the good kind. The kind that are golden on the outside with a thick crust but light and fluffy on the inside.

I spread them out on my plate, dumping pepper on them with reckless abandon.

My ears are still ringing from the club, and my head is still a little fuzzy from trying to figure Jeremy out. My heart is still in my chest from my not-so-meet cute with Ronan.

He sits across from me, his arms folded over his chest as he leans back in his seat, watching me add more and more pepper to my fries. The longer I keep going, the more concerned he looks. "What do you want to know?"

"Well, first of all," I pick up a fry, feeling the crispy shell break between my fingers. "how do you know about my parents? Why were you at their funeral tonight?"

His eyes narrow a fraction before he wipes his face with his hands, his warm eyes sparkling with annoyance. "I was told I had to come get you. I know Jeremy. Knew he was going to take you in."

"But you somehow also know that I didn't have anything

to do with their deaths?" I drop the fry, my head tilting to the side. Something about this isn't adding up, and unease swirls in my stomach. I can feel my phone buzzing in my pocket.

Ronan's eyes run over my body, finally resting on my lap. "See who that is," he demands, a muscle in his arm popping through the sleeve of his button-up.

"I don't know who the fuck you are, but you're certainly not someone who can tell me what to do," I bark back, whipping out my phone regardless.

> Where did you go?

> Sydney, the guy you were with looks pissed.
> Where did you go?

> Please pick up.

> I hope you're okay.

> I swear to God if I find out you're dead in a
> ditch somewhere I'm bringing you back just
> to kill you myself.

> Sydney please for the love of everything
> please pick up. I know things have been hard
> with your mom and dad and all but I'm here
> for you.

> Did that man say something horrible?

> Did you go home with some random person
> you met in the bathroom line again? Jesus
> Christ, Sydney, I'll never let you live it down.

> Please just let me know you're not dead.
> Who's going to help me pick up girls? You're
> the Barney to my Ted, the—

"Who is it?" Ronan interrupts as I read the long string of texts, his voice clipped.

I shoot him a scowl before going back to my phone.

I'm okay, I type back. *I had to get out of there. I'm safe, I promise.*

"Sydney." Ronan snaps, his elbow slamming against the table. I look around, ensuring no one notices my ill-behaved friend. It's one thing to be running from the law, apparently. It's entirely another to act foolish in the middle of a diner full of drunk college kids. I'd look so uncool, and that just won't fly.

"It's my best friend. He was there and saw me leave."

He rolls his eyes. "Did Jeremy know he was there with you?"

I shrug. "I'm not sure. Maybe? If he's an agent worth anything, he probably knows. Adam was with me the entire time we were at the funeral. He followed us to the club but stayed his distance."

Ronan nods, looking at his own phone he holds in his lap. I try not to notice how tight his shirt is, his stomach muscles rippling as he rolls his eyes in irritation.

"What's going to happen now?" I ask him, biting my nail before picking up another fry.

He sighs, closing his eyes as he massages his temples. "I need to make sure that no one is coming for you, and that includes Jeremy."

I look around the busy diner. "Does that mean I can go home?"

That's all I want to do right now. It's been a long day and an even longer week. The only thing I want to do right now is go home, get in the bath, and curl up with Shiloh before falling asleep for the next two days.

Not that I have that luxury. My boss wants me in the office at 8 a.m. sharp tomorrow; dead parental figures be damned.

"You can go home for the moment," he tells me sharply, back to looking at his phone. His wavy black hair falls into his face as his face twists in concentration. He scrolls briefly before biting his lip, his nose scrunching at whatever he's reading. The freckles that dot his nose are cute, but his attitude is atrocious.

Usually, I wouldn't give men with no facial hair a second glance, but something about him makes me stop and look. Really look.

"We should get you home soon, though," he sighs when he finally looks up, meeting my eyes.

I nod, placing a twenty on the table and climbing out of the booth.

My feet hurt like a bitch in these heels, and my shoulders desperately need to be rubbed. I stretch, yawning as Ronan follows close behind. I feel the heat of his body on my back, the brush of his suit jacket on my arm as he puts it on.

"Are you okay?" he asks as I stop for a moment, fidgeting with my shoe.

I wave him off. "Yeah, these heels are just killing me."

He nods, taking the lead as I thank our waitress on the way out.

The October air hits my face, nipping at my skin. Although being kidnapped in the middle of a date—if you can call it that—has sobered me up, I can't help but feel the alcohol hit me once again the second the fall air nips at my skin.

"Do you need help?" Ronan asks, his brow arched.

I shake my head, but after taking another step, my ankle seems to have other ideas. I groan, adjusting my shoe again.

"Give them to me." He says as he steps in front of me, reaching for them.

I gape. "I'm not walking barefoot in the city. Do you know how many people spit on these sidewalks? It's a lot."

He pauses, looking at me like I'm crazy. "That's what you're worried about stepping on? Spit? Not needles or glass or other, I don't know, rats?" I don't like the judgment in his tone, but the second I open my mouth, he cuts me off. "We're going five steps and waiting for an Uber." He seems angry, and that makes me happy for some sick and twisted reason.

"Fine."

I bend over to remove my shoes but don't get far before I'm picked up bridal-style in his arms. I flounder, surprised. "What are you doing?"

"You were taking too long. This is easier. Shut up and relax."

"I hope you know I'm not sleeping with you," I tell him as I watch him.

My head rests on his shoulder, and I watch as his jaw works, biting back something undoubtedly nasty. Instead, he ignores me, looking down the busy DC street.

I stay silent this time.

We get back to my apartment quickly, and I'm thankful that there's no one there. No cops, no family members trying to bother me, no one. I have my peace and quiet.

"I'm coming up with you," Ronan tells me, and I roll my eyes. Apparently, I don't. God has favorites, and I am not one of them.

I haven't decided whether I trust him or not. I feel stupid for doing so, especially because he wouldn't answer a single question I asked him, including *how the hell he knew my address*, which, to be honest, I figured was because he's probably some type of private detective. Unfortunately, I've had my fair share of run-ins with those, so I'm familiar with how easy it can be to figure out where someone lives.

No matter how disconnected from social media I am, and no matter how careful I am about giving out my address anywhere, someone always manages to find it. But none of them have ever been like this.

They mostly asked if I knew how to get in contact with my

parents. It turns out it's hard to get ahold of you when you're murderous criminals.

But the man didn't answer a single one of my questions, not even when I asked him what his favorite color was. I'm sure it's purple.

"I'll be fine by myself," I say, unlocking my front door.

"It doesn't matter."

"You really need to tell me what's going on, Ronan, or I'm just going to call the police. You have to understand how fucking weird this is."

He sighs again, and I can't help but wonder if he sighs a lot normally or if it's just me. It's probably just me, and for some reason, that gives me some sense of joy.

"I can explain later, but for now, you need to get some rest," he tells me, shutting the door behind me.

Thunk.

Ronan's head whips to the bedroom, his eyes wide as he whips something out of his back pocket.

"Is that a fucking gun?" I ask, talking myself out of smacking it out of his hand. There are a couple of things not allowed in my apartment, that being at the very top of the list. I hate guns. There's nothing about them I enjoy, and I'd much rather use these fists of steel to protect myself.

Not that they would be much use, but I decided a long time ago that if it's my time to go, it's my time to go.

He brings his finger to his lips, telling me to be quiet before he starts creeping toward the bedroom.

I follow close behind him, careful to keep quiet as we make our way across the hardwood floor of my family room to the closed door on the other side.

Ronan positions himself outside the door, his gun poised in front of him, pointed at the ground as he motions for me to get behind him. I do, looking around.

"I think I should tell you now that I have a cat, and if you shoot him, you're a dead man," I whisper, and he looks at me, eyes hard as he continues.

Slowly, Ronan opens the door, peering inside for a moment before stepping in.

Suddenly, from the dark comes a small chirp.

"What the hell is that?" Ronan asks, putting his gun down.

I roll my eyes, stepping into the room and bending over to pick up my small grey cat. "I told you, I have a cat," Petting his soft head, he lets out a small chirp. "Now put your gun away, you trigger-happy twit; you're scaring him."

His forehead wrinkles as he looks around, unconvinced.

"Everything is fine," I assure him as I move into the room. Sitting Shiloh down on the bed, I sit on the corner, watching Ronan check every nook and cranny. "Why am I so important to you?"

Ronan freezes for a moment before tucking his gun back in his pants. Finally. "I've been told to keep you safe until they can rule out your involvement," he says simply as he looks me dead in the eyes. I stare at him for a little longer, the silence sitting heavy on our shoulders as Shiloh rubs his head against my arm, his gentle purr settling my racing heart.

That doesn't make sense. I know it doesn't make sense. Yet, things revolving around my parents rarely ever did. Did they make sure that I would have protection in the event that they passed? Were they in trouble when it happened, and now I'm in danger? Was their death even an accident?

I didn't allow myself to think about it in the days after finding out they had died. In fact, I don't let myself think about them much at all. To me, my parents are just people who I spent a lot of time with growing up. I don't have a significant emotional attachment to them. and although I always wished them well, I knew that was a battle I would never win. Having them respect me. Having them be good people.

I knew what they did. I knew what they were capable of. I've seen it with my own two eyes, burned in my memory.

I never wanted to be them. I never wanted anything to do with it.

But for the first time, Ronan has me considering what their deaths mean. I haven't spoken to them in a long time, and I doubt they'd ensure I'm protected even while alive. I'm positive I wasn't left anything, either. The most I was bothered to do was show up to the funeral, and even then, Adam and I were only there for a little while. I bounced the first chance I got, which was clearly not my finest decision.

There's some sort of freedom in that, right? In knowing that you're not your past. That when it came down to it, no one can use you as an example of nature versus nurture. You chose peace. You chose to be an exemplary person.

You chose the safe route.

"I'm going to stay out on the couch," he tells me as he turns, his eyes narrowing just slightly at Shiloh, still sitting comfortably in my arms, purring away.

I shrug, heading into the bathroom for a shower.

THREE

RONAN

SYDNEY IS everything I thought she would be. Annoying, entitled, and hard to work with.

Jerry's feelings about her aside, Sydney's cushy life shouldn't irritate me as much as it does. But looking around her apartment, seeing all the luxuries she's had in this life splayed about, I can't help but feel a nudge of irritation for my friend who had nothing.

I settle into her couch, sinking into the cushions. It's like sitting on a fucking cloud. Despite all the money we have now, our couch isn't even this fancy.

The walls are wrapped in a silver, textured wallpaper, and I can't help but wonder if she asked to put it up. If that's even allowed here, or if she just simply doesn't care about damages or her security deposit.

Because it was a large deposit. She pays a lot to live here.

Hearing the shower turn on, I look at my phone, letting myself settle a little bit. I've been on high alert all night, and I just really want to sleep. Something I know isn't going to come easy, if at all.

Despite my distaste for her, something is interesting about Sydney. Something that draws me to her. I think it's just the mystery. Why would someone completely write off their parents and then go to the funeral? She didn't seem comfortable. Instead, she was unhappy and hapless.

But she knew people there.

I watched from the corner as she schmoozed with some of her parents' top clients. Some big politicians. I'm not even sure she knew who they were exactly. Old family friends, distant family. They were all together, talking like her parents weren't responsible for thousands of lives lost. Many of whom were innocent. Many who only ever wanted to do good in this world.

I don't blame her for not doing something about it. The fact that she didn't seem to ride her parents' coattails is probably one of her only redeeming qualities. But I want to know why.

There has to be a reason, and I'm going to get to the bottom of it.

My phone vibrates, and I sigh, instantly knowing who it's going to be.

Are you with her?

"What do you think?" I mutter, rolling my eyes as I answer her.

Yes, I'm at her place now.

Getting up from the couch, I head to the kitchen for water. I know which cabinet her cups are located in already, but I use the time to snoop, opening each one and looking for anything suspicious. You'd be surprised where rich people decide to hide important things.

But I don't find anything.

All she has are green Pottery Barn monstrosities she

would call plates, gold-foiled wine glasses, and glassware that looks like they cost forty bucks a piece.

Rolling my eyes, I continue to the drawers, pulling them out one by one. I find the same as you'd expect. Random notes here and there, a bill or two tucked under tape and highlighters, a takeout menu, and a really impressive drawer full of fancy spices. One of the only really odd things was an entire spice jar full of saffron. How anyone could have so much, I have no idea. That must have cost a fortune.

There are some things that memory loss can't take from you, and money insecurity is one of them. No matter how much money the agency gives us, I'll never understand rich people. I don't remember anything from the past, but I do enjoy the humor in knowing I was definitely poor.

"This hasn't helped much," I mutter, finally just grabbing a glass and filling it with tap water before leaning against the counter. I drink it in one go.

My phone buzzes again, and I set the glass down to check it.

> You need to bring her in. Tomorrow.

A groan escapes me as I throw my head back. "That's not what we talked about, Jer," I whisper angrily as if she's here with me.

> What are you talking about? That wasn't the plan.

> Well, it's the plan now. Get with it, get the information we need, and bring her in.

> The very second she's there, she's going to shut down, and we won't get a single thing out of her. She's sassy. Just like you.

That sounds like a you problem. Deal with it.
Get the information and bring her in. I want
her here tomorrow.

I can't begin to describe how much I loathe this situation.

You could say that my job requires a whole lot of acting. But never as much as it does right now. There's so much riding on this one woman, and yet there's nowhere I'd rather not be.

I need to figure out how to get as much information from Sydney as I possibly can before bringing her in. We probably won't get any at all from her afterward. But it occurs to me that gaining her trust quickly will require me to actually be nice to her.

But how do I prove myself an ally in less than a day?

We'll see, I guess.

Moving around the room, I check out her bookshelves. Almost all classics, but they're all well-loved. A stack of movies sits by the TV, and some magazines are on the coffee table. A journal and colored pencils sit on a desk in the corner, and she has a couple plants lying about, though they mostly look dead.

Sydney's door creaks open, and a small grey head peeks out. The second his big green eyes meet mine, a menacing hiss is sent my way.

Settling back on the couch, my glass of water next to me, I prop one of her pillows against the armrest, getting comfortable and allowing myself to drift to sleep.

FOUR

SYDNEY

THE SECOND I WAKE UP, I thank God that the night before was a dream. Because it was a dream, right? That's the only explanation.

There's absolutely no way that all of that happened.

But the second I sit up and look around, I notice the door propped open, a blanket strewn over the couch haphazardly, and Shiloh nowhere to be found.

Getting up, I don't even bother checking myself in the mirror. I know I'm wearing clothes and don't owe anyone anything more than that. If someone's in my house, they'll have to be happy with this.

But what I don't expect to see is Ronan, the man from the night before, at my stove, making bacon.

The meat sizzles in the pan, the smell wafting over me as I relax just a little. Sure, this means that last night *wasn't* a dream, but I almost feel more at peace knowing he's here and not just a figment of my imagination. I don't like the man. He's rude and frustrating and could definitely be lying to me through his stupidly perfect teeth. But then again, maybe he's not, and he's really here to help me.

The funny thing about my parents and their job is that I'll

never know. Anyone that's associated with them, anyone at all, could be here because they want to kill me or because they want to protect me. Or they could want to use me. I'll never know which one.

There's one reason I've stayed far, far away.

"What are you doing here still?" I ask because I'm not sure what else I should say.

"I told you I was watching you through the night." He barely looks up from the stove, concentrating on what he's doing.

He wears the same clothes he had on the day prior, but this morning, his hair is disheveled, and his black shirt is wrinkly. It's cute.

"Okay, well," I look around, spotting Shiloh on the couch. His ears are back as he watches Ronan move around the kitchen. "I don't think we need protecting anymore."

He puts the pan of eggs down with a clank, his eyes moving up slowly to meet mine. They're hooded, and I can't tell if it's because he's annoyed or he likes what he sees. "Well, I was told to stay here and watch you. I think you just have to deal with it for now."

"What makes you so sure that I won't call the police on you right now?" My chest puffs out, and I cross my arms over it.

"Well," he starts as he returns to work on breakfast. "I assume you'd rather not spend the next couple of days in jail as they question you about thousands of lives lost," he says without looking back up.

"How do you know I had any involvement at all? Who would be capable of that?"

I don't quite remember what I told him the night before and whether he knows the full extent of what I know about my parents. In reality, it's not that much. I've worked incredibly hard to forget a lot of it, and what I do remember was still a long time ago. A lot has happened since then.

A lot of terrible things, clearly.

But what type of terrible things would make me have to go into some kind of witness protection, I'm not quite sure.

Is it still witness protection if I'm being protected *from* the FBI?

"I still don't know who you are or who you work for," I tell him as I take a seat at the counter. The cold metal of the chairs bites into my exposed thighs.

"You don't need to know that just yet," he says as he grabs two slices of toast from my toaster, placing one each on the two plates in front of him.

"Why not?"

"It's just better if you didn't know," he shrugs.

"Okay."

Handing me a plate of breakfast, I eye it, not sure if I should eat.

"If I wanted you dead, I had every opportunity in the world to kill you while you slept," he says, his voice monotone.

"Yeah, but it would have been obvious I was killed. You could just slip me something here, and no one would know."

Ronan rolls his eyes. "That's not how it works. I could have made it look like an accident last night, too."

I take a forkful of eggs, eyeing them warily before taking a bite. "I still don't trust you."

He takes a bite of bacon. "The feeling is mutual."

And yet, somehow, out of everything we've spoken about, out of all the words, that makes us both crack smiles.

A couple minutes of silence follows until Ronan sets his fork down. "It may kill me, but I want to apologize for last night. I know that you had nothing to do with your parents' deaths, and you didn't have anything to do with their, well, business. I just need to make sure you're safe. I can't really tell you why yet, which I understand makes things a little complicated," his knuckles tap the counter twice as he looks at the ceiling, and I can practically see the gears turning in his pretty little head. He doesn't know how to speak to me. "I just know that your parents weren't in a great place when they passed away and that you're a person of interest in, well, many things at the moment. There's a lot of people who may want you dead."

I decide to play stupid. "Why would anyone want me dead?"

"Why wouldn't someone want you dead?" he asks me, his eyes burning holes into mine.

"Well, I'm not sure."

"You're the daughter of two of the most powerful people in this world. Two people who have used that power to hurt many people, Sydney. I understand that you haven't had contact with them in a long time, but you have to understand the gravity of the situation and how many people wanted them dead. Now that they are, what better way to get revenge than to go after the daughter?"

"And why does law enforcement want me?"

He shrugs. "Like I said. They either think that you may know something about their deaths, or they want you to figure out what your parents did and where the bodies are, so to speak."

"I don't know where they are," I tell him stiffly, setting my fork down, my appetite lost. It's a lie. I do know where some of them are buried.

"Do you think it's partially your responsibility to make things right?" he asks, throwing me off.

"I think I would if I could, but they've been doing unthinkable things for a very long time, and I escaped when I could. There's not much more I could have done."

"You could have turned them in."

I shake my head. "I would have been dead in minutes. They knew every step I took. No matter how hard I tried to make it for them, they always found me. They knew exactly where I lived, who I spoke to, where I was at every given moment. I'm not sure how, but they did. There's no way I could have turned them in and lived."

"They wouldn't have killed their own daughter," he scoffs.

I roll my eyes. "You've been standing here for the last couple minutes telling me about how horrible my own parents are, people who raised me. I know how horrible they were. I lived it. And yet you're going to stand here and tell me that you knew them better? You think you can sit here and tell me that they wouldn't have taken me out if it meant that they'd live to see another day outside of a jail cell?"

Ronan's jaw sets as his eyes narrow at me, and my hands turn to fists at my sides.

"You don't know a thing about me,"

His head turns as he rubs his chin with his hand, contemplating his next move. "I don't mean to make it seem like I know you. I just, I'm sorry." he apologizes. Part of me believes it and another part says to not let my guard down. "I'm here to make sure you're safe. Part of doing that means that I need to know everything you were involved in. How close you were with them. Who may want to kill you, if anyone."

Pushing my eggs around my plate, I consider his words. I get it. I do. I just think he could be so much better with his delivery.

I sigh, leaning back in my chair. "I don't know much about what they did, like I've said. I've seen things, sure. But honestly, I haven't wanted to deal with any of it. I ran."

He nods, taking another bite from the plate in front of him.

"I remember my parents used to hold meetings while I was around. There was always a commotion. Always threats. They were both a team. They were a team when it came to taking down clients, business partners, and the like. They were also a team when they told me off. Told me I wasn't enough. Told me I was worthless to them if I chose to run. But I did. I never looked back."

I leave out a lot, but he hasn't earned that level of honesty yet.

When he doesn't say anything, I clear my throat. "What are we going to do about Jeremy?"

"We're not doing anything about him," he tells me as he finishes, placing the plate in the sink and washing it.

"Well, I don't want to get arrested, and I certainly don't want to keep you around for the next few days."

"You're not going to be."

"How do you know?"

Ronan turns, brushing his black hair out of his face with his hand. I keep my eyes focused on him and away from the bulging muscles of his bicep.

"If you haven't been arrested yet, you won't be. They want information from you but don't have probable cause."

"Then what was he doing talking to me last night?"

He dries his hands on my kitchen towel, refusing to look up. "Getting probable cause."

The man was trying to trick me into saying the wrong thing. The second I did, I'd be brought in for questioning. I'm aware of the law, and I'm pretty sure that kind of deception is illegal, but I'm not quite sure.

"So they can't come here and just arrest me for shits and giggles," I nod in understanding, grabbing my water bottle from the counter and taking a swig. It's been sitting there for days, and when I make a face at the stale water taste, Ronan grabs it, pours it out, and fills it with fresh water before placing it in front of me again.

"Thank you," I say, opening the cap and taking a sip. "So what do we do now?"

The second I ask, Ronan's phone rings in his back pocket.

Pulling it out, he makes a face. Holding up one finger, he starts the call.

"Yes?" he asks before walking into my bedroom and closing the door behind him.

But what he may not know is that I'm a nosy fucker.

Getting up quietly, I gently pad over to the door, pressing my ear against it.

"I just need more—no, you're not listening to me. I think just a little—" His voice cuts in and out as I try to listen, and I can tell he's pacing the room.

His voice stops, and a loud groan is all I need to hear to send me back to the couch, waking Shiloh up as I pretend I've been here the entire time.

"You'd be a really shitty spy," Ronan tells me as he walks out of the room, his eyes dark and moody.

"I'm not sure what you're talking about."

"Sure. Anyways, we need to go somewhere."

"Where?" My interest is piqued. I'm always down for a cool adventure.

"Somewhere. I can't say right now."

"Oh, that sounds ominous. I'm not sure how I feel about that."

"It doesn't matter how you feel about it. The real question is, do you trust me?"

I think about it for a little while as I eye him. His beautiful eyes look almost onyx, and they never leave mine. I feel myself caving under the intensity of them. "I'm not sure," I answer. But I think I do. I'm not sure why. I feel like I shouldn't. But there's just something about him that makes me feel safe.

He could have slit my throat easily last night. He could have poisoned my food this morning. There are so many moments he could have harmed me, yet all he did was rescue me from a terrible situation.

I think I have to trust him. But my sense of self-preservation has never been high.

"I think you do. So, because you trust me, you're going to do exactly what I say, okay Princess?"

A chill runs through me. "Don't call me that."

A smirk creeps onto his handsome face, and I hate it.

"You're going to get your things. We're leaving in five minutes. You hear me? Five minutes, and we're downstairs getting into a car."

"What about six?"

"Five."

I salute him, heading to my room. I'm not sure how long we will be away, but I assume it won't be long. I grab my backpack, stuffing it with some essential items I may need. If I'm not allowed to know what's happening, the least I can do is be prepared.

Next, I fill Shiloh's bowls with food and water. It's all he should need, and if I happen to be away for longer, I'll just have Adam feed him.

Shit, Adam. I text him to let him know everything is okay and I have some things to take care of for my parents' estate.

Sliding the backpack on, I head back to Ronan, who already has his shoes on, ready to go.

I kiss Shiloh's soft little head on my way out.

The walk down to the front door is silent. Even Ronan's footsteps seem too muted. It's unsettling, but I push the thoughts back. It's like he floats over the surface, and something about it reminds me of a predator.

"You sure you can't tell me anything about what's happening?" I ask him.

I understand that I'm an idiot. I understand that a lot of people wouldn't trust this man. I'm not sure why I do.

I think I should be a little more scared of death than I am.

"Nope," his jaw pops, his voice dripping with annoyance.

Okay then.

Heading out the front door, we only have to wait a couple minutes before a black car pulls up to the curb. Ronan opens the door, not bothering to let me in first.

Which means he knows that I'm going to follow him. He knows he has the upper hand, and I won't run. For some reason, that fact eats at me.

And yet, I still do. I still climb in the car without a sound, despite everything in me telling me not to.

The car doors lock.

"Now that you have me in here, can you tell me what's going on? Where we're going?"

"What's happening is that your parents were very bad people, and we've been working on bringing their empire down for quite some time," Ronan says, his voice void of emotion.

"Who is this *we*?"

"You'll see soon enough,"

"Ronan, tell me now."

"We, meaning us," a voice from the front says.

The driver's voice.

"And who are you?" I ask as we come to a stop in traffic.

The woman takes her glasses off, whipping out a cigarette before lighting it slowly, taking a drag before she turns to me.

And I see myself staring back.

FIVE

RONAN

I ALMOST FEEL BAD.

Almost.

Sydney's body goes rigid as her eyes grow wide. A range of emotions run through them, and I can't help but feel unsure of this. This would be a shock to anyone in normal circumstances, but as someone going through what she is right now, it's probably so much worse.

"Who the hell are you?" she asks, her voice small. She clears her throat, trying to act tough.

"Jerry," the woman in front says, taking another drag from her cigarette.

I try to suppress my annoyance with Jerry and focus on what's happening in front of me. With my aggravation for the other redhead in my life right now, sitting next to me. We weren't supposed to bring Sydney in yet. She wasn't supposed to find out so soon.

We were making progress. Slow progress, but progress nonetheless. I knew she wasn't telling me everything she knows. I just needed a little more time to push her—a little more time to make her trust me.

I should have handled the situation better from the beginning. Instead of coming off strong, I should have been friendlier. When I'm undercover working, I'm always friendly. I'm capable of it, that's for sure. I should have made her feel better.

But something about that makes my actions somehow seem more sinister than they already were. No matter what, my job has been to lure her into a false sense of security. To trick her. To deceive her trust. But being nicer to her, making her believe I'm someone wildly different than who I really am, seems worse.

But then again, why do I care?

Sydney is a means to an end. We're here to get information from her and drop her off at home. She won't be in our lives long. She's necessary collateral in our mission, which is bigger than every single one of us.

Sometimes, people have to suffer for the greater good. That doesn't make it okay, and that doesn't mean you can't feel horrible about it, but it's the truth.

The car seems to heat up as Sydney sits in her confusion. Her white fingers twist the bottom of her blue t-shirt, her neck almost as red as her hair as she watches Jerry in the rearview mirror.

Jerry glances back at her, a slight smirk on her lips as she flicks her cigarette out the window.

I wish she wouldn't smoke in the car with me. We've had this conversation before. But there's no controlling her. If you ask her not to do something, she'll just do it more.

I stopped asking.

"There's some things we have to ask you," I start finally.

Sydney's head whips my way, her eyes narrowed. Fury radiates off her shoulders in waves; her hands balled into fists in her lap. "I'm not answering a single thing."

Jerry clicks her tongue from the front. "I'm not sure that's going to go over too well for you, Syd."

Sydney's eyebrows draw together in befuddlement, her shoulders hunching just slightly. I can see the dozens of questions in her eyes, but there's not much I can say here. There's not much I can say in general. She's just going to have to deal with that and trust us.

Which would be a whole lot easier if I had more time with her.

"What is this?" she asks me, her eyes pleading as they grow larger and larger, glistening in the late morning light.

I shake my head. "We'll be able to tell you a little more when we reach our destination."

Her hands start to shake, her fingers reaching for the door handle as her body whips around. She throws herself against it, hoping it'll open.

Jerry's eyes meet mine as she looks back, and I know she wants me to handle it.

Gripping Sydney's body, I bring her back into her seat, holding her down as she thrashes. But I don't hold her tightly enough.

A searing pain starts in my cheek as her palm connects with it, her eyes staring daggers at me.

"Don't. Touch. Me," she hisses, the palm of her hand held in her other as she massages her red skin.

"I wouldn't have to touch you if you wouldn't try to escape a moving vehicle," I inform her, annoyance clear in my tone. "What were you trying to do, anyway? We're in the middle of nowhere."

She looks around, surprise on her face as if she thought we were still in the city.

Instead, all she can see is the blur of trees as we pass them, a neighborhood off to the left.

"Where are we going?" she asks.

"You're lucky we're not blindfolding you," Jerry snarks as she reaches for her phone. She has one leg propped up on the seat, her knee resting against the door, her left hand gripping the wheel as she texts the others.

The car drifts into the opposite lane, and I have to snap at her to get her attention back where it's supposed to be. Jerry isn't exactly known for being a safe driver.

Meanwhile, Sydney has stopped shaking, but her head whips around, trying to figure out where we are.

"We're about ten minutes west from DC," I tell her. "We have about ten more minutes to go."

"Where are you taking me?" Her eyes land on mine, and I can't help but feel a little pang in my chest as I see they're filled with tears.

"We're taking you to our place. You're going to be fine."

The rest of the ride is silent. The soft beat of whatever music Jerry plays thrums through the speakers as I anxiously tap my fingers on my jittery leg. I just want to be home, where we can get this over with and get this girl back to her place and away from us.

Not that I think that she would do any better there.

Even if we get all the information we need from her, she will still have problems at home. She's still going to have people after her. If she's lucky, it'll only be the FBI. The Agency wants nothing to do with her; they don't even know we're talking to her if I'm being honest. But the criminal enterprise her parents established, well, that's another story.

I'm not sure what anyone would get out of catching her attention. If anything, I think it would go poorly for them. But that doesn't mean that they can't take her out, just to make sure their lives are easier down the road.

For good reason, Sydney Quinn would have a high price on her head.

Finally, after what feels like an hour, we pull up the dirt road leading to our compound. The trees thin around us, leading to a large clearing. The giant warehouse stands before us, completely secured by a tall metal fence.

Opening an app on her phone, Jerry plugs in the key code, scans her finger and her eye, and presses the button to open the gate. It groans for a minute before letting us through.

Sydney looks around, her mouth open slightly as she gapes at what's before us.

Pressing another button, the large garage door to the compound opens, and Jerry pulls inside, parking beside her usual 1970 red Challenger.

Sydney stiffens, looking ahead, eyes wide.

Jerry turns the car off and opens her door, catching my eyes as she nods. I climb out as she opens Sydney's door, leaning against it with her hand on her hip.

And she runs.

It doesn't take long, and if I'm honest, we were both probably expecting it to happen. Only a moment after that door was opened, Sydney is out and halfway through the compound door.

Jerry rolls her eyes as she sighs. "Go get her."

"Why don't you? You caused this," I say, spreading my arms out wide.

Her eyes turn hard. "Do it."

There's no use arguing with her.

Instead, I roll up the sleeves of my white shirt and run after Sydney, who hasn't gotten super far. About halfway from the compound to the gate.

It doesn't take long to catch up to her. Hooking my arm around her waist, I pull her into me, trying hard to keep her thrashing to a minimum. Mostly to make sure I don't get kicked in the balls.

"Please make this easy," I tell her. "I don't want to do this. We just need some information, and you'll be home."

"I trusted you," she spits. "Who the *fuck* is that in there?"

"I know. I know. She'll tell you, please."

She thrashes more, her elbow meeting my gut as I double over. Losing my balance, I fall, bringing her with me.

Pinning her down, Sydney scowls at me, hurt and pain clear in her eyes as dirt and gravel tangle her hair.

"Fuck you," she says, and before I know what's happening, she spits in my face.

Spits. In. My. Face.

My mind blacks out as I set my feet under me, standing up. Wiping the spit from my face, I crack my neck before leaning down, grabbing Sydney by the arm and waist, and hoisting her over my shoulder.

Turning around, I head back into the compound as she continues to scream profanities at me, her legs pushing against my arm as I keep them still.

By the time we're there, she's calmed, giving up. The moment we cross the threshold, the door closes.

I don't put her down until I reach the couch, dropping her on the plush material with a thump as she gets the wind knocked out of her.

Stepping back, I stand beside Jerry, who sits in the chair opposite the couch, staring at her.

Sydney's hair is a mess, sticking out from every direction. Her bare face is red and puffy, her eyes glistening with tears.

A little tinge of regret pings inside me, but I push it down as far as I can.

I've killed men and felt less.

This is necessary.

"Now that we've gotten *that* out of our system," Jerry starts, "we need to get down to business so that you can go home."

"Who are you?" Sydney asks, betrayal in her voice as her eyes flicker to mine.

"I'm Jerry," the woman beside me says as she leans against her armrest, crossing one leg over the other as her combat boot twists in the air like she's discussing how to braid hair at a sleepover.

"Are you going to expand on that?" Sydney asks, her hands busy in her lap as she massages her fingers.

"Well, I think it's pretty obvious we're related."

SIX

SYDNEY

I CAN'T EVEN BEGIN to understand what's going on right now.

The woman in front of me has long, thick black hair with natural red roots, like she just hasn't been to the salon for months. Freckles cover her heart-shaped face, and her piercing green eyes are the same ones I stare at every time I look in the mirror.

It's my face.

We have the same face.

The only difference is my natural red hair, and while her nose is slightly crooked, mine isn't. I can only imagine it was from her getting punched. I wish I could have been the one to do it.

I take a second to look around, trying to figure out what my next move is. When we first pulled up to this warehouse, I was a little worried I'd be murdered and left for dead on a dirty concrete floor. Although that's still a reasonable possibility and something to certainly distress over, the inside of this building is nothing like I thought.

It looked massive from the outside, but it looks even bigger inside somehow.

I sit in the middle of one of the largest rooms I've ever seen, lined with dozens upon dozens of cars—the expensive kind, not that I could name any of them. New, old, it doesn't matter. They're here, parked in rows like some type of car museum.

It's beautiful and unsettling, and I wonder why they have so many.

But I think there are bigger, more important questions to ask here.

To the right of me is a kitchen nestled against a wall that goes up about two stories high. Its industrial design perfectly fits everything else. I can't help but admire the beams running along the walls and the large metal staircase leading up to a platform that runs across the length of the warehouse, leading to different rooms.

If I weren't terrified out of my mind, I may find the place way cooler.

Scaffolding sits on the right, wrapped in caution tape, warning people away from the space. The second floor's metal railing looks like it's just been put in.

I can't hear anything else around me at the moment, but I'm not sure if it's because the place is quiet or if the blood rushing to my head is drowning out any other noise.

The smell of rubber, gasoline, and... lavender? Surround me, and I find the scent oddly calming.

"I'll tell you whatever I can as long as you tell me who you are," I tell her finally, crossing my shaking hands over my chest to keep them still. My lower abdomen starts to constrict, and I close my eyes for a moment, hoping and praying it goes away.

"Well, sister, mommy and daddy dearest have been up to no good, and we need you to tell us everything you know so that we can fix it," the woman in front of me, Jerry, I think I recall her saying her name was, says.

"Sister?" My breath catches.

"Twins, actually," she says as she examines her nails, a bored look on her face.

"Twins?"

"Yes, that is what I just said."

Ronan rolls his eyes next to her, his arms crossed over his broad chest. My eyes drift to his face, and the second I see the small smirk slide onto his lips, I think I'm going to be sick. How could I trust a complete stranger?

I didn't.

I didn't, but I still let my guard down. But what other choice did I have? I knew it was a risk. I knew that there were evil people out there—bad people who would possibly come after me. Bad people most likely associated with my parents. I should have just gone home by myself. I shouldn't have told him a goddamn thing.

We all have regrets in this life, and this one may get me killed.

It occurs to me that my lack of self-preservation doesn't seem to extend to real-life or death situations. I've been chasing a high most of my life now, and although I think I want danger and destruction, what I really want is the threat of it—without the actual life or death possibility.

Ronan's smirk paired with Jerry's steely gaze lights a fire in me. I'm unsure where it came from, but I feel it creep through my body, lighting me up.

They look at me like I'm weak, but I'm far from it. I've lived through worse than getting kidnapped by someone.

I'm better than this.

I straighten against the back of the couch and my shaking hands start to slow. My shoulders roll back.

The least I can do is become their worst nightmare.

"I haven't talked to my parents in years," I tell Jerry, ignoring the fact that she said we're twins. I'm curious, but not curious enough to let it show.

"I know," she replies, flicking a fuzzy from her black cargo pants onto the floor. "That doesn't mean that you don't know anything."

"I know very little about them. I've worked for years not to have any association with them."

"But you share their blood."

"You do too, apparently."

Jerry is silent for a moment, her head tilted to the side as she studies me. I can feel her eyes piercing mine, and for a moment I want to look away. "You spent your childhood with them. That means something, and I'm sure you know more than you've told Ronan."

I shake my head, a plan forming in my brain in real-time. "I'm not going to tell you guys anything unless I get some answers, and even then, I won't lie, I'm not sure how much I'm going to be able to tell you. I really don't know a ton."

My muscles coil as Jerry turns to Ronan, annoyance written across her face…

And I bolt.

Running as fast as I can toward the back of the warehouse, I'm pleasantly surprised to find that it's darker behind the kitchen wall.

Weaving between the cars, I hope they either underestimate me or are just slower than Ronan was outside.

Whipping open a car door, I slide into the backseat, the cool leather feeling soft and welcoming under my touch. I don't dare to sit on the seat and instead curl up in the footwell, looking up through the right window as I hear Jerry and Ronan walk around.

"Where is she gonna go?" Jerry laughs, and here, without looking at her, a shiver runs down my spine at how similar we sound.

"I don't really think you want to risk it, Jerry," Ronan tells her.

"She's gotta come out at some point. Let her be."

"It's not going to take that long to look through the cars
—"

"Let her be. The place is locked down. No one is getting in
or out without us knowing. She's not going anywhere; she'll
be here later. You may just want to lock your door tonight so
she doesn't creep in and slit your throat for betraying her."

"I betrayed her because you made me," he says, venom in
his voice. Like he cares. He didn't.

"You were going to betray her whether you had more time
for her to trust you or not, Ronan. I'm not sure why you've
been so pissed about this. She would hate you more if you
had more time with her." It occurs to me that they have to
know that I'm not that far and can hear them; they just simply
don't care.

"Maybe we wouldn't have even had to bring her in.
Maybe she would have come willingly."

Footsteps retreat, echoing through the space. I make a
mental note to ensure I'm not making too much noise when I
leave and to keep my steps light.

The two continue to bicker back and forth. I don't care
what they have to say, or what they think about me or their
betrayal. I just want to go home.

Home.

Where Ronan knows I live.

I wish I could text Adam.

Wait, my phone!

I start feeling around my pockets for it but realize that it's
in my purse, which was left in Jerry's car when they brought
me in. The second I started thinking something was wrong,
Ronan swept it toward him. I was so caught up in everything
that I didn't even think about it.

I think this is the only time I've been let down that I don't
share my location with anyone. It's too risky for me, despite
knowing that even if I don't share it, my parents would have

been able to find me if they had really wanted to. It wasn't hard for them.

I let my head hit the seat next to me as I groan internally, wishing things were different. I'm still the scared little girl who couldn't run away. This time though, I'm an adult who continues to let her guard down when she shouldn't. My only comfort is knowing that if I didn't come willingly, I would have likely been forced.

But that's not quite unfamiliar, either.

It's been what feels like hours but has probably only been one. Everyone has gone to bed from what I can tell, and I start getting fidgety.

There is no way I'm going to sleep here, waiting until the daytime when they're both awake and walking around. Where I can be seen and found way more easily than at night.

I'm also not waiting here another day. Cramped in this car, my knees tucked under my chin as I listen to all the sounds this old place has to offer. Besides, I'm sure that they'll get pissed off at some point and come to find me, making sure that I'm still here.

It takes me a couple of seconds to build the courage to get out. I keep telling myself I can do it. To just not think about what comes after. I just need to get past this. To open the door. After that, things are easier.

I get up, careful not to rock the car, and reach for the handle. It feels good in my clammy hands.

Holding my breath, I pull it, popping the door open quietly.

While the light didn't come on when I got in, I was prepared for it to upon my exit. I'm pleasantly surprised that it doesn't.

Climbing out silently, I only think about leaving the door open for a split second before I get too anxious about an alarm going off or a light coming on, and close it as softly as I can, bumping it with my hip for good measure.

Crouching, I make my way through the mess of cars before coming out into the space. I could creep around the outskirts of the compound, but it's much too dark here, with only the moonlight filtering through the tall windows at the top of the building, and I worry that I'll bump into one and set off an alarm.

Taking another deep breath, I tiptoe my way across the room, looking around as I do.

Finally, I'm at the kitchen with only halfway to go.

Click.

I don't have to guess what the sound comes from. I've heard it too many times throughout my life.

Eighteen years ago

I close my hands as I hold the cool metal in my hands. It feels far too big for me. Too heavy. My arms shake as I try to steady myself, holding it straight out like my dad told me to.

Target practice, he says, is one of the most important things I have to work on before I can work with them.

I don't want to work with them, though. But I do want to make them proud. I wish I could tell them that without getting smacked.

"Remember what I told you," my dad says, happiness shining in his eyes.

"Hold my breath when I pull the trigger," I repeat. My dad says it's one of the most basic rules. My breathing causes me to move, even just a little, and my aim will be off. But other things prevent my aim from being accurate, too. Like this gun being too heavy.

"I think it's too heavy," I tell him, looking at my feet.

"You don't have the luxury of thinking it's too heavy. Having to hold it still will be good practice for you."

He makes me hold it in the air until my muscles burn. Every single time my arms lower even a fraction of an inch, I'm forced to put them back up.

My body burns, my eyes water, and my brain clouds with fog.

After an hour, my father looks at me with what feels an awful lot like shame, taking the loaded gun from my head and weighing it in his hands.

And suddenly, the barrel is in my face.

"Now, next practice."

Looking to the left, the barrel of a gun fills my vision. It's, unfortunately, a fairly familiar sight, and for once, I'm almost happy to have seen it a few too many times. My stomach lurches, but my anxiety stays at bay. Maybe it's the training, or perhaps it's adrenaline.

Ronan levels me with a stare, and my eyes naturally drift over him. He's still wearing the pants he had on from yesterday, but he lost the suit jacket. Instead, his sleeves are rolled up, exposing his thick forearm. An expensive-looking watch sits on his opposite wrist, but I can't seem to see what brand. Watches have never been my thing, but it looks so natural on him that I almost think I could come around to them.

"You wouldn't," I whisper, my hands still up as my eyes return to his. The space is dark, and he looks dangerous. Lethal even. I really think he could if he wanted to.

He doesn't say anything.

"You need me."

"Do I? You said you don't know anything else," he whispers in reply, a predatory smile creeping over his lips. His eyes don't leave mine once, and I think I need a whole therapy session just to unpack why that bothers me.

"I think you and I both know that I know more than I told you."

He grins, and it's the grin of a man who knew I was full of

shit the entire time and is finally being proved right. His eyes finally sweep over my body, setting my skin ablaze. His forearms ripple as he's momentarily taken out of the moment. "We can do this the easy way or the hard way, Sydney. And I'd rather not do it the hard way."

"That depends."

"On what?"

"What the easy way is."

"The easy way is you come with me up to my room where you'll sleep tonight. Tomorrow, you'll tell us everything you know, answer all of our questions, and maybe, if you're lucky, we'll let you go home where you can get scooped up by other psychopaths who may want you out of the way," he tells me.

I sniff, my head tilting as I lower my hands slowly, crossing my arms over my chest. "At least buy me dinner first," is what I decide to say, and only after the words leave my mouth do I think, *hey, saying that may not be the greatest idea you've ever had*.

I'm not sure where the newfound confidence has come from, but I'm happy I'm not as terrified as I was.

"The hard way," Ronan continues, his gun still pointed at my head, his arm unwavering, "is I bring you down in the basement, throw you in one of our cells, and keep you there until you eventually get so hungry you have no choice but to give us what we want. Or die."

My eyes narrow as my spine straightens. Neither one of those options sounds good to me, but what choice do I have?

"Why are you doing this?" I ask him quietly.

He shrugs. "We have to stop what your parents started. You know what they've done is horrible. I'm not sure why you're fighting so hard."

"People tend to fight against what they don't understand," I tell him. "I don't know who you are, or what this place is or who Jerry truly is to me. I don't know anything right now. I'm not going to work with you like this."

Ronan considers this, running his other hand through his hair as he lowers his gun just slightly.

But he doesn't say anything.

We stare at each other, and I swear he can see right through me. He can see everything I've been through, everything I've hidden deep inside. I know he can't, but I know that at some point, if I stay here, he's going to tear me open little by little, and he will. He'll know everything soon enough.

It feels violating. It feels exciting.

"I choose the easy way," I murmur, dropping my gaze. Me and basements don't work. I wonder if he knows that somehow.

But mostly, I know when to stand down.

"Good girl," he says, and I'm just about to open my mouth when he tucks his gun into the back of his pants, leans down, and scoops me into his arms, setting off for the stairs.

"What are you doing?" I seethe.

"I'm carrying you to my room. I'm not letting you go first because you don't know where you're going, and I'm not going to go first and give you time to run again. This is the next best option."

I'm smart enough to stop arguing as he climbs the narrow metal stairs. It dawns on me that all he has to do is toss me over the edge of the railing, and I could be dead.

On the first level, he kicks in one of the doors and brings me inside.

The warm smell of whiskey suddenly wraps around me like a hug as Ronan tosses me roughly onto the bed.

"Get some sleep," he says. "I'll explain everything I can tomorrow, okay? Will you just do what I ask if I promise you that?"

I nod. It's all I can ask for right now. Some answers.

SEVEN

RONAN

SYDNEY FINALLY FALLS asleep in my bed, cocooned in my comforter. It's getting chilly here, and she's been sweaty with fear all night. I really hope she doesn't get sick.

My thumb runs across my lip as I watch her from the loveseat in the corner of my room, measuring the steady rise and fall of the blankets. I shouldn't care about her health.

I've been a Fallen Angel for, well, I would say as long as I can remember, but for me, that's only about ten years. A spy that infiltrated his own government. An informant. I've worked hard to build up my resume, gaining the trust of my peers.

But I'm watching them all, keeping them in check.

Most importantly, I'm keeping a close eye on the politicians and high-powered individuals who belong to a specific secret society within the US. We're not sure what they're planning. Not even quite sure who is part of it, but we know it's there and they have connections we can only dream of knowing.

But they don't know about us. We're sure about that after we took out Senator Bernard Huxley just a few months ago after he kidnapped his daughter, a Fallen Angel whom he killed years ago, and didn't understand what was going on. He wanted answers for the secret society. Thankfully, he didn't get any. Not that it would have mattered. He was dead before he would have been able to hand over our secrets. We weren't even the ones to kill him.

I lean back in the chair, thinking about what will happen in the coming days.

Jerry has had a chip on her shoulder since the moment I met her. She's one of the few of us who remembers life before the Fallen Angels, and there's a good reason for that. Although Sydney is a means to an end, and although I think she's annoying, I also think that she's fairly innocent. Just someone trying to live her life. Someone trying desperately to leave the past in the past and to not let it creep into her future.

But some people can't run from our pasts like we can. Like I have.

While I've had my memories wiped, my past is a kaleido-scope of color I'll never possibly recollect. Some don't have that benefit. Some people have to live with what's happened to them.

And I feel pity for them.

I'd rather run.

I think Sydney and I are similar in that way.

Sighing, I get up from my spot and head for the bathroom, swiping a pair of sweats and a T-shirt on my way by my dresser. Closing the door softly so as to not disturb her sleep, I slip off my clothes, turning on the shower in the process. It's been a long day, and all I want to do is close my eyes for a few hours before I have to get up and have what is likely to be another difficult, taxing day as I deal with whatever bullshit Jerry throws my way.

Don't get me wrong, I adore Jerry. We all do here. She's like the sister none of us have. She's family, the glue that keeps us together. But with that comes a lot of bullshit. A lot of things are just thrown at us without a care in the world because she knows she'll get away with it.

It's how she started to lead us. We never elected her to the spot. None of our handlers gave her the position. She took it.

You have to respect it.

Stepping into the cold shower, I turn the shower handle, warming the water up. I need my muscles to let go of the built-up stress.

I need to relax.

I also need to stop thinking about Sydney.

Something about her makes me want to go soft on her, and it feels unnatural. I've never gone soft on anyone, especially not when they're standing between me and a mission I need to complete.

Yet she is. And all I want to do is tell her that things are going to be okay and give her all of the information Jerry wants to keep from her.

What we're doing suddenly feels unfair, despite the fact that we've brought men here to die before, promising them a life after they spill their souls to us, only to leave them to starve in the basement, burying them out back in the woods, never to be found.

We were trained to be soulless. To do what is required of us without question. To feel nothing as we spill blood. *It's for the greater good*, they say to us. For the most part, they're right.

Some of what we do really is for the greater good. But at what cost?

What settles my soul in those cases is that the men deserve it. Every single one of them. Sometimes, the world is just simply better without horrible people.

But Sydney isn't horrible.

In fact, she's not half bad at all.

I've been trying far too hard to dislike her, it occurred to me tonight as I waited in the kitchen until I heard the soft pop of a door. She's not half bad. Honestly, she's easier to deal with than Jerry. Sure, she's infuriating sometimes, but I've dealt with much worse.

I like her spunk. Her attitude. The way she settled down tonight, her feisty side coming out. I like someone challenging me. Telling me no.

I'm not sure when the switch happened, but I think it was when she spit on me. Through the rage, I couldn't help but think of how strong she is to fight back. I admire the balls she had to do it.

Stepping out of the shower, I grab my towel and dry off before pulling on my clothes. Leaning against the counter, I look at myself in the mirror.

We just have to get through the next couple of days, and it'll be back to normal.

The mission is simple. The second we have the information we need, we'll go on our separate ways, never to speak again. She'll go on trying to forget, and suddenly, we'll be a distant memory one day.

I grab a small blanket and head back to the loveseat, stretching my legs out in front of me as I sink into the back cushion, closing my eyes.

———

A loud knock on the door wakes me from my sleep.

Shooting up, I look around the room, noticing Sydney still peacefully asleep in bed.

I head to the door, opening it just a crack to find Jerry, looking as rested as ever.

"I want you guys downstairs in ten," she demands, looking past me into the room.

I yawn, wiping my hand across my face. "How do you even know she's in here?"

Her head tilts, irritation clouding her eyes. "I'm not an

idiot. I know you wouldn't have left her down there. Plus, you look like shit. Clearly you didn't sleep well."

She's got me there.

"I'll be down soon," I say, rolling my eyes.

Pushing off the wall, she gives me one last look before heading back down the stairs. I can hear the others in the kitchen making breakfast.

Groaning, I turn back toward the bed as I wonder how the hell I'm going to get Sydney up.

It starts by nudging her. When that doesn't work, I try yanking the comforter from her.

"Go away, Adam," she moans, rolling over on the other side of the blanket and weighing it down.

I know who Adam is. Why he'd be waking her up, I'm not sure.

Rolling my eyes, I head to the bathroom, filling a cup sitting next to the sink. Returning to the bedroom, I don't wait a single second before throwing the contents onto her head.

And that does the trick.

Screaming, Sydney sits upright in bed, her eyes throwing daggers at me as she seethes.

"What the *hell* was that for?"

"You weren't waking up," I smirk, setting the cup down on my nightstand before rifling through drawers and finding a pair of jeans and a T-shirt.

"My shirt is wet, you asshole,"

I look back toward her as she pulls her shirt from her body. Sure enough, the entire top half clings to her. "That's unfortunate," I tell her, turning back before I can focus too much on the hard peaks of her nipples showing through it.

"What am I going to wear?"

"That sounds like a you problem. Figure it out. It'll dry eventually." I cringe at how much I sound like her sister.

"Can I at least take a shower?"

I think about it for a second, almost inclined to say yes. Maybe she wouldn't be as much of a bitch.

But we don't have time.

"Not right now. If you tell us everything we need to know, then maybe. But Jerry wants us downstairs in a couple minutes."

She groans as I pass by the bed and into the bathroom to change, flopping back down on my mattress. If she weren't so infuriating, I think it would be cute.

It's definitely over ten minutes by the time we're downstairs, and judging by the tense look on Jerry's face, she's not pleased with me about it.

I shrug, not knowing what else I can really do.

Sydney drops into the chair Jerry was sitting in the night prior, immediately crossing her arms over her chest with a huff. Her hair is tangled, and her shirt still wet, clinging to her body. My eyes linger a moment too long, and I mentally slap myself out of it.

There's no interest there.

"Nice of you to join us," Jerry tells her as she leans back against the couch, her arms outstretched on either side of her. To the right sits Brandon and Elena, sitting a little closer than they usually do. Upon seeing my eyes on them, Elena narrows hers, scooting away just an inch. Zach is to the left of Jerry, his oversized shirt swallowing him whole as he shoots a smile at Sydney.

The light tapping of toenails alerts me to Maverick's arrival. Jerry's Doberman, a rescue she took from a terrible man a couple of years ago. He's one of the sweetest dogs you'll ever meet, but he looks intimidating as hell.

Walking up to Sydney, Maverick sniffs her once, his ears flattening as he looks back at his mom and back to Sydney, almost confused. Sydney sits, exhausted, and watches as the dog decides she's not worth the brainpower and goes to sit beneath Jerry's legs.

"Are you guys going to tell me what this is?" Sydney asks, bored.

"Are you going to tell us what we want to know?" Jerry replies in a mocking tone, annoyed.

Sydney doesn't flinch. She's her parents' daughter. It just took her a bit to settle. "I could possibly do that if you told me what it is you wanted to know."

Jerry's eyes narrow as she grinds her molars and watches her, the room silent.

"This is Elena," I start, figuring introductions are the best place to begin. "That's Brandon and Zach. We have one other person who lives here full time, Kim, but she's out on a mission right now and isn't going to be back for quite some time."

Jerry looks over at Zach, a pout on her full lips. "Did you scare her off?" she asks, humor in her voice.

"I didn't do anything!"

Brandon rolls his eyes. "They got in a fight before they left, so she's probably going to take even longer to come home."

"We resolved it before she left; everything is fine."

Elena props her head on her hand, looking at Sydney. "They do this all the time."

"*What* other time has this happened?" Zach throws up his hands, exasperated.

Jerry thinks for a second. "Literally any time either of you go on a mission. There's always drama. Every time."

"I don't mean to be a bitch," Sydney starts, and something tells me that the next thing that comes out of her mouth is going to be *super* bitchy. "But I don't give a shit who these people are. Tell me what I have to do to get out of here."

Jerry claps her hands in front of her, a smile tugging at her lips as she pulls her pack of cigarettes from where they're tucked between her thighs, taking one out and lighting it. Brandon and Elena scooch away quietly. "Well, sister of mine, as I said last night, mommy and daddy dearest weren't exactly upstanding citizens. They got into a lot of trouble. Trouble that I now need to clean up."

"I know they weren't good people," Sydney tells her, hurt creeping into her voice. "I grew up with them. Why don't we start by you telling me what the fuck happened to you."

This isn't going to go over well.

"Well," Jerry starts, cracking her neck, "as you know, mom and dad grew up in a cult. A cult that wasn't exactly, should I say, fond of women."

"I knew they grew up in a cult, but I didn't know any of the details. They wanted me far away from them."

"Yeah, well, they're not exactly the voice of morality either," Jerry says, her voice dripping with sarcasm. "The cult, much like many, was incredibly invasive regarding women's bodily autonomy. Their choices were never their own, and the cult had to involve themselves in every single aspect of their existence. That included what happened when they had kids.

"Instead of just simply, let's say, leaving, mom and dad conformed to it until it was too late. Until your mother decided that they went too far. That moment was when they made her give me up at the hospital. A hospital in which they controlled."

"Why would they make them do that?" Sydney asks, crossing her legs underneath her as she leans forward just slightly, her eyebrows drawn together.

"Because cults don't like powerful women, and the more women are born into the cult, the more opportunity for women to come into power." Jerry shrugs as if it's the simplest answer in the world. "There are some people who are simply stuck in the past, and this cult was packed full of 'em. You think the US Government is bad?" Jerry scoffs, "This was another level."

"Why didn't I know any of this?"

"Fuck if I know." Jerry shrugs. "The cult only allowed one girl. Women could have as many boys as they possibly wanted. But only one girl. If they already had one girl, they were forced to have an abortion or to give the kid up. One thing was clear, and it was that women weren't allowed to have any chance at power. No chance at growing within the cult."

"But they left somehow."

"From what I heard, your mom felt terrible for giving me up. She was sick over it, but dad told her to knock it off. That it was what they had to do. That I would never know anything different. Like that would make it okay."

Sydney looks down at her hands, contemplating this.

"Things were fine until I turned twelve and was bounced from my foster home to another one. They weren't as nice there," Jerry tells her, her eyes never once leaving Sydney's. "I ran away the second I could. For years I'd be bounced from foster home to foster home, suffering abuse at the hands of some lame man who shouldn't be trusted with children, only to run away again. Eventually, I wasn't dragged back.

"I was around seventeen and looking for a job somewhere. At that point, I had been on my own for a month, homeless. Then I met Veronica, who brought me here." She gestures around her. "I met Ronan then, and we became friends. He was nineteen. We were just babies, trying to figure things out."

"What is this place?" Sydney asks, now fully leaning forward on her forearms, taking in the story.

"I think it's your turn," Jerry tells her.

"What do you want to know?"

"What's your earliest memory?"

Sydney thinks for a moment, pondering the question as

her hands start to rub together in her lap. Her tongue peeks out to run over her bottom lip before she bites it, nervous. "I don't know," she tells her, her voice small.

"That's bullshit."

"No, I really don't. I've tried to block everything from that time out. I remember mom and dad used to take me to the country where they'd just abandon me to run in the field. I remember my nanny running after me. I also remember the day my nanny, well," she takes a deep breath, closing her eyes. "I remember when the nanny was caught. I don't remember what she did. All I remember was her body dropping in front of mine, and asking dad why she was bleeding. Whether I should call someone to help her."

"Was that the first time you saw them kill someone?" I ask her.

Sydney nods, her eyes squeezing shut even tighter. "It was the first time but far from the last."

"Do you know what they did for work?" Jerry asks.

"I know that the company they work for is a front," Sydney says with a nod, tipping her head back to the ceiling. "I know that Atlee Enterprises is a front for something horrible. I don't know the specifics. I've tried running from it my entire life. I didn't want to know about it. Do you think they were still tied to the cult?"

Jerry shakes her head. "They may still have had ties to it. I know dad had a few business partners, but they left the cult a couple years after giving me up. Mom couldn't take it anymore, and if there was one thing that dad loved more than the cult, more than all the money and power that came his way, it was mom. They wanted to make their own way."

"How do you know this?" Sydney asks her sister.

Jerry shrugs. "I've followed them my whole life. Researched. They're not exactly subtle people. They're famous in the criminal underworld. Infamous, really, among criminals. No one liked them, yet they had all the respect in the world."

Sydney considers this, nodding.

"And who are you guys? What do you do?"

Jerry looks at me, considering what she should tell her sister. If it were up to me, it would be everything, but I'm not sure why. Sydney doesn't deserve it. Not more than anyone else we question. And yet, something about her seems so familiar. Well, I know why *that* is. But I mean something... I don't know. I don't like the woman, but I think I'd have some serious problems telling her no if she asked really, really nicely. If she lost the attitude.

Maybe it really is just because of Jerry. I've been under her thumb for so long that I don't remember what it feels like to be my own person. To make my own decisions.

That being said, I wouldn't have it any other way.

"Well," Jerry starts, standing up and placing her hands on her hips. Maverick looks up at her, annoyed at her movement. "I think this is where the other part of this comes in. We need your help to take down their criminal enterprise."

Sydney looks suspicious, leaning back in her seat again as she watches her sister intently.

"I was hoping you'd know more than I do about how the company is run, who is in charge, and how to get it from him, but you don't. Thankfully, I know enough to have come up with a plan." She flicks her cigarette ash into the dish on the coffee table.

And now it's my turn to be confused. She never told me that she had a plan, and I'm usually the first one she runs things by.

"And what is this plan?" I ask her.

Jerry gestures to Sydney. "You two are going to get married."

EIGHT

SYDNEY

I COULDN'T HAVE HEARD that right.

"What do you mean we have to get *married?*" Ronan asks, his hands curled into fists at his sides, his eyes shooting lasers at the woman in front of him. The other three on the couch look at one another. Although they don't look surprised, they do look befuddled.

"I mean exactly what I said." Jerry tells him. "You two need to get married. I already arranged for someone to come here to get the papers signed. The second that happens, we can start taking down the empire."

"Why is that necessary?" I ask.

"Well, you know daddy dearest loved his old pal Jeffrey? They go way back. In fact, all the way back to the cult. But the thing is, Jeffrey never really changed his opinions on women. Neither did dad, really."

I close my eyes. I know Jeffrey. I just don't want to think about him. "What does that have to do with me? What does that have to do with getting married to—" I look him over, and he eyes me, his nose scrunching as if he smells something revolting. My eyes narrow in his direction. "—*him.*"

"Women weren't allowed to run the company," Jerry tells

me, sitting back down and crossing one leg over the other. "At all. You're the sole heir of the company, and yet it's written into their will and all contracts that you are not to take it over unless you're married. There has to be a man at the head of the company for it to be passed along."

"Who's at the head of it now?"

"Jeffrey Wright."

I shiver, immediately feeling like I'm going to be sick. If there's one thing I've never wanted, it's to be involved in that company. If there's one other thing, it's to never be in the presence of Jeffrey Wright ever again.

"I'm not going to do it," I tell her, my back straightening.

"I'm not doing it either," Ronan tells her, and I get a small amount of pleasure knowing he seems just as thrown off as I do.

"I don't think you two understand that neither of you have a choice. We've been working on taking this company down for the past three years. We didn't know much about it until recently. Only a couple of months ago, really. This is what needs to be done."

"If you know everything about it, why don't you just drop all the information off at some journalist's doorstep?"

"I don't think you understand exactly how powerful these people are," Jerry says, her voice steely. And I believe her. I don't know. I don't even remotely know. I've worked hard to keep it that way. But I know how powerful mom and dad were. At least for a time. "The second this gets out to the press anywhere, they'll be as good as dead."

"And we won't be?"

"We have something else on our side," Jerry says, looking at the others.

"What is that?"

"The CIA."

My blood turns cold. "What is going on here?"

"Welcome to Project Fallen Angel, sis."

"I need to go back home." I get up, my heart beating out of my chest. I can feel the blood racing to my ears, my neck getting hotter and hotter as my shirt suddenly feels ten times too tight.

"There's no going home. The second you go home, you're dead."

"You told me I could go home after I told you what I knew," I hiss.

"And I thought you knew a little more. I can't use anything you know, so now we're going to plan B."

"Who the hell are you. Tell me the truth," I say, stepping to the right and slowly drifting backward.

"Project Fallen Angel. Top secret black operation by the CIA. We're stationed all over the country to keep everything in check."

"But, that's ill—"

"Illegal since 1947. Yes, I know." Jerry rolls her eyes as if this is something she's heard dozens of times. I doubt anyone would get this far with her, though. Not unless they were going to die after she told them.

This isn't something you tell someone who will be a free woman after this.

"It's not exactly a secret that the CIA doesn't exactly do what it's told. There have been dozens of projects conducted on US soil since the National Security Act was signed."

"Project MK-Ulta," Elena says, and my head whips to her. I had forgotten she was there, too focused on the story my sister was telling me.

"Project SHAMROCK was a big one, but that was kind of a sister project of Project MINARET from before the act was signed," Zach says, stretching his back.

"Hell, in the 60's, they had Operation CHAOS," Brandon states, throwing his hand up before slapping it on his leg.

"Okay, that's enough," Jerry barks, annoyed at the explanations. "The CIA has never once done what it was supposed to. Why do you think they would start now?"

"What do you do?" I ask, half curious and half terrified.

"We all do different things. Elena is an informant, Zach gathers intel, Brandon does, well, I'm not actually quite sure what Brandon does, if I'm quite honest with you. Ronan is a deep cover agent and an informant."

I look them over, watching their faces as they watch me intently, trying to figure out what I'm thinking. For a moment, just a moment, I forget that I was just told that I have to marry Ronan.

I have so many more questions, but they'll have to wait.

Anxiety grips my stomach, twisting it as pain starts up in my lower abdomen. I feel like a knife is scraping my insides, and I close my eyes, trying not to show fear. I don't have time for pain right now, especially when it's my own body turning against me.

"I need to go home."

"You can't do that," Jerry says, her voice monotone. "If you're not killed, you're going to get arrested. You're going to be put in this very same position, except you won't get a chance to fix what your parents did wrong. No. You'll be arrested, put on trial for their wrongdoings, and you'll be put in a jail cell for the rest of your pathetic, miserable life, where you'll likely die. Here, I'm giving you a chance to really do something good with your life. To make a difference."

I feel my eyes well with tears as I look around, desperate to go anywhere but here. I just want to go home, back to my bed. Back to Adam and Shiloh.

And a deep, deep hatred for my parents claws its way to my heart, sinking in and slowly taking over. They left me with this. I've tried to run for so long, and they left me with this anyway. This mess. Something that could so easily ruin my life.

"Do you know what their company does?" Jerry asks.

I shake my head. I don't. Not really.

"They hire mercenaries for high-powered individuals. They don't ask questions. They just do. Someone wants a competitor taken out? Done. Someone wants a climate activist who's been grating on their nerves dead? They make it look like a suicide. After all, there really is a mental health crisis in this country. These people have no regard for human life and no empathy for a single individual. All they see is the price of death. The money they get for taking someone out. That's all they care about. Do you know how many good people have been murdered by them? How difficult they've made our lives as people who have to keep these idiots in control?"

I shake my head.

"They've taken whole families out, Sydney. Entire bloodlines. Just because some man sitting in a leather chair somewhere asked for it to happen. Our parents have wiped out whole families, do you understand that? They've approved that call. They've exchanged cash for it. And you know what? Mom and dad didn't have the fucking *balls* that Jeffery Wright does. However horrible they were, triple it. Jeffrey knows what he's doing. He has an in with way more politicians. Way more powerful people. Mom and dad stuck to murder for hire, but Jeffrey Wright is going to dabble in world conflicts."

I feel my skin grow clammy as my vision grows blurry. I don't want this. I don't want the responsibility; I don't want the hurt that this is going to cause.

I feel like I'm running from something I shouldn't. Like this is my responsibility to fix, but I know it's not. At least, that's what my therapist would say.

If I changed, well, every single part of this story for our session.

I black out.

Fifteen years ago

The sun beats down on my face as I lay in the tall grass. The sound of birds chirping and construction vehicles surrounds me, and I try my best to stay in the moment.

This peaceful moment. A moment where nothing else exists but me and nature.

I wish it would swallow me whole.

"Sweetie?" I hear my mom call from up the hill. I turn, finding her standing there, wiping her hands on a towel.

It wasn't long ago that I heard the gun go off. I'm not sure who it was this time or what they did, but I know they probably didn't deserve it.

"Yeah?" I call out.

"We're going to have dinner in ten, okay? Jeffrey's here."

I nod, my blood running cold as I turn back around and plop my body back down on the hard ground.

It seems like my peace is over for the night.

We'll be leaving tomorrow, and I can't help but imagine the day I get out of here.

The only thing I'll miss is this place.

Back home, I have no friends. My parents send me to an elite private school. You're only supposed to be surrounded by the best, *they would say to me. But what friends I do have don't actually like me. They're made to be friends with me to get their parents in Mom and Dad's good graces, hoping that, at some point, they can help them.*

I don't think any of them actually know what they do. What actually happens in their home, at work, and even here.

But I do.

And it's something I wish to forget.

We've been coming here for as long as I can remember. Twelve years of my life, and this has been the only place I feel like myself. Like I can be normal.

I fist the dirt in my hand, feeling it sift through my fingers as I let it go. Tiny pebbles scratch at my skin.

I don't know why this place feels more home than home is. There are far more bodies buried here. More secrets.

But here, I can get away from it. I can pretend I don't see it.

I try not to think about how many bodies are buried underneath me.

I come to with a start, blinking away the stars clouding my vision. My hand reaches out, and I can almost feel the grass beneath me. Instead, I feel concrete.

Sitting up with a start, my eyes wide, I look around at all the faces looking at me, wondering what's wrong.

I don't feel like talking to them anymore. I have nothing else to say, nothing to hide.

"I don't have anything else to say to you," I tell Jerry, who sits perched on the edge of the couch, her body propped up on her elbows as she leans toward me, her head tilted. "Please let me go."

"We can't; I'm sorry," she says, sounding anything but sorry. "You and Ronan will get married tomorrow, and then we're taking this company down."

"Jerry, I've run from this my whole life—"

"Like a coward."

I stop, the words caught in my throat. "I've done everything I could."

"No, you haven't. You ran the second you could, but you still benefitted from them, didn't you? You were able to afford a fancy new college because of your connections. I'm willing to bet that you still get paid by them, don't you?"

I sputter, unsure what to say. She knows the answer. If she's bringing this up, she knows.

"You've benefited from who your parents are, what they do, and how much money they make. You still receive blood money from them. Doesn't that make you feel bad? If you really wanted to run?"

I close my eyes, sinking into myself. "They were controlling. They knew where I was at all times. It was their form of control. I couldn't get a job unless they approved, but I had to live—"

"You didn't *have* to do anything, Sydney. You're a coward. A selfish coward who will make absolutely nothing of herself unless she grows some fucking balls and stands up to them."

"They're *dead!*" I scream, my chest heaving as my entire body shakes, my skin heating.

The others have left, I'm just realizing, leaving only Jerry and I here. But there's no doubt in my mind that they're off listening somewhere.

"And you will be, too if you don't get your head out of your ass and see things for what they are," Jerry seethes, standing up to tower over me.

I push myself up more, climbing to my feet.

But she's right.

I've let fear control me for my entire life. Let them hold money above my head, let them control me as I swore I was free. I was never free. I'm still not free, and I don't think I ever will be.

"I want to go home," I tell her, my shoulders slumping.

She shakes her head. "It's not going to happen. Ronan!" she calls. "Take her upstairs."

NINE

RONAN

"WE'RE NOT FINISHED with this conversation," I tell Jerry as I grab Sydney, bringing her upstairs. "I'll be down in a minute, and we're sorting this out. This is my life too, Jerry."

She rolls her eyes, flopping back down on the couch.

Sydney is like putty in my hands, all but given up. The dark circles under her eyes age her, and I feel an unfamiliar twist in my stomach, like a knife.

I tell myself I just don't like seeing women upset.

"Hang out in here while I figure things out, okay? I got this; I'll get us out of this mess," I assure her, but my voice lacks confidence. I'm not sure if I can talk my way out of this. I'm not sure if I can really help her. Once Jerry has something in her mind, she's like a dog with a bone. She's not going to risk it. She's not going to drop it. Not ever.

If this is the only option she thinks we have, we're screwed.

Sydney nods, looking up at me with her large, scared eyes. She tries to play tough, but I can see right through it.

This woman just wants to be free. If turning her head from the ugliness of her world is the only way to do that, then that's how it has to be.

"There are towels in the cabinet in the bathroom. Go take a shower and wash off."

She nods again, heading off in that direction.

Not wanting to take any risks, I grab the angled stopper from behind the door. Closing it, I shove it into the opening on the bottom from the outside, effectively locking her in the room if she tried to run while I wasn't watching her.

Heading back downstairs, I take a seat opposite Jerry.

"Are you going to tell me what the fuck that was?" I ask her, fuming.

She shrugs, tossing her black hair over her shoulder. "I'm pretty sure you know what that was. It's time we stop this. She's the only way we can get in. This is the fastest, most effective way of taking them down, and you know that."

"That doesn't mean I have to agree to *marry* your *sister* against her will—against *my* will, to get that done."

"Actually, it does," she says as she crosses her legs underneath of her, her posture cool and collected. The very opposite of what I'm feeling.

"Jerry, there are other ways."

"What are they?"

"I don't pretend to know the answers. I have no idea, but I know there's something better than this. She doesn't have to be involved."

"She's going to be involved no matter what," Jerry snaps, her eyes turning cold. "She's taken money from them. She still gets money from them to this very day. You saw those statements. She's getting funded by them, and even if she were innocent, even if somehow there's another way and she can go off on her merry way and forget about all of this, there are still people out there who are likely to take her out for this very reason."

"What do you mean?"

"You think those men don't know that the second she gets

married, if someone knows who her parents were, or if she comes around to the idea of what they do, that she won't take it? Do you seriously hear how fucking stupid you guys sound?" she asks, throwing her hands up. It makes me think that the others weren't exactly for this idea either when she ran it by them. "If those men standing at the top of that fucking company had any sense . any sense at all, they'd kill her. It's the one and only way they can be sure that she'll never burn that company to the fucking ground."

I sit back, thinking it over. I know not to argue too hard with Jerry when she's like this. But I also know that although I wish she didn't, she has a point. Even if we let her go home, she really would be killed at some point. And what's worse is that she wouldn't see it coming. If she's so intent on not having anything to do with her family, she's not going to be looking at what's right in front of her.

She has a lot worse to worry about than marrying me.

"The second this is over, you guys can get an annulment. Or a divorce. Whatever works," Jerry assures. "It's not like you have to be stuck with her for your whole life." I open my mouth to reply, but she isn't done. "Not that it matters."

"What's that supposed to mean?" I ask.

"You're acting like you're waiting for someone. Like you're dating someone, and I'm asking you to marry this girl."

A surge of anger shoots through me. "*That girl* is your sister. I don't like her any more than you do, but if you're asking her to be a part of this and risk her life, I think you need to be a little more appreciative of what she's doing."

Jerry rolls her eyes.

"And I don't have to be actively seeking a relationship in order to feel bad about being forced to marry someone, Jerry." In fact, I haven't had a single relationship the entire time I've been here. They never interested me. I was here for my job. Besides, bonding with someone is a little hard when you're in this kind of work. Whoever I'm seeing can't come over here, and I have to make sure my stories are lined up at all times.

I've thought about it, sure. Which is why I know that relationships just aren't for me. Not now and not ever.

I have my hand for other needs.

With a flick of her wrist, Jerry turns around, heading to the kitchen to grab a water.

"Jerry, we're not done talking," I say as I follow her, watching as she reaches the fridge. I feel like I've been saying that a lot lately. Without a care in the world, she takes a bottle of water out before jumping on the counter, taking a sip as she swings her legs.

"We're done. This is happening. Preferably tomorrow, but if it has to be pushed another day, that's fine."

"And what am I supposed to tell Sydney?"

"I don't really care what you tell her," she says, setting the bottle next to her. "I just care that it gets done. She may be freaking out right now, but that girl has a moral compass that doesn't let up. She'll come around and help."

"How do you know that?"

"You know I've kept watch on her for years. You want to take down my parents' empire, and she wants to make things right. The second I called her out, I saw the wheels turn. Just watch. She's going to come around."

I shake my head, feeling as if I can combust. "That's not the point, Jerry."

"I'm done arguing," she says as she jumps down, heading to the stairs. I grab her arm, forcing her to look at me again. She looks at my hand, her gaze drifting slowly up to mine. "That girl has a heart of gold. You never have. Don't go soft on me now, Ronan."

With a shake of her shoulder, Jerry is on her way. Without a second glance, she ascends the stairs to her room.

I stand in the middle of the compound, wondering what the hell I'm going to do.

If Jerry makes us do this, I know Sydney is going to make my life a living hell. I've seen that side of her. No matter how much we may try to break her, she's going to come back.

Seething, I head up the stairs and back into my room, finding Sydney sitting in a towel on my bed.

"What are you doing?" I ask her.

"You told me to take a shower."

"That doesn't mean you can just sit around naked," I snap, but quickly realize it's not her I'm angry at.

I watch her face as it falls, her eyes drifting to the floor. I'm just about to apologize when her head snaps up, her eyes suddenly hard. Steely. Wicked. "I assume there's no way of getting out of this, is there?" she asks.

I shake my head, confirming.

She nods, biting her lip, her eye contact unwavering. "I guess we have to get comfortable with each other then," she says as she stands. Before I know it, the towel is on the floor as she runs her fingers through her hair.

I stare at her, not giving her the reaction she wants, but I won't lie and say that her body doesn't stir something in me. All muscle, curves, and temptation. "I don't think that will be necessary," I tell her, heading to my dresser to get her some clothes.

"You don't want people thinking we're strangers, do you?" Her head tilts, a smirk tugging at her lips.

Running my hand across my forehead, I turn back to her. "Out of all the women I've ever been with, I'd put you last on the list of women I want to touch," I bite back and instantly feel horrible.

But she doesn't back down. Instead, she crosses her arms over her chest, narrowing her eyes.

Whipping out a pair of sweats and a t-shirt, I toss them at her before leaving the room once more.

I've told a lot of lies, but none have ever felt as false crossing my lips.

. . .

Ten years ago

The building in front of me stands tall, its walls crumbling around it. Surrounded by broken-down cars, abandoned, shredded tires, microwaves, and TVs, the place looks like any other abandoned warehouse in any city.

"We're here," the woman beside me says, clasping her hands in front of her.

"This is where I'm going to be living from now on?" I ask, wondering how the hell that could be.

"You're going to fit in just fine, I promise."

I don't believe her.

My lips press into a firm line as she gets out of her seat and swings the back door to the van open, the summer heat hitting me like a wall.

I've been awake for a month now, running through the CIA Project Fallen Angel program with ease.

The first week was used to create my background. I chose my new name. I was told why this job is important and even taught about the Fallen Angels' history, who it was created by, and what they've been working on.

The second week started training. Every day I would be training with someone, learning to fight. There were multiple days when I was taught about torture. I was waterboarded, prodded, threatened, and almost beaten to death.

But I came out of it okay. Stronger.

Mentally ready for what was to come.

The rest of the month was a mix of it all. I met with various people from the project and was placed with the DC Fallen Angels.

So far, there's really only one person there full-time. Others are coming soon, but they come and go as they wish.

Jerry Flannigan.

I wasn't sure what to make of her initially, and I'm still unsure.

I hope living with her proves different than our first meeting, as that went, well, poor.

Jerry has a knack for being an asshole, I was told, but she means well.

Means well, my ass.

Unlike most of us, Jerry never got her memory wiped. She had a choice, they said.

I haven't entirely made up my mind on whether I'm jealous of this or not. On one hand, I think it's incredible to understand where you came from. Only having a month of memories makes me feel like a ghost. Like I'm not a real person. I'm almost twenty, and yet I know nothing.

Nineteen years of memories are just gone.

Who am I? Who was I to others back home?

Why am I here?

What happened to me?

Part of me desperately wants to know, while another part doesn't. Another part of me understands that there's nothing natural about this.

I was told that I died. That the CIA found me and gave me a second chance at life.

But who are they to play God?

Who are they to determine when someone can get another chance? When they can breathe another breath.

Sometimes if someone was meant to die, they were meant to die.

And I was meant to die.

I was told that this would be a natural thing to think about. To ponder. To stress about. But I'm not sure. This doesn't feel natural. This doesn't feel good.

This feels like I'm suffocating.

Veronica leads me through the large metal doors of the compound. The place is empty except for a small kitchen space in the middle and a makeshift living room in front of it.

There is only one floor with what looks like hurriedly made

rooms to the right. The walls are plywood, the doors just cutouts covered by a tarp.

The place looks absolutely insane.

"This can't be real," I mumble, swiping my hand through my short hair.

"We're working on it," Jerry says as she steps out of her room, the crinkling noise of the tarp echoing through the large space as she does.

I'm not sure I'll ever be able to sleep here.

"Working on what?" I ask, eyeing her as she pulls on a sweater. It's the middle of summer, but for some reason, this place feels cold.

Pulling on a pair of worn-out combat boots, Jerry hops on one foot, steadying herself on the makeshift wall. The entire structure moves.

"We're working on making the space more livable. It's going to take some time, but I pleaded with the Agency. They're sending some people to start working on it soon."

Oh?

I take a look around. "Why is it a warehouse? Other compounds are real houses."

Jerry shrugs, her red hair spilling over her shoulders. "Who knows. It's scary, looks abandoned, and it's out of the way."

Reasonable.

Veronica comes up behind me, a grin on her face. "How do you like it?" she asks.

I don't answer.

Jerry winks.

TEN

SYDNEY

THE SECOND he leaves the room, I allow all the panic I've felt to take over again. My hands shake as I feel electrical shocks make their way down my legs. Grabbing the clothes he tossed at me, I pull them on, feeling bloated and in pain.

I have a life at home that I'm not ready to give up. I have friends—well, one friend. A cat. A job. Not one that I care much about, that's for sure, but I don't want to just leave all of that in the past.

And I don't have my phone to tell Adam to feed Shiloh. I can't just leave him to starve. If I died in that little apartment, I'd happily let that little man eat my corpse to keep him full. I'd do anything for him.

I've never had anything stable in my life. Not family, not jobs, not relationships. Nothing. Everyone has left me; everything has fallen apart. Every single boyfriend I've ever had has chosen jobs over me. Every single friend other than Adam has left because of my instability. The only thing I've been able to rely on is the money coming in from my parents, a desperate attempt to keep me tied to them. But what choice did I have when I was constantly mysteriously losing my job?

How can I run from that? Or when I was so buried under medical debt that I couldn't breathe?

In the back of my mind, I've always thought about where that money comes from. But when it's my only choice of survival, I'm not sure what else I can do.

I was good with it. It may look like I'm well off, but I save every penny I can, hoping that one day I can somehow cut them out for good until I figure out how to really get out from under them. The key is making it look like I spend it. DC has a lot of rich people, and at the end of a semester, there's almost always nice, expensive things left out at the curb for people to take. That's how I found my dream apartment for cheap, too. The college girls that rented it before I moved in wallpapered the place, and instead of paying to take it down, the landlord tried to sell it as is. Turns out that a lot of people don't want silver walls. To me, it was charming, and I was able to swindle him into giving it to me for much cheaper.

But cheaper is still DC prices, meaning it's not cheap at all. But it's what I needed. I needed the extra security in the building. I didn't feel safe without it. I got my apartment for cheaper than it's worth, but it's still a pretty penny. It's the one thing I choose to spend a large amount on. If I didn't, I wouldn't be able to sleep.

I've been there, done that.

I don't want to feel bad for the money, but I do. I know where that comes from. I know how it's earned, and I do feel somewhat responsible, even if I shouldn't.

Groaning, I run my fingers through my hair, thinking about what I should do. There has to be something in here that I can use. Something that can get me out of this mess.

I don't know how much time I have.

I race to his closet, throwing it open and looking along the ground to find something. Anything. I have no idea what I'm looking for, but this is the only chance I have. These people aren't going to let me go home.

Ronan keeps his things neat. His closet is full of mostly black slacks hung neatly over hangers, black suit jackets, and white button-up shirts. The floor is lined with various shoes, so shiny they reflect the little light above.

Crawling along the back, I run my fingers across the floor, along the baseboards, and under shoes before standing up and doing the same to the ledge above. Not even a speck of dust comes away on my fingers, and I start to lose hope.

Closing the door gently, I go to his dresser, opening the smallest to find rolls upon rolls of neat black socks piled neatly. I move my fingers under them, careful not to displace them too much, but needing to see if there's anything there. Everyone keeps shit in their sock drawer, right? There's gotta be secrets in here.

But I don't find anything. I move on, opening each drawer and finding, well, not much. Every drawer is neat, and every drawer is full of simple, neutral clothing.

There's nothing fun, much less anything I can actually use.

I can feel my panic growing in my gut as I move around the room, snooping around everything I can see. Finally, I move onto the bed, peeking underneath.

And there's a box. Interesting.

Pulling it out, I run my hands over the smooth metal, holding my breath. Popping it open, I finally find something that may be of use to me.

A key.

It's a car key, that much I know. It looks weird. Like something you'd see in a sci-fi movie. Like a key to some sort of spaceship. Or at least, that's what I think of. It's black with a silver crest in the middle, broken up as if the crest were made out of a 'W.'

I don't know what it's to, but it's my only shot right now.

I quietly pocket it, careful to close the box back up and place it *exactly* where it was before I messed with it. I don't need him barging in here, huffing and puffing and accusing me of stealing his shit, even if that's exactly what I'm doing.

I need to get home for a bit, at the very least. I'm not naïve. I know that they'll find me again. I know that if they don't find me, someone else will. I get that my life could be in danger, and if someone associated with my parents doesn't find me, I'll likely be taken in by the FBI and questioned.

But I *need* to go home first, and I know they're not going to let me.

Tonight, I'm getting out of here. At least for a little bit.

───

It's been hours, and Ronan hasn't returned. I tried the door, but there's something tightly wedged in the bottom of it, preventing it from moving inward much at all. At least, not without significant effort and a lot of noise as the rubber catches on the concrete.

I still don't think I totally understand who these people are and what they do. I haven't even processed that Jerry is my twin sister completely. She was never brought up, and the more I sit with that information, the more awful I feel that she was out there, bouncing from foster home to foster home while I at least lived in a house. No matter what happened to me there, it's better than what she went through.

The thought of the CIA operating within the US isn't surprising. Like they said downstairs, it's happened before. But as I sit with it, it makes more and more sense. I know more than most that there's a deep, seedy world out there, and it's reasonable that people would want to ensure that world is kept in check.

And I start to wonder what really happened to my parents. I mean, I figured they pissed the wrong person off. That much wouldn't be surprising in the slightest. But I wonder who and why. Am I going to have to deal with them? Are they going to be after me?

Either way, I'm not really excited to stick around and find out more about them at the moment. I need to get home. I need to tell Adam what's going on, and most importantly, I need to feed my damn cat.

Wait, scratch that. I can't tell Adam about this. Not specifics, anyways. I just need to tell him something came up. That I'm fine. That I'm going to be gone for a little while. I just need him to feed Shiloh for me. Just to stop by every couple of days. Or better yet, to take him to his place. I don't need any trigger-happy idiots barging into my place looking for me only to find my cat.

I don't want to get him in trouble or put him in danger, that's for sure.

I lay on Ronan's bed, sprawled out, my arms outstretched as I look at the ceiling, counting the number of times the fan spins in a minute.

It doesn't help the time go by any faster.

Finally, after what feels like hours, I hear the door open, and Ronan's annoying face peeks in. When he spots me, he frowns, and the words he spit at me before he left come rushing back to me.

Asshole.

I saw the way he looked at me. He can pretend all he wants, but he liked what he saw.

I just wanted him to leave so I could rip apart his room.

I look out the high window, noticing that, at some point, it got dark.

My plan is happening sooner rather than later. Now I just have to figure out whether I want to do it the first opportunity I have or if I want to wait for him to go to sleep.

"Any news?" I ask him nonchalantly, sitting up and crossing my legs.

"Nope," he replies, grabbing clothes from his dresser. His

eyes linger a moment too long on his stack of boring black t-shirts, and a sliver of panic runs through me. Did he notice something was misplaced? Did I mess something up? Is he going to know I was looking for something?

But he doesn't say anything, at the very least. Instead, he just takes a shirt, digs in another drawer for shorts, and heads to the bathroom.

"I'm taking a shower," he says as he passes, the scent of whiskey following him.

I nod, keeping silent as I watch him disappear into the room.

Getting up quietly, I tiptoe to the door, opening it just a touch. Just enough to look down into the main living area. The lights are off, and no one seems to be around.

Perfect.

Waiting for him to go to bed is a gamble. I don't know if he's a light sleeper or not, and I'm not going to trust my gut enough to find out. It's gotten me in enough trouble.

Silently backing away, I turn back and grab my shoes, quietly putting them on before pressing my ear against the bathroom door, making sure I hear the sound of water splashing against the floor from him moving around. I don't want him to come out as I'm leaving, having forgotten something.

When I'm satisfied, I turn back to the door happily, feeling for the key still tucked in the oversized sweats Ronan gave me to wear. They slip down my hips slightly, but they'll work until I get home and I have my own clothes.

Opening the door just enough to slip out, I close it quietly behind me, careful not to make any noise that would alert the others to someone being up. When it's closed, I rush down the steps. I'm not going to have much time, especially when I start whichever car this belongs to.

When I'm finally in the main room, I click the button on the key fob once, praying that it doesn't make the car beep.

Instead, the interior lights come on as the car unlocks. I take a deep breath and head to the back of the room where it sits.

The thing looks insane. Like the bat mobile but more conventional. The red paint is glossy, reflecting the moonlight from the windows up on top of the walls perfectly.

It takes me a moment to figure out how to open the door, but when I do, it opens upwards like a wing. I've never been in a car like this.

It's odd that he had the key to this hidden away in his room. I wonder if they hide the keys to all of the cars. I don't think it would make sense, would it?

Despite mom and dad being rich, they didn't like drawing too much attention to their money. Something about drawing unnecessary attention their way and legal battles. Instead, they invested it into my education and their extracurricular activities. We didn't have fancy cars, especially none like this.

As I climb into the seat and figure out how to close the door, that familiar pain in my abdomen starts again, and I close my eyes, praying that it'll go away. I don't have time to deal with it right now.

I know that I have to get going, but I take a moment to breath. The second I start this, I have to go. And how do I even open the garage door? I should probably figure that out before I start this up.

Looking around, I silently pray that there's a garage opener around. I almost give up before I find a small rectangular object in the glove compartment: two buttons with up and down arrows on it.

Perfect.

Okay. One, two… three.

I turn the key in the ignition and immediately have a heart attack as it roars to life, the headlights flashing on. There's no way that someone didn't hear that.

Shit.

Looking around, I have another heart attack as I realize

that it's a stick. I don't know how to drive stick. Who the hell has time to learn. Who would buy a car with a stick, even? What's the point?

But I'm shocked when I shift it into drive that it works like any other car. I'm not going to complain. I don't know what fancy things this car has, but I'm not going to complain about it.

A door on the second floor opens, and Zach's head peeks out, his eyes wide.

I have to go now.

Clicking the garage opener, my leg shakes as I watch the door open. It's slow. Much too slow for this, as another two doors open. I should have been out of here by now.

When it's finally open just enough, I hit the gas, shooting through the space as the engine thunders. I'm thrown back in the seat, surprised at how fast the acceleration is. I'm going to have to get used to that and quick.

Before I know it, I'm flying out the front door and swerving on the unstable dirt road leading out of it, my headlights illuminating the gate ahead of me.

Shit!

Clicking the garage opener a couple of times, I'm unsurprised that it doesn't work. But I don't have any time to think about what I'm going to do. Instead, I drive through it.

Metal scrapes against the hood of the car, making me wince as the gate blows apart on impact. I don't know how fast I'm going—too scared to look away from the road—but it's fast enough.

I pull onto the road just as I see headlights flash behind me.

ELEVEN

RONAN

THIS SHOWER IS the one and only peaceful thing about my day.

I'm angry, stressed, and annoyed, but as the water sluices over my skin, I forget about everything for just a moment. Just one peaceful moment.

But that moment of peace is effectively eviscerated the second I exit the bathroom, finding my room completely empty. No menace in sight.

Grinding my teeth, I throw open the door, finding the others rushing down the stairs yelling.

"What's going on?" I ask as the nippy air hits me. The garage door is open.

"She took the Lykan," Zach yells as he runs for a car.

"What do you mean she took the Lykan? The keys are hidden."

Zach spreads his arms, exasperated. "Do you want to take a look for yourself?"

I don't have time to go back and find out how. Instead, I take two stairs at a time, nearly tripping as I head for my Camaro.

She could have chosen any of the cars in this room. Every single one of them has the keys *in* them. Yet somehow, she chose that car. The one car that the police have been looking for. She took the one goddamn car that'll get her arrested instantly if she passes by a goddamn cop.

Gritting my teeth, I watch as the others stop and watch me. "I fucked up. I'll get her," I tell them.

"And the car?"

I shake my head, making no promises.

Turning the key, the engine purrs to life, and I grip the wheel in my hands, flexing my shoulders.

It's going to be a long night.

Five years ago

"I can't believe we're doing this," Brandon says with an eye roll as we look over the sea of people in front of us.

"It's the biggest mission of our lives," Zach breathes out, a glimmer in his eye that I can only describe as insanity.

If the Agency found out what we're about to do, they'd be pissed.

And why we're doing it, I don't even know. Jerry doesn't even know.

But I'm excited for it. For one of the first times in years, I feel a glimmer of pure excitement.

A lust for life.

"Brandon, you go talk to the guards. You know your lines. Zach, go do, well, whatever the hell you're good at. Distract everyone. I'll go get the keys and find my way in, okay?"

They both salute me before walking in opposite directions as I watch below.

The car is beautiful. A deep red with black trim, this is one of the most beautiful cars in the world.

And one of the most expensive.

"What are you about to do?" a voice asks from behind me as a firm hand is placed on my shoulder. Cigarette smoke wafts over me, and I roll my eyes.

"Why are you here, Jerry?"

"You think I don't know what's going on in my own compound?"

"I trust that you wouldn't want anything to do with it."

"That, my dear friend, is where you're wrong. You're about to steal that thing, aren't you?"

I nod. "Three million on the low end. People pay more for it."

"How many are there?"

"Seven."

She whistles.

"She has a twin turbocharger and can accelerate from zero to two hundred in under 9.4 seconds."

"You guys know you'll be in deep shit if you're caught, right?"

I look to my right, taking her in.

She dressed for the occasion, that's for sure. In a blue form-fitting suit, Jerry looks stunning.

"What are you here for?"

She smiles at me, winking her charcoal-lined eye. "Hunting."

Right.

"Are you going to have any problems getting it out of here?" she asks, turning her attention back to the car in front of us.

"No. It has a seven-speed dual clutch, so it basically drives like an automatic."

Jerry makes a face. "Who would possibly want that?"

"Rich people,"

She nods.

"It has a satellite navigation system we can use, but we're going to have to hack it to make sure that we're not tracked. That's going to be the biggest feat. Other than that, it's just wicked cool. A great addition to our collection."

Over the last five years, Jerry and the other new Fallen Angels and I have bonded over stealing cars. We're not totally proud of it, but it's fun and we can get away with it. It's something to pass the time, and that makes it good enough for me.

We've collected twenty so far, filling half of the bottom floor of the compound with our expensive, free toys.

Jerry has always secretly worried about our little extra-curricular activity considering it's not exactly Agency-approved, but we have to do something for us, and this is what I choose.

"You want to help?" I ask.

She shakes her head, her eyes stuck on a blonde down below. "No, I have business to attend to," she says with a smirk before prowling away. She shakes out her now black hair, letting it sweep behind her.

Taking a deep breath, I make my way down the stairs behind her, heading for the car.

"Are you lost, boy?" a man asks. He's older, probably around sixty, and he wears a three-piece suit. His question is reasonable. At twenty-four, I'm sure he doesn't understand why a kid is here looking at cars he cannot even possibly afford.

But I'm not here to buy them.

"I was just wondering if I could look in the Lykan," I say, beaming at the beautiful thing.

"We only let people actually interested in purchasing do that," the man states, looking me up and down.

I don't look poor, that's for sure. In my best suit, I cross my wrists over my waist, tapping my Rolex.

"Well you see, I'm trying to convince my father to buy it, actually," I smirk, running my thumb across my lips. "You know men with old money, they need so much convincing."

The man's eyes widen when he realizes that there's a possible sale happening, and he changes his tune. "Yes, of course. Let me show you to it."

When he lets me in it, I wipe my hand over the wheel, feeling how comfortable it fits in my hands. When the man looks away, I quickly grab the jammer from my pocket, placing it under the dash.

When this is over and I take it, it'll keep it from being tracked.

I spend a few minutes in it, taking videos and pictures to send my fake father. When I'm done, I slide out, thank the man, and head off to find Brandon and Zach.

And then we wait for the end of the event.

Hitting the gas, I'm out the door in seconds and racing to catch up to her. Out of all the cars in that room, this is one of the few that can possibly keep up with her while also lying relatively low. People tend to notice a McLaren racing through the streets of DC. While my Exorcist Camaro is nothing but normal, to an everyday person, it looks to be.

It doesn't take too long for me to catch up with her, flashing my headlights. We're going around two hundred miles per hour, and I can see the distant lights from the city through the trees.

I would wonder how she was able to figure out how to work the navigation system, but in my experience, women figure out everything. I don't know how they do it, but they do.

A moment later, flashes of red and blue go off behind me, and I curse, hitting the wheel with my palm. We're going much too fast for them to catch up to us right now, but the city streets are a much different story. She's not going to know what to do.

We cannot get caught, no matter what.

So I speed ahead of her. I don't bother turning on my signal for the empty street, rushing by her before pulling in front. She hits the brakes, scared she'll drive into me, and I can see her surprised, annoyed face through her windshield illuminated by my taillights.

She looks in her rearview mirror, watching the cops get closer and closer, and I speed up, hoping and praying she knows what I'm doing. We need to get away from them. If the cops get her, she's doomed.

Sure enough, she keeps up with me, and soon we're entering the city, slowing down significantly as cars rush by. Moving over into one of the other lanes, I hang back, opening the passenger window so I can yell over to her. She looks at me, her eyes narrowing as she hits the gas, but is only stuck behind another car stopped for a red light. I keep up with her, motioning for her to open her window.

After what feels like ages, she finally does, not saying a word to me.

"You need to listen to me, okay?" I tell her. "I'm going to get you out of here, but you need to do *exactly* what I tell you to do. Up here, there's going to be a road to the left. Let me go first and follow me. Take the turn no matter what, do you hear me? The second we're around that corner, pull into that parking garage and jump into my car, got it?"

Her eyes soften just a touch, realizing that I'm trying to help her. She nods, her fists white as she tightens her grip on the wheel.

Looking behind us, the police are catching up.

The light turns green, and I continue ahead. She slips in behind me, practically touching the bumper of my car.

The light turns yellow, and I can see oncoming traffic ready to go.

Speeding up, I turn the wheel as fast as I can, hoping that Sydney has stayed with me this whole time. I hold my breath until I see her behind me, following me still. It would have been easy for her to just keep going, leaving me in the dust.

We may be getting somewhere in the trust department. Or maybe that's just desperation.

Turning quickly into the parking garage on the corner of the street, I don't bother taking a ticket, instead flying through the gate, breaking it in half. I'll worry about cameras as soon as she's safe in my car.

Pulling to a stop, I wait for her to pull up beside me, not bothering to park in an actual space. We don't have time. We don't have a choice.

Turning the car off, she takes the key out of the ignition, throws the door open, and takes off toward me. She fumbles with the handle for a moment before she's able to open it, climbing quickly inside. The second her feet are off the ground, I'm off, racing toward the other side of the garage before the police can surround it, not bothering to look both ways before pulling onto the street.

Sitting behind a string of cars at another red light, we watch as a string of police cars pull onto the road behind us, the inside of the garage flashing red and blue, the sirens echoing around us.

My fingers grip the wheel tighter. "What. The. Hell. Were you thinking?" I hiss, looking at her for the first time since she climbed in.

Her skin is pale. It's paler than it usually is. She looks like she's going to be sick, and although I've seen her shake with fear before, I can't help but feel sorry for her now.

"I wasn't," she says simply, her eyes wide as she stares ahead.

"Where were you trying to go?" I ask her.

Her head turns to me, her eyes distant. "I was trying to just go home. Just to feed my cat."

"Sydney, how many times do we have to tell you that there is no normalcy for you anymore? You can't just drive through our fucking gate in a three-million-dollar car to go home to *feed your fucking cat*," I tell her, shaking my head. "Has anything we've told you over the last couple of days made it through your head?"

"Nope," she replies honestly, and I can't fault her for it.

"Your parents were horrible people, Sydney. It's time that you face that and do something about it. Running away isn't going to help you."

I don't think she thought a single thing through.

"I knew you guys were going to come for me," she says, slowly coming out of her daze. "I just needed to get home for a couple minutes."

"You could have asked us."

She pauses, thinking that one over.

"You would have brought me to my place?" she asks.

I shrug, annoyed. "I'm sure we could have set something up."

She slumps into her seat, crossing her arms over her chest.

"We're going back to the compound right now, but I'll see what I can do, alright?" I ask.

She nods, looking out the window as the city lights fly by.

"How long have you been working on this case?" she asks eventually.

I consider the question for a moment. It's been a really long time. "I'm not sure," I say honestly. "They've been on our radar for a really long time, but it was only a couple of months ago that we got a break in the case, and we were able to find out some intel on how it operates. Jerry has known that her parents were controlling it, but she didn't quite know how or where."

"Have you guys been watching me for a long time too?"

I shake my head. "No, we knew that you weren't really involved. It was only when they died that we realized that you're our last hope. Honestly, them dying is the best thing that could have happened for the case. We had an in, no matter how we went about it. You're their daughter, and by blood, you're to take over the company. Well, as long as you have a husband."

Sydney scoffs, rolling her eyes dramatically. "I should have known there would be some kind of fucked up requirement."

"When was the last time you talked to your parents?"

She thinks for a moment. "I'm not sure. I think it was a couple of years ago. They kept trying to come back into my life, but I kept shutting them out. That didn't stop them from trying. I've lost so many jobs because of them. I had no choice but to take their money. With that came a couple of conversations."

I nod. She said as much back at the compound.

"Listen. I don't like this any more than you do. But this is big, okay?" She looks at me as her hand goes to her lower stomach, pressing against it. "Are you okay?"

She nods, looking back out the window without answering my first question.

About five minutes later, she breaks again. "Why were the cops after me?"

I chuckle sardonically, running my fingers through my hair, pulling at the ends. "That car was a three-million-dollar car. We stole it."

She gasps. "Why would you steal it?"

"Well," I start, smiling. "Almost all of those cars in that warehouse are stolen, actually. But that one was significantly harder. There was a car show up here, and it was brought over from the UK for it. We found out and decided that we wanted it for our collection. I think there's only seven of them in the whole world." I shrug.

She pauses, looking me over. "Doesn't the CIA have an issue with you stealing cars?"

"You have to understand that Project Fallen Angel is an extremely illegal black operation, Sydney. No one knows about us. We don't exist to most of the CIA. We're not *employees* of the CIA. We're literally used as necessary collateral. They don't want to risk their agents' lives, so they risk ours."

Her eyes widen as she lays her hand in her lap. "Wait, why would you sign up for that?"

"Well, we don't really," I explain. "Most of us don't

remember what our lives were like before we were initiated, but one thing we all have in common is that we were basically dead. We were at the end of our lives, for one reason or another, left without family. The CIA only chooses the best people for the job. People who won't be missed. People who have no one to look for them."

"But you don't remember anything from the past?"

I shake my head. "Not a thing."

"Nothing about your parents?"

"Nope."

"That sucks."

I nod. It does suck. But I think it would suck to know, too.

"So yeah. If we get arrested, we have to deal with the consequences. The CIA won't bail us out, but they're also not going to slap us on the wrists for doing something bad. They don't care as long as we keep our mouths shut."

"I have to think that at some point you can become a liability, though, right?" she asks, and I find it almost cute that she's actually showing interest. That she's been actually speaking to me.

I let my guard down a little bit, letting her in. The anger in my head clears, and I start to notice more. The almost spicy scent of her sweaty skin filling the car, like an expensive perfume I've only smelled at galas. But those rich women always wear far too much, suffocating me. Sydney wears just enough to notice it. Just enough to make me want to lean in and breathe it in.

Snap out of it, Ronan.

"Since we technically don't exist, the second we become a liability, they just take us out," I say with a shrug. It's the truth. They don't care about us at all.

Sydney turns in her seat, trying to catch my eyes as I watch the road ahead. "And you're okay with that?"

"Why wouldn't I be? They gave me life. They provide me with a roof over my head and an interesting enough job. We get paid more than you can ever imagine just to do their dirty work for them. We're pawns, but we know that, and I think we're all okay with it."

"Jerry, too? How does she remember the past?"

I bite my lip, wincing. "I don't think that her story is mine to tell," I say simply, unsure of what else to add. Jerry is a complicated person. I adore her, but she's not an easy person to get along with, and what she told Sydney earlier in the day was only part of everything.

She's complicated, and I'm not the person to explain it.

"What do you do then?"

I explain my job to her. Or at least as much as I can. I work in the government as a low-level aid to one of the secretaries of state. I listen in on conversations, give him advice sometimes, and plant information. Whatever I have to do for a specific job. I'm there to make sure that things are running smoothly and report back to the Agency.

Sydney nods and sits back, staring ahead. Blowing out, she knocks her head against the back of the seat. "I'm in so much trouble, right?"

I nod. She's so screwed.

The second we get out of the car, Jerry is in her face screaming, the police scanner in her hand crackling.

"What the fuck were you thinking? Do you really think that you could just run from us? That you weren't going to get stopped?"

"I was hoping I'd get further, yeah," Sydney says, pushing against Jerry's chest.

"You could have died, and then we'd be screwed. Do you understand that?"

"I understand it plenty." She rolls her eyes, trying to move around her.

Jerry goes to smack her, but I move between them easily,

stopping her. "It's been a long night, okay, Jer? Why don't we talk about this in the morning?"

"You could have gotten arrested," she tells me, her voice small.

Jerry doesn't have many weaknesses, but one of them is us. Especially when we're in trouble. She'd lay down her life for us, of that I know. She cares about each and every one of us, and I can't help but love her for it.

But this isn't the time to worry. "I'm back; everything is fine," I assure her.

She looks me over as I feel Sydney's body heat against my back. "You left your phone here," she starts, her voice hardening again. "I already called Stella and asked her to take out the cameras in the city."

I nod. Stella is one of the best hackers in the entire country, stationed at the Texas Fallen Angel compound.

"If she wasn't able to take them out in time, she said she erased any footage."

"Thank you,"

"I didn't do it for you," she snaps before turning around and heading back to her room.

I let out a breath, taking a step forward. Zach, Brandon, and Elena are left watching us.

"I assume the car is toast?" Zach asks, frowning.

"For now," I reply. "But we'll figure out how to get it back." I hear Sydney squeak from behind me, and I turn to her. "What?"

"I'm sure you had other things on your mind, but just so you know, the hood got pretty banged up."

Of course, it did.

Sighing, I look at the others, realizing just how annoyed they all are, before pushing Sydney softly toward the stairs. "Go upstairs and get some sleep," I tell her.

She eyes me warily before nodding once and finally, for the first time, doing as she's told.

Something in my chest squeezes. Something changed in that car, and I don't like it.

TWELVE

SYDNEY

THE SECOND I get into the room, I lock the door, praying that Ronan doesn't try to come in, and I break down crying.

My chest aches, my body aches, and I can't stop shaking as everything hits me all at once.

My life has never been normal. Never been something to be desired. And yet, somehow, everything has come crashing down on me faster than I ever thought possible.

And I'm hurting.

I've been hurting for a very long time.

Every feeling I've ever had for my parents rushes through me. Hatred. Despair. Confusion. Indifference. Guilt. Resentment. Bitterness.

I was only a kid. I was a kid subjected to watching men be murdered in cold blood in front of me.

They were training me to take over, they said. They had to toughen me up, they'd tell me.

I didn't need to be toughened up. I needed to be protected. I needed to be loved.

When other kids were having sleepovers, I was learning how to put a hit on someone.

Memories I worked so hard to forget rush to the forefront of my brain, flashing before my eyes as I squeeze them shut, sobs taking over my body, making me feel like it's not mine.

I don't want to be here.

I've had those thoughts before. But everyone has, haven't they?

I think so.

Laying on Ronan's bed, I curl up into myself, pulling the comforter over my body as I shake, my back aching.

And at some point, I fall asleep.

A soft knock on the door wakes me from my sleep. The sun shines in from the high windows, warming my face.

Realizing I locked the door, I sit up in bed, stretching before climbing out to open it.

The second it's open, I go back to the bed, not bothering to look at who it is before climbing in, seeking comfort in the soft blankets.

"Are you okay?" Ronan asks, peeking in.

"Are you?"

He nods, opening the door wider and entering. He looks around, his hands tucked into the pockets of his sweatpants as he thinks about what to say.

"Just say it," I tell him, sighing.

"We have to get married," he tells me, wincing.

"You said that yesterday."

"Yeah, well, it's confirmed. I tried to get out of it one last time. To come up with some kind of a plan that wouldn't require that, but it's the easiest way to do this."

"So that you guys can complete your mission," I deadpan, repeating their talking points back to him.

"I believe it's mutually beneficial," he says as he shrugs sheepishly.

I scoff. "Oh, do you now. How did she manage to convince you?"

His head tilts to the side. "Now that your parents are dead, there are two paths for you. Paths that their successors are weighing. You can go on your merry way, living your life like nothing is happening, but one day, you'll get married, and they're going to kill you and your family so that you can't take over. And that's the best option. The worse path is that you simply go home, and they kill you in your sleep, making it look like an accident. Either way, they're going to take you out. They have to."

I consider this. They've said as much before, but I won't pretend it's starting to sound like the likely outcome the more I learn about my parents and the way their empire is run.

He moves closer, sitting on the edge of the bed. "We do this, you can live your life in peace after. Finally. You'll actually be free, and you'll be free knowing that you did something right. That you did what you could for everyone your parents have hurt. I complete this mission after years of trying, and you get to go on with your life as if none of it happened. Got it?"

Everything within me tells me to say no. To tell them to get out of my way and go home. But I know he's right. I've known that they've been right. They don't need to know that, though. I nod, biting my nail.

"Okay. Let's go downstairs and talk to Jerry, okay?" he says carefully, offering his hand. I look at it, my face twisting in displeasure.

"Just because I'm agreeing to this doesn't mean that I want to, for one. Two, I'd rather not speak to Jerry."

"You're going to have to at some point, and that point is now, Princess," I bristle at the pet name, "I told her that I yelled at you enough for us both, okay? She doesn't have to know it's a lie."

A wicked feeling builds in my chest. No matter how tough

Ronan pretends to be, he's soft. He's soft now, and he's always going to be soft.

And I can use that to my advantage.

I may be agreeing to do this, but that doesn't mean I have to make it easy on him.

"Fine," I say finally, whacking his hand away as I climb out of bed once more, pulling a pair of socks on.

"Are those mine?" he asks, his thick, dark eyebrows furrowed as he looks at me pull them on.

"Yeah," I reply simply with a shrug.

His lips thin as he rolls his eyes, standing up and heading for the door. Opening it, he turns back to me. "You coming?"

"I'm not doing it unless you bring me back to my place so I can get Shiloh," I tell Jerry as I put my fork down.

Elena made everyone eggs, toast, and bacon for breakfast, and although I won't admit it, it's one of the best meals I've ever eaten. Or maybe I'm just starving.

Jerry considers this, her chin propped on her hands as she watches me from the other end of the table. Ronan sets down his fork roughly, throwing himself back in his seat with a groan.

"Done," Jerry says simply, and Ronan's head shoots up, looking at her.

That was easy, I think, trying my best not to throw my hands up in victory.

"We'll leave right after we finish here," she tells me as she takes a bite of her particularly burnt toast.

I nod, getting back to work on my own food.

We all eat in awkward silence before the three others start talking about their latest assignments, casting me sideways glances as they make sure what they're saying in front of me is okay.

"The Agency doesn't really know the extent of your involvement," Jerry tells me when I send Ronan a questioning look. "But I trust you understand that if you run your mouth, none of us would hesitate to kill you."

I gulp, understanding just fine. Of course, she would. From what Ronan told me the previous night, they wouldn't risk their lives for mine.

When we're all done, Zach takes the dishes into the kitchen as he and Brandon get to work cleaning up, and Jerry motions for me to follow her. I don't look back at Ronan as I do, but I can feel his piercing eyes on me.

She wastes no time climbing into her red Challenger and pulling out the door.

It's the first time I'm seeing the damage I caused in the sunlight, and I wince, realizing that it's way worse than I thought. The entire gate is a mangled mess, parts of the barb-wire fencing on top laid out on the ground.

"You're lucky a tire didn't pop," Jerry mutters as we drive through the mess. She doesn't say the silent part out loud. I'm lucky that *Ronan* didn't have a tire pop. Going at the speed we were going, he would have been toast.

The burnt kind.

Like the slice she *put back in the toaster* after Elena placed it in front of her, attempting to *burn it more*. What kind of psychopath am I dealing with here?

…says the woman from a family of murderers.

"Thank you," I say softly as we pull onto the road.

She looks at me, tucking her black hair behind her ear as she reaches for a pack of cigarettes from the center console.

"I'm not doing it for you," she snaps. "If this is what will get you to actually work with us and stop putting our lives in danger, then so be it."

I nod, looking out the window. I have a feeling there won't be much getting through to her. Bonding may not be in the cards for us, and I have to accept that.

But ten minutes into the drive, I get antsy.

"How did you find out about mom and dad?" I ask.

Jerry sticks her hand out the window, letting it sit there as we drive along the rural roads. "Mom visited me once or twice," she says, her voice not giving anything away as she speeds along the road, swerving a couple of times for small critters that find their way in her path. My stomach stirs, and I pray that I get back without vomiting.

But I'm also surprised. "She did?"

"Yep. Felt guilty. Wanted to see me. Still wasn't good enough for her to take back, though. Still wasn't good enough for her to help."

I sink into my seat, feeling horrible.

"If I had known, I would have—"

"You would have what?" Jerry interrupts, cracking her neck as her black hair falls into her face. "You would have fixed it? You couldn't even stand up for yourself, Sydney. You wouldn't have done a fucking thing for me."

As usual, she's right. She's right about it all.

But I can't help but feel a deep, unwavering melancholy inside of me at the thought of growing up with a sibling.

Of not being alone all the time.

"I just wish things were different, is all," I whisper.

"We all do. Just have to focus on the future."

"I hope you know that my life wasn't easy with them," I start, but I'm once again cut off.

"I don't want to hear it," Jerry snaps, her eyes flashing to mine. "I understand they were horrible. Got it? I don't want to hear it. You were loved. You were funded. You were educated. You were clothed and fed. That's more than I ever got, understand?"

I nod, turning away once more. I get it, and she's right to be mad.

I would be, too.

"I had no one. So much so that Veronica had me initiated into the project without even wiping my memory. No one was in my life before, no one would be in my life after. No one was going to come looking for the girl who was never loved to begin with," she hisses, her knuckles turning white around the wheel.

I don't have the heart to argue with her because I don't know. I don't know if she had anyone.

And although I had people, I'd never felt so alone.

———

"Grab the cat; you're not bringing anything else," Jerry tells me as she exits my room. Shiloh purrs happily in my arms, attempting to rub against my face.

"What do you mean?"

"I mean that all of your clothes are ugly, and you need to look the part of Ronan's wife. None of those are going to help you."

I try not to be offended, but I am.

"I like those clothes," I tell her, rearing back.

"Well, I don't, and I'm the one controlling this mission. Someone will take you shopping today or tomorrow, and you'll get some proper clothes. You're not going to go around to dinners looking like a homeless rat."

I look at what she's wearing right now. From the two days I've known her, it's basically the same. Combat boots, pants with endless pockets, and a tight-fitting shirt underneath a flannel.

"Says the wannabe Kim Possible," I mutter as I grab Shiloh's food.

"What was that?" she asks, her head snapping to me.

I shake my head, smiling at her. "Nothing!"

The second she looks away, I roll my eyes.

When Shiloh is in his carrier, and his things are placed in

bags, we make our way downstairs, packing her car with everything.

I didn't take much. My cat, some undergarments that Jerry disapproved of—why they'd matter beats me—and a few of my sketchbooks so that I would have something to do when I'm left in a room for hours at a time by myself other than snoop.

And finally, we're on our way back to my new home. For now.

THIRTEEN

RONAN

THE SOUND of the other three behind the kitchen playing pool distracts me as I look over Jerry's paperwork from the last week. It's her least favorite part of her job despite it being, well, *most* of her job.

Jerry is here to oversee us. To make sure everything is running smoothly and to ensure that everyone is safe. Not every compound has someone like her, but since we're at the epicenter of American politics, we get a lot of Fallen Angels coming and going. With that comes the responsibility of keeping track of every single visit, every mission, and every misstep.

Our lives depend on it.

I wasn't lying when I told Sydney that we're used as pawns. It's something that each and every one of us has had to accept. It's just life. We owe our lives to the Agency, and they can take it away without a second thought.

Life is rarely fair, but it wasn't fair for any of us to begin with.

The sound of the door opening knocks me out of my daze, and I watch as Jerry's car rolls into the room, parking in its usual spot. The smell of exhaust hits my nose, relaxing me a little.

A second later, both doors open, and the two women exit the car bickering, shattering my moment.

"I just don't see why I wasn't able to bring my clothes," Sydney says, frustrated.

Jerry rolls her eyes. "Because they're ugly."

"You threw my sweater out the window!"

"Because I told you *not to bring it,* and you didn't *listen!*"

"Jerry, I don't *have* anything else!"

They continue arguing, throwing insult after insult at each other as Jerry rounds the car, roughly handing Sydney a carrier.

"Take your mut upstairs to Ronan's," she demands, turning away from Sydney as if she can't stand to look at her face for more than a moment longer.

Sydney's eyes narrow, her lips set in a firm, thin line. "He's not a mut. He's a domestic shorthair," she seethes before spinning on her heel, heading toward the stairs, muttering "idiot" under her breath. Jerry makes her way to me, her hands crossed over her chest.

"I'm not gonna tell her," she tells me. "You need to take her shopping," her voice is filled with displeasure.

I shake my head, putting my hands up. "Why do *I* have to take her shopping?"

"Because you two are about to be a married couple to anyone who isn't in this building right now, and you have to start pretending to act like it. I'm not her bitch, she's yours. Take care of it," she hisses, making her way past me and into the kitchen to grab a drink.

Well.

I watch Sydney make her way up the stairs, lugging the carrier with her.

I'm allergic to cats.

I'm not horribly allergic. I was able to be around the thing at her apartment, and it didn't bother me much. I just may need to take a Benadryl or two at some point.

"When you get back, Paul will be here," Jerry tells me as she leans against the counter, peeling an orange.

"Do you even have a marriage license?" I ask her, annoyed. I thought we'd have at least a little more time.

Jerry levels me with a stare, her head falling forward an inch. "You're kidding, right? You know we can get around having one."

I throw my hands up, trying to find the words to describe how frustrating this entire situation is.

"But," she adds, shrugging one shoulder and popping a slice into her mouth. "I did get one legally. Just… expedited."

I'm not even going to ask.

Done with the conversation, I head up to my room. The second I open it, I find Sydney and her cat on my bed, cuddling.

"I owe you so many treats," she tells him as she pets his fuzzy little grey head, nuzzling his face with her nose. I stand back against the doorframe, arms crossed over my chest as I watch her, a smirk fighting its way onto my face.

It's cute. I won't lie.

"Hey," I say, scaring her. Her head whips to mine, her eyes large as she and her cat look me over.

"Hey. You've met Shilch. The little man." She gestures to the indeed little man next to her, now licking his paw, never once breaking my eye contact.

"I do recall meeting a cat," I tell her stiffly.

"Well, if you're taking me shopping, we should probably stop at the store on the way home, too. Jerry wouldn't let me stop for food, and she wouldn't let me put his litter box in her precious car. Something about the smell not coming out of the seats for the next ten years. Like I'm about to dump dirty litter all over them or something." She rolls her eyes and scoffs as if someone not wanting a used litter box in the back of their car is the worst thing in the world.

I can tell she hasn't been around car people.

"We can stop," I smile, moving into the room and taking a seat on the end of the bed. I reach out to pet Shiloh, but he narrows his eyes at me, his little ears falling back as he looks at me like I'm the scum of the earth.

How one cat can pack that much emotion into one look, I'll never be sure.

Shaking my head, I look at Sydney. "Are you ready then?"

She looks down at the dirty jeans she's wearing before pulling on her thin, form-fitting white top. "I think so. I don't have to look too fancy, right?"

"No, you're fine."

That's half a lie. Where we're going, she should probably look a little more decent. I'm almost positive she had plenty of nicer clothes back at home. Jerry just wanted to embarrass her.

I've never liked these places. The white walls, the gold accents, the smell of overpriced perfume being pumped through the walls.

I really don't understand why someone else couldn't bring her here.

Sydney has spent a total of one hour in just this *one* store. While I would have preferred pulling things off of hangers, checking out, and figuring out what fits later, Sydney has decided that she wants to truly make an event of it.

I consider myself a fairly patient man, but it's running thin.

I lean back in the seat, draping my arm over the back as

Sydney steps out of the changing room in yet another all-black outfit.

"Are you allergic to color or something?" I ask dully.

She looks at me through the mirror as she adjusts the sleeves of her blouse. "I just like the color. Plus, I feel like it fits the theme, you know?"

"What theme?" I ask, leaning forward.

Her eyes meet mine through the mirror. "You know," she says, her head tilting, the glint in her wide green eyes almost charming.

"I'm not sure I do."

She looks around, making sure no one else is around us. "Spies," she mouths, shrugging.

My jaw hangs on the floor.

"You know that we're spies, not fucking ninjas, right? You know those are two separate things?"

"Spies wear all black, too!"

"In the goddamn movies!"

"You mean to tell me that Mission Impossible isn't a good depiction of espionage?"

"They don't even always wear black in Mission Impossible."

She smirks. "How weird is it watching Mission Impossible while being a spy? Like what predicament did you end up in that had you watching that."

She's so *aggravating*.

Instead of answering, I get up. "I'm grabbing you some clothes. You're going to try them on, and then we're getting out of here."

Sighing, she turns back to the dressing room and retreats inside without another word.

It only takes me a couple of minutes to come back with my arms full of clothes. Knocking on the door, she opens it, looking at them.

"You're supposed to look the part of an important businesswoman. Someone who would be with someone in politics. Someone who's taken seriously."

"You said you're a low-level aid, Ronan. That's hardly a position you need me looking like Jackie Kennedy for," she deadpans, and I freeze, squeezing my hands together as I attempt to calm myself down. "And black can't do that?" she asks, looking up at me from under her lashes.

"Not when it's obvious you're trying to look like a ninja, no."

She nods, taking the clothes.

I head back to my chair, wiping my hands down my face as I silently pray this will only take a couple moments.

Flopping back, I rest my head against the back of the seat, staring up at the ceiling, wishing for all of this to be over.

When I hear the door open, I look at her.

And then look some more.

"What the fuck are you doing?" I ask, dumbfounded.

"I need help."

"What could you possibly need help with?" She holds up one of the dresses I handed her.

Because in front of me stands a woman dressed to the nines in lingerie.

I try not to look. I do. But my eyes can't stop noticing how her curves look in the black, lacy material. I swallow.

"And why did you need to come out here in this?"

She looks down at herself as if just now realizing she's wearing lingerie before her gaze finds mine again, her eyes wide and innocent.

I know she's just fucking with me.

"Well, I wouldn't want to come out here naked, would I?" she asks, tilting her head. Her red curls fall around her shoulders as she holds the dress out to me.

The dressing room is in the back of the store. No one would see her unless someone came in, which is still a likely scenario considering they're open.

Taking a moment to mentally slap myself out of it, I get out of my chair, taking the dress from her hands. The expensive, silky material feels too fragile in mine.

"What do you need me to do?"

"Help me put it on."

"And you were wholly incapable of doing that yourself?" I ask as I yank it over her head. The second my fingers brush her arm, a zing runs through me. A small electric current that makes my stomach twist.

Moving her hair over her shoulder, I pull the dress down over her hips, feeling her shiver every time my finger makes contact with her skin. She watches me in the mirror, her eyes never once leaving mine as her chest rises and falls steadily.

It takes me a moment to realize why this feels so weird to me.

I haven't touched a woman like this. Not that I remember.

But that's the only reason I'm feeling this. Yep. The only reason.

Zipping her up, I move my hand around her neck, watching as her head tilts just a bit, her breath hitching as I move her hair back, shaking it out.

"You look beautiful," I whisper, dipping down to run my lips over her neck.

"Wha—what are you doing?" she asks, leaning into me.

Moving my hands down to her hips, I grip them, pulling her into me. "Don't make this mission more difficult than it has to be, Princess." Her eyes narrow, her back straightening. "If you fuck with me, I'm going to hit back ten times harder. Only one of us is going to come out of that fight a winner, and it's sure not going to be you."

I back away, retreating to my chair. She watches me the entire time, a scowl on her face. It would be cute if she weren't ruining my peace.

I arch an eyebrow at her through the mirror, and with a grunt she retreats to the dressing room. There's a commotion from behind the door, and I realize that she likely can't get the zipper down herself.

And the thought of that is fucking hilarious.

If she's going to play with me, then game on.

"So you've clearly murdered people, right?"

I glance at her from the corner of my eye, already completely spent.

It's been a long afternoon. Hours upon hours of shopping later, plus one grocery store haul, and we're finally heading back to the compound. Jerry texted me hours ago that Paul was there hanging around, to which I told her to kindly eat a dick.

She said she'd rather chew off every single one of her fingernails than ever do that.

If she wanted this to be quick, she should have brought Sydney herself.

"That *is* part of my job description sometimes, yes."

"So all of you have killed people?"

I sigh. "I liked it better when you weren't talking to me."

Or when she was sad. Anything was better than this.

"I liked you better when I thought you had good intentions," she shoots back, examining her fingernails.

"I always had good intentions."

She lets out a sardonic chuckle as she looks out the window.

And I think she's going back to ignoring me.

"You know, you'd look so much hotter with a beard."

My eyes snap to hers. "What the hell does that mean?"

She doesn't answer.

Running her fingers along the cool leather of the car, I clear my throat, not knowing what to say next. What do I say to someone completely unwilling to work with me on this?

"You know we don't have any other choice, right?" I say finally.

Her eyes flash to mine, and an icy cold feeling settles in my bones. "I'll only do it if you grow a beard," she says, her arms folding over her chest as she slumps back into the seat. My knuckles turn white around the wheel, my teeth grinding together so hard I feel like one may break.

"I have to keep it shaved for work," I tell her through gritted teeth. It's like she's trying to make our lives as difficult as humanly possible. I have no idea how I'm going to survive this.

"And I don't want to do this. I'm not marrying someone with a baby face." She reaches over the center consul and grabs my cheeks between her fingers, squeezing them with a shake before I smack her hand away, swerving on the road ahead just slightly. "Grow a beard, or I'm not doing this," she says.

I've never met a more infuriating woman in my entire life, from what I remember, and I've been under Jerry's thumb for the past ten years.

"You don't have a choice, Princess."

"I could literally throw myself out of this car right now."

"That would certainly be a *choice*, I guess," I grumble, rolling my eyes. "We'll talk about the beard later."

I just wish we were back at the compound already.

FOURTEEN

SYDNEY

RONAN IS fun to mess with.

At least, that's what I'm telling myself is happening. We're just messing with each other. Back there? In that dress? Just something to piss him off.

And I love it.

I'm not happy about any of this, but there's a certain level of acceptance that comes with understanding your debt to the world that comes after the grief over the normal life you've so desperately yearned for. A deep melancholy that settles on your soul like the weight of the world pushing down on you.

I've accepted that this is my responsibility. My path.

I can either accept it, make peace with it, and live my life as I always have along the way, or I can be miserable.

I can be weak and pliable, or I can be powerful and stand my ground. They'll just have to live with it.

Seeing myself in those clothes made me realize that my life is never ever going to be the same. Until the very day I die, things are going to be different. Whether that be I live the rest of my days as a failure, I die young, or I succeed, and I'm finally free of the weight of the past, everything will be different. And that's okay.

I'm tired of running. I'm tired of panicking.

The rest of the ride is silent as Ronan hums softly. I see his jaw working, and it sends a little bit of joy through me that I can get under his skin so easily.

When we pull into the complex, a man immediately stands from his place on the couch, scowling.

Ronan sighs. "That's Paul. He's a minister for the Fallen Angels," he informs me.

"Why can't we just hit up a courthouse somewhere?" I ask, unbuckling.

"Because Jerry doesn't always do things the legal way," is all he replies before getting out and unloading the trunk of his car. I watch him, my hand on my hip.

"You guys took your sweet time," Jerry says from the second floor as she exits her room, skipping down the steps with a cigarette between her teeth. I don't miss the look Ronan shoots her. "Take her shit upstairs and come back down, okay?"

Jerry pats Ronan's back before turning to me, a wicked grin on her face.

"Sydney, this is Paul. Paul, this is Sydney."

Paul looks me over. He's handsome. Maybe in his early thirties, he digs one hand into his black slacks as he runs a palm through his sandy blond hair.

"You guys really are sisters," he says as he looks between us.

Jerry chuckles, watching Maverick trot over to sit next to her, scratching him between the ears.

"This isn't going to take long. I have dinner with someone, anyways," Paul says, his voice laced with annoyance.

"That's fine with me," I reply, shrugging.

Ronan exits his room, making his way back downstairs. He changed out of his more formal outfit and into a pair of form-fitting jeans and a blue Henley. He looks more handsome than I'll give him credit for.

"If you guys can come over to the island, please," Jerry says, stepping behind it with a paper in her hands.

Ronan and I take a seat on the other side as Paul stands at the end, watching all of us grimly.

"Now, I want it to be known that I'm trying to do this the right way, okay guys?" she jokes, casting a sideways glance at Paul. "I could have gotten away with not having Paul here, but instead, I took him away from a very important dinner, right, Paul?"

He rolls his eyes, gesturing for her to get on with it.

She places the paper between Ronan and me and points to the lines we have to sign. "Sign that, and you're golden."

Ronan holds his hand out for a pen, and Paul quickly plucks one out of his jacket pocket, handing it to him. I watch as he signs it before pushing it over without even looking in my direction.

Grabbing the pen from his hand, I quickly sign my current name on the requested line. *Sydney Quinn.*

"Wait, so is this really legally binding? Is my last name going to be different?" My eyes widen as I realize what all of this really means. I look at his signature, trying to figure out what my name will be. I feel like I'm waking up in Vegas.

"Miller. You're Sydney Miller now," the man next to me says. I look him dead in the eye, silently challenging him.

"That's the most basic name I've ever heard."

"But it's yours."

Paul claps his hands together from his position next to Jerry, yanking the piece of paper away from us before we can rip it to shreds. My eyes don't leave Ronan's deep brown ones, determined not to be the first to look away. "Well, congratulations are in order for the lovely couple. I truly hope you guys have the best marriage."

Jerry clears her throat in front of us, but I still watch him, a smirk growing on my lips. "Yeah, we're done here, Paul. You can go now," Jerry tells him.

He doesn't need to be told twice.

Ronan's gaze burns inside of me, and if I didn't know he hates this as much as I do, I could mistake the look in his eye for desire.

"If you two would stop eye fucking each other, we have some more business to discuss," Jerry eventually snaps, ending our stare-down. "Thank you. In just two days, you guys are going to be going to a dinner. It'll be your first outing as a married couple, and you have to act the part. Spend however long you have to together to figure it out."

"What exactly do we need to do?" I ask.

"You need to pass as happily married and in love. I'm going to give you guys your cover tomorrow. You'll have to memorize it."

"Cover?"

"How you met, how long you've been together, who Ronan's family is, the like," she replies.

I nod, thinking it over.

"There will be important people in attendance, including one Jeffrey Wright. This is the start of the whole entire operation, and it's imperative that we ace this. Do you understand me?"

I nod, understanding alright.

If we can do this, I think that bringing the enterprise down will be easier than I initially thought. The second it's over, we can both go back to our lives.

"One last question," I say as Ronan makes a move to get up. "Can I have my own room?"

Jerry's eyebrows shoot up, her head coming forward slightly as she throws up her hands. "What part of act like a fucking married couple do you not understand? I don't give a single shit what you guys have to do to get through your time together, but being separated for everything but missions isn't gonna help."

So that's a no.

Nodding, I get up, following Ronan up the stairs and to his bedroom.

He sits on the end of his bed and yawns, disturbing Shiloh.

"I have one side of my closet clear. You can hang your things up in there. I'll clear out a drawer or two for you tomorrow," he tells me, laying back.

I look around for the bag containing Shiloh's things.

"I already set him up in the bathroom when I came up here," he adds.

Nodding, I get to work putting things away as I feel him watch me.

When I'm done, I sit next to him, tired and cold.

"Oh!" he says, sitting up. Grabbing one of his bags, he digs into it, producing a small velvet box. "I almost forgot. Jerry ordered it for you."

I take it from him, opening it up to find one of the biggest oval diamonds I've ever seen situated on a thin silver band.

"Holy shit,"

"Jerry said she stalked your Pinterest."

"Of course she did." Why would she have respected my privacy? That's so unlike her.

I take it out of the box, placing it on my left ring finger before examining it.

It's beautiful.

But something inside of me hurts.

I always wanted this. Ever since I was a little girl, I wanted this life. Find someone to love me, have kids, and grow old together. But this isn't love. This isn't even like.

Part of me wishes he picked it out himself.

"Thank you," I tell him. He smiles, a dazzling look on him, and grabs a pair of pajamas before heading to the bathroom.

Stripping out of my clothes, I slip on a pair of underwear

and an oversized shirt from Ronan's drawer as I slip into bed, pulling Shiloh into my chest.

Ten minutes later, the bathroom door opens behind me, and I feel Ronan's body get into bed.

"What are you doing?" I ask him, turning over.

"It's my bed. You think I'm going to sleep on the chair again?"

"I mean, yeah, that's kinda what I was thinkin'."

Ronan rolls his eyes. "Shut up and go to sleep. I'm not going to touch you."

I turn back over, finding comfort in Shiloh's soft purrs.

Ronan Miller.

Uptight. Mean. Entitled.

Probably a murderer.

Definitely a thief.

In desperate need of a beard.

And now, on paper, he's my husband.

Twelve years ago

"Sweetie, it's incredibly important that you understand how important finding someone to live your life with is."

I sit in my chair, my legs crossed as I pout, placing my chin on my hands.

"I don't want to go, mom."

"He's a good man! Has lots of connections. His father is very wealthy."

That doesn't mean anything to me.

"You know, one day you're going to regret all of this attitude," my mother tells me, brushing her beautiful red hair. *"Someday, you're going to wish that you had listened to us. Do you hear me?"*

I roll my eyes.

I don't want a husband anytime soon. If it were up to my parents, I would be married the very second I turned sixteen. A child bride. I would be wedded off to an older man. Someone who would most definitely creep me out.

He would be polite at first. Nice even. But over the years, he would turn wicked.

I've seen it happen to my own parents, and even then, they were well into that process by the time I was able to form memories.

I don't want that for myself.

What I picture is Prince Charming. Like from one of my books. A man who looks at me like the moon hangs above my head. Like I have everything to offer.

Like he thinks that I'm powerful. Like he believes I am powerful.

That's the kind of man I want. Someone who will love me and shower me with affection.

I want that more than anything.

But I'm not going to get it here. No. Here, I'm going to get a wrinkly old man who smells and wants me to wash his feet.

No, there's nothing for me here. Nothing to keep me here, either.

And I can't wait for the day I can leave.

FIFTEEN

RONAN

THE FIRST THING I think when I wake up is that someone is in my bed. I've never woken up with someone before. A jolt of panic runs through me before I see the mess of red hair and remind myself that Sydney is here.

My arm is draped over her small frame, my face practically in her neck. As I move over, a small moan exits her mouth as she sprawls out, scaring Shiloh in the process. He sends a glare my way, like it's my fault his mother nudged him.

I almost want to wake her up, but I don't. Why don't I?

Maybe because she looks so peaceful. I've never looked at her like this. Never noticed the light sprinkling of freckles across her cheek or the way her blond eyelashes curl naturally.

The spicy scent of whatever perfume she wears wraps me in a gentle haze, sucking me in. Is it perfume, or is it just her? Did she bring it from her apartment? Does she keep it in her bag? I make a mental note to check at some point. I tell myself it's not because of *her* but simply because I like it.

Sometimes, we can get so wrapped up in what we know that we forget that other people exist outside of our bubble.

My entire life has been my job. Has been sacrificing myself for the greater good. Letting myself be taken advantage of. I've been okay with that.

But with that comes forgetting that some people are just human. They're doing the best they can, and that should be enough.

Sydney holds the sins of her parents close to her heart. That much is blatantly obvious. But her decision to run from it, to turn her back on what she cannot control, is natural.

Her soft curls frame her face like the sun, and suddenly, all I want to do is run my fingers through it.

I don't know what's coming over me.

Maybe I simply don't want to wake her up because I know the second she does, she won't shut up.

Yeah, that's the reason.

But I don't really get a choice because the second I move, her eyelids flutter open, her green eyes bright but exhausted.

"Hi," she says, a small smirk on her face.

"Hey," is all I can manage to respond.

"Seems like someone's excited to be awake,"

What is she talking abo—oh. "Don't flatter yourself," I roll my eyes. "It's only natural."

"Mhm," she says, stretching her arms above her head as she yawns. Her giant ring sparkles in the sunlight.

I wish I picked it out for her. The fact that I didn't eats at me. There's a proper way to do things, even if this isn't real.

But I also wasn't going to lie to her.

"So what's the deal with today, big guy?" Sydney asks, her eyes on me. I get up, stretching.

Her eyes immediately find the line of exposed skin as my shirt rides up, and as I remember her little stunt in the dressing rooms yesterday, I decide to have a little bit of fun. Test the waters.

I take off my shirt, watching her the entire time I do it as

142

her intense gaze makes its way up my torso before finally meeting mine.

"I'm not sure," I say with a shrug. Her eyes sear my skin. "Tomorrow is that dinner we have to go to, but I'm not comfortable telling you how that's going to go because your sister is a bit of a loose cannon. Plans can sometimes change at the drop of a hat."

"Do you know what's going to happen after the dinner?"

"That's all up to whether Jeffrey Wright buys our schtick and how fast it takes him to reach out afterward."

She nods, her eyes drifting down again.

"Hey, eyes up here, Princess," I smile as her head whips up, her eyes narrowing.

"I don't like it when you call me that,"

"And I don't like it when you ogle me like some piece of meat," I tell her with a chuckle. It's a lie. Deep down, I love it.

"You ogle me too," she throws back.

I lean onto the bed, leveling her with a stare. "You're not my type,"

"You're not mine, either,"

"Glad we're on the same page."

The rest of the day goes by in a blur. I don't see much of Sydney, but I can feel her presence. Whenever she walks into a room, a chill goes down my spine.

I've shot people square in the face and tortured people for information, and yet, for some reason, this girl is what consumes my mind. This infuriating woman.

It's just because you don't remember ever being with a woman, I tell myself. That's not to say I haven't envisioned myself with one. Haven't fantasized about it. But I'm not one to play with women's emotions. I'm not going to pretend that something is what it's not, and I'm not going to go to a woman's apartment for a quick fuck when she doesn't even know my real name. That's not what I'm about, and it never will be.

I think that's part of the reason I keep pushing Sydney away. Everything about her draws me in. The way she looks at me, the way she holds her breath when I move past her, the way she flirts. But I know that this is a job. This is life or death for a lot of people, and the second this is over, she's going to go home a free woman without me while I'm stuck here taking orders from her sister.

Not that I'd rather be running the place. I'll gladly take orders from Jerry for the rest of my life if it means not having to deal with some of the bullshit she deals with every day. That being said, the similarities between the two also throw me off.

While Sydney would like to pretend that they're nothing alike, they're both loose cannons. Both hot-headed and temperamental. Both infuriating and also endearing. Jerry has been jaded by the past. Lonely for most of her life, and although Sydney never quite had it as bad, I think their grievances with their parents are closer than the two of them may think.

Throughout the day, I watch as they interact with each other. The changes are subtle, but they're there. Jerry smokes in the family room, Maverick by her side as she watches Sydney pace around the kitchen, finding something to eat as she rubs her stomach. Jerry's brows furrow, catching the movement.

"Are you pregnant?" she asks, suddenly extremely concerned.

Sydney's head swivels at the speed of light, a look of confusion clear on her face. "What?"

"Your hand."

Sydney looks down, noticing what she's doing.

Chuckling nervously, she takes her hand off, placing it on the counter. "No," she says simply.

Jerry narrows her eyes as if she doesn't quite believe her.

"I'm serious. It's just cramps."

Looking like she almost believes her, but not quite, Jerry turns back to her phone, letting Sydney be.

But that's more interaction than they've had before, and there was no arguing or yelling involved. That's progress.

Maybe something can come of this, and Jerry can have a family for once in her life. She's had us, and we're more than enough for her, but I think that having a tie to a real sibling would do her a world of good.

Maybe take a little bit of the chip on her shoulder off.

As the hours pass, I find myself more and more in my head.

We just have to get through the next couple of weeks, and it will all be over.

"Can you take Mav for a walk?" Jerry asks, holding his leash out for me.

She usually does it herself, but she's been unusually annoying lately.

"And take Sydney, her face is infuriating me."

Sydney looks up from the couch where she's curled up with her sketchbook, her forehead creased.

I swipe the leash from her hand, getting up with a sign.

Turning to Sydney, I motion for her to follow me.

We head outside without a word, and I make our way over to the small door in the large gate surrounding the area leading into the woods.

Sydney tucks her hands into the pockets of her pants, looking around.

"The place is nice," she says quietly.

I like this Sydney. The quiet one. The one that doesn't argue.

At least, that's what I tell myself. I like the other one too. The one that will push back. The one who's angry all the time. The one who would set the world on fire if she could.

I like that one too.

I nod, watching as Maverick sniffs every single leaf he sees on the ground.

"It's nice. Wasn't always that way," I tell her.

She pulls her arms tighter around her, looking up. "I'm not sure what I'm doing here."

My head swivels to her. "What do you mean you don't know what you're doing here? I feel like it's fairly simple. We've spelled it out for you," I all but hiss.

Her eyes flash to mine before looking at the ground as she carefully avoids tripping over a log. "I just mean that I don't know what I did in life to end up here. What went wrong."

I know that question. I know that question more than I think most people would understand.

Because most of us haven't done a single thing wrong. Most of us have no idea why we're here. Why we're subjected to this.

I wish I knew the answer.

"I don't know where it all went wrong, Sydney, but I know where you could make it right."

She sighs again, her shoulders slouching as what can only be described as remorse clouds her face.

And I feel for her.

I do.

I don't want to, but I can't help it.

And I hate it. I hate that there's just something about her that feels comforting. The woman who stole my car. The woman I kidnapped. It's only been a couple of days, and yet she feels like home.

No.

Why do I even think that?

It's because she looks like Jerry, I tell myself.

But I don't have feelings for Jerry. I never have. The fact that she doesn't swing my way isn't even the problem. It's just that I simply look at her as family. A family that none of us have ever really had.

But Sydney feels like that, plus more, and I have to shove it back.

I have to.

This is our job.

This is the way I live. I mess this up, I'm good as dead.

But I can't help it.

And that makes me hate her.

SIXTEEN

SYDNEY

YESTERDAY PASSED IN A BLUR. Nothing really happened, but it served as a moment of settlement for me. A moment of peace and security.

No one yelled at me. I wasn't forced to stay in a room, and out of the way, I wasn't pushed around. I was just able to exist, and that was enough for me.

But there's still that little feeling in the back of my mind that makes me think that I'm being lured into a trap. That's how I got into this mess to begin with.

"How are you feeling?" Elena asks as she sits next to me, a bowl of granola in her hands.

I shrug, moving my soup around my bowel with my spoon, looking down. "I'm getting by," I tell her.

"Jerry told me to help you get ready for the dinner tonight. I don't have all the details, but I'm sure you're going to do great,"

I nod, tucking my hair behind my ear. "I hope so."

I've never been in this kind of position before. I've never gone undercover, never had such stakes attached to my actions. I don't know what I'm walking into when I get to that dinner or how Jeffery will react when he sees me. I haven't seen him in a long time. So long, in fact, that I barely remember what he looks like.

But I know it's also something that I have to do, and I know that I have the guts to do it. Everything will be okay, and we'll be home before we know it, ready to deal with this head-on.

"I hope you and Jerry can learn to get along," Elena says suddenly, leaning back in her seat as she swipes a braid from her forehead. I look at her, curiosity radiating from me. She puts her hands up, shaking her head slightly. "All I'm saying is that I've known Jerry for a long time, and she's never been this nice to an outsider."

"This is her being nice?" I ask her, dropping my spoon as I stare at her, mouth agape.

She chuckles. "Yeah, surprising, right? You should have seen her when she first met me. Mean as a dog."

I can picture it. "Why was she mean to you?"

"I messed up my first mission," she tells me, taking another bite before taking a long sip of water. "Not my finest moment. I'm one of the newest people here, but I've still been here a long time. She had an established relationship with everyone here. I almost put their lives in jeopardy." She shrugs.

"I'm sorry," is all I can think to say.

She smiles. "Why are you sorry? It was my own problem. I should have known better at the time. My point is that Jerry has a big heart, no matter how tough she tries to make herself seem. She's been trying to find a family for herself for years, and when she finally found it, she refused to let go. Anything that threatens it is her enemy." She pauses for a minute, looking me over. "I think that you two are more similar in different ways than you think, and eventually, you'll be able to talk about it."

I ponder her words. "I don't expect her to forgive me. But I do hope that at some point she does."

Elena looks at me as if she feels bad for me, her large brown eyes searing into mine, and I sink into myself.

"Finish eating and come meet me in my room," she tells me as she suddenly gets up.

"Which room is yours?" I've seen her come down the stairs, but I never paid attention to which room she was coming out of.

"Fourth room, just knock, and I'll get the door."

———

"How many dresses did you guys buy the other day?" Elena asks as she examines the array of dresses spread out on her bed.

I shrug. "I figured if I was going to be kidnapped, I might as well make the most of it, you know?"

She smiles, picking one of them up.

"Stand over there," she says, holding the dress up to me.

"I don't know everything about tonight, but I know it's a black-tie dinner. There's going to be some type of fundraiser, but I'm not sure for what. There will be speeches, a dinner, of course, and the last one I went to had dancing."

"You went to one of these?" I ask in surprise.

"You have no idea how many shady business deals go down at those dinners. They have them all the time. There's usually at least one of us there at all times."

I nod, pursing my lips. "That makes sense."

"I think you should go with the silver," she says as she shoves the shimmery fabric in my arms.

"You think it'll look good enough?"

Elena nods. "It's gorgeous, professional, sexy; you'll look amazing in it."

I smile, sitting down on the end of her bed. "If you don't mind me asking, do you remember your life before this?" I've been thinking a lot about all of this. About what it means for the world. I didn't know that this project existed, and neither does anyone else. And it should stay that way. But what's going to happen when Atlee Enterprises gets taken down? What's the next step? I assume they have a million other issues they work on weekly. I mean, Ronan did say that they only really just had a break in the case. But it makes me wonder how much really happens.

She shakes her head, sitting next to me. "No, I don't."

"Do you ever feel like your life was taken away from you?" I've also been trying to figure out why what happened to the Fallen Angels feels wrong. How are they supposed to know that they were taken from bad circumstances? For an agency known for doing shady things, I don't quite understand why all of them have such trust in the system that's controlling them.

And then I think about me. Growing up. Also stuck in something I couldn't control, spiraling further and further until I couldn't breathe. Until I had no choice but to run. To get out however necessary.

Elena thinks for a minute, looking at her hands. "I like to believe that I didn't, but that doesn't mean that it's true. There are people here who know the truth about what happened to us. People I trust. I don't want to know what happened to me; I don't want to feel that pull of curiosity. I shut that out a long time ago. But for the most part, I believe what we do here is necessary and good, so I don't tend to dwell on the past. What's done is done; there is only moving forward."

What's done is done; there is only moving forward.

My lips thin as I rub my fingers together, finally realizing how exhausted I really feel. A mental exhaustion that comes on like a train, hitting me at one hundred miles per hour, knocking me off my feet.

"I just want this to go well. I don't want to disappoint anyone," I tell her, my head falling to the side as I rest it on my shoulder.

"You won't," Elena assures me, taking my hands in hers. She lays her head on my other shoulder, breathing with me.

We stay like that for a few minutes, just existing in the space we take up, contemplating the meaning of life and what human existence is.

"Thank you for being kind to me," I whisper finally, and her head shoots up.

"Why wouldn't I be kind to you?"

I shrug, wincing. "I don't think it's a surprise to say that I was a little shocked coming here. I didn't know any of this existed, of course. Jerry doesn't like me, and neither does Ronan."

She scoffs. "Ronan doesn't like a single person in this world, baby girl, but the way he looks at you is something new."

"What do you mean?"

She grabs my shoulders, spinning me toward her. "I'm saying that that boy isn't nice to anyone. He keeps to himself. He's a lone wolf. He hangs out with us, sure, but none of us know a lot about him."

"He hasn't told me much, either."

"But he will."

"How do you know?"

"There's something about the look in a man's eye that'll tell you everything you need to know."

Elena helped me get my dress on and did my makeup, and I don't think I've ever felt more beautiful.

The form-fitting silver dress falls around my feet, its shimmery fabric reflecting in the light. The bodice hugs my curves perfectly, lifting the girls just enough to still be perceived as classy by snooty politicians, yet still makes me feel sexy.

My hair falls over my shoulders in waves, with two

chunks from either side of my face braided and tied at the back of my head in a bun.

I look in the mirror, examining the magic Elena performed on my face. A dark smokey eye makes my green eyes stand out, a hint of silver at the inner corners. A neutral lip to balance it out.

Thanking Elena profusely and leaving the room, I make my way to Ronan's room, my heels in hand. I don't even bother to knock; instead just barging in.

Ronan spins on his heels, his eyes widening as he sees me. But it's me that can't take my eyes off of him.

Dressed to the nines in black dress pants, Ronan's perfectly ironed white button-down shirt sits untucked and open, revealing his chest. I've seen his chest before, sure. Just the other morning, he was completely shirtless before me. Mouthwateringly gorgeous in a way that sends heat plummeting into the depths of my belly.

But a man in a suit is a whole new level of sexy, and Ronan has it perfected.

His dark eyes gleam with delight as he catches me looking, his lips quirking up in a smirk. His black hair is tousled slightly, and when he turns his head to grab his belt from the bed, I notice his stubble. Like he hasn't shaved in a couple days.

It's not because of me, though, surely.

His bicep bulges in his shirt, and I lick my lips, attempting to desperately get a grip on myself.

"Sorry for barging in like that," I tell him, closing the door finally.

He chuckles as he loops the belt through his pants. "No, you aren't, but that's okay."

I shake my head, smiling. "No, I'm not."

"It's okay to check me out. I won't hold it against you."

I roll my eyes. "Sorry, pal, I'm not interested."

He looks up, his eyes darkening as the corner of his lips lift in a wicked smile.

And suddenly, I find him right in front of me. His hands go to my stomach, pushing me back.

"You can admit it, Sydney."

I breathe in, closing my eyes. His scent surrounds me. Whiskey and sin. "There's nothing for me to admit, Ronan."

His head dips down, his eyes level with mine as he comes closer, brushing his lips against mine in a feather-like touch. "What are you trying to do?" I ask him, keeping my composure.

"I'm trying to *win*," he says, and it snaps me out of my daze in an instant.

"Fuck you," I spit as I try to shove him off, but I'm only shoved back into the wall, my breath knocked out of me.

"You're the one who started this. I'm the one trying to finish it."

The air is electrified with something I don't quite understand, an unavoidable doom that leaves my brain fuzzy, my hands shaking as they press into the wall.

"I'm not one to break, Ronan. You can do whatever you want to me. There is no game."

He scoffs. "That's bullshit, and you know it."

I meet his eyes, biting my lip as I press into him, my lips on his neck. "I wouldn't be so sure about that, husband," I whisper. I push him off of me, heading to the bed where I sit, watching him stand there, something that looks a lot like fury flashing across his handsome face.

"I don't know what you're playing at, but it's not going to get to me."

"You won't admit that you're attracted to me," I start.

"Because I'm not."

"Meanwhile, you're ticked off that I won't admit I'm attracted to you." Ronan opens his mouth to argue, but I put my hand up, silencing him. "I think you need to ask yourself why you really care that much."

His mouth shuts, and after a few seconds of staring at me, he starts buttoning his shirt, looking anywhere but at me.

———

"We're here to take care of business and nothing more. I may have to talk to some people I know, but you need to keep quiet unless you're talked to, okay? Most of the time, wives talk to each other, but most don't mingle with the men."

"Am I going to have to walk around with you?"

"Of course, just don't get us into trouble."

I feign shock. "I would never," I tell him, pressing my hand to my chest. He looks at me from the side, smiling.

"This is really important, Sydney."

I nod. "I know. You want to get this over with so I can go on my merry way. We have a grand divorce. I take half of your money and skip town."

He shakes his head. "I hope you know that that isn't going to happen."

"You mean I won't be properly compensated for the emotional stress I've endured while married to you?"

"What emotional stress?"

"I don't know. I'm feeling pretty stressed out." At least that much is true.

I was given a lot of information about the dinner before we left, including who I can expect to see there. Ronan flashed some photos of coworkers of his that may be there.

Jerry was late in handing us our files that contained our covers, and I had to memorize everything quickly. Ronan said we couldn't bring them with us.

"Who are you?" he asks.

"Sydney Miller. God, that's such an ugly name," I make a face.

He ignores me. "When did we meet?"

"About a year and a half ago." Short enough that it's reasonable the relationship isn't as public as some, but long enough that there shouldn't be too many questions asked on why we got married so soon.

"When did we get married?"

"Two days ago."

"Good girl," he says, nodding.

I like the sound of that.

"Okay, well, what do we do when we see Jeffrey?" Ronan had told me a little of what to expect, but we hadn't explicitly talked about what I should say when we see him. That is if we even speak to him. He said that there's a good chance we don't and that this dinner is just to be seen.

"You talk to him. Answer his questions. I trust you to be smart about what to say if I'm not there. You show off that rock on your finger. Show everyone that you're mine."

"This isn't a pissing contest, Ronan. I'm not yours."

"Right now, you are. To every single man in that room, you're mine."

As much as one part of my brain hates the sound of belonging to someone, the other part doesn't hate it. In fact, I love it.

I hide behind my hair, afraid he'll see the blush creep down my neck.

We come to a stop in front of a large mansion. Before I make a move to get out, his hand lands on my thigh.

"You're going to behave, right?"

I smile, my teeth grinding together. "Ronan baby, husband of mine, light of my life… you should know better than to ask that."

SEVENTEEN

SYDNEY

I'VE NEVER SEEN SO many rich people in my life, and that's saying something.

Although my parents had regular visitors at the house, and despite going to the private school I attended, I've never been around such riches.

Guards meet us at the door, and Ronan hands him an invitation, giving him our names. The man scans a code on the invitation, which brings up a photo of him. Once they're sure we are who we say we are, he lets us through.

The entryway is unlike anything I've ever seen. Beautiful marble floors are adorned with the most beautiful double staircases I've ever seen, leading up to a landing against the back wall. A giant, beautiful cubism painting hangs against the wall, a rock sconce on either side of it, casting a light glow over the surface.

To the right is a dining hall, the walls covered in dozens of art pieces, while a small stage is set up against the main wall, a microphone sitting on top of it.

People dressed in the most expensive dresses I've ever seen line the entryway and overflow into the dining hall, the low hum of conversation radiating through me.

"Oh wow," I say, starting to fidget with my simple silver necklace sitting against my chest.

A firm, warm hand envelopes mine, bringing it next to us. I look at our intertwined hands, my gaze lifting to meet his.

"We got this, okay?" he asks, his voice low. "We have to turn it on now; remember the goal." Although he's completely serious and borderline intense, his voice is sweet. Relaxing. He just wants me to calm down so I don't blow the mission. I know that. But I love it.

Ronan gives me one last look before he starts walking in the direction of a large, greying older man in the corner, lightly tugging my hand along.

The brunette he's speaking to looks at us, her eyes wafting over my dress before she notices Ronan and smiles.

I shouldn't feel possessive, but I do, a shimmer of jealousy thrumming through my veins despite there being no reason for it being there. He's not mine, and by the way the man moves to face us, his hand on her lower back, I think she's taken.

"Steven!" Ronan greets him, shaking his hand with a smile. "This must be Allison?"

"It's good to see you out and about, Ronan. This is Allison, yes." The man has a large smile on his face, his teeth chipped and yellowed.

Allison, at least half his age, leans into him, plastering a smile on her face as she acts the part.

I've known that there are many young women who will marry an older man for financial security, and I get it. I do. I would never judge. It's just not something I'd ever be able to do. The idea of having to put on a performance every second you interact with them, pretending to enjoy the touch of a creepy older man as he infantilizes you, makes me want to throw up in the corner.

I watch her as he grabs her waist, palming it with his big,

sweaty hand, and miss what he's said to me until Ronan's hand squeezing mine breaks me out of my trance.

"This is Sydney, my wife," he tells the man in front of us, a twinkle in his eye. It's one of the first times I've heard him say it, and it sends a shockwave through me.

I've always wanted to be called that.

I just never thought it would happen like this.

I smile, offering my hand. "Hi, nice to meet you," I tell him, careful to stay friendly while not slipping into my customer service voice.

I don't know that bitch.

"I didn't know you were married," Steven says, taking my hand and shaking it. His palm is clammy, yet his skin is still rough against mine.

"Just got married the other day, actually," Ronan smiles at me, and my breath catches. "When you know, you know, right? Had to lock it down."

Steven chuckles, turning back to Allison. "It was so nice to see you guys here; enjoy your night!" he says before directing her away from us.

"That's one of my bosses," Ronan tells me, dipping down to whisper it in my ear. He stays there, playing with my hair as he kisses my cheek.

"Boy, you're laying it on thick, aren't you?"

"Do you want to get this over with or not?" he asks, pulling away just slightly to graze my lips with his.

"Is anyone even watching?"

"And if they weren't?"

"If they weren't, I would think you like touching me."

"I like touching you just as much as I like touching any woman,"

"I'm pretty sure that's the opposite of what you've told me in the last couple of days,"

"We all lie,"

I pull away, narrowing my eyes. "What's happening here?"

"We're playing a part, Syd."

My hands start to shake, my chest heaving slightly. "This doesn't feel like a part for some reason."

His eyes meet mine, a grin on his face as he looks over my shoulder. I can tell when he sees someone he knows, and he puts on the mask. I can tell when he's pretending. He's been flipping between acting and not since we got here.

"Who do you see?"

"Your friend."

Grabbing my arm, Ronan turns us around to walk in the other direction, making sure we come face-to-face with Jeffrey and his wife, Rebecca.

"I'm so sorry," I say as I brush his shoulder.

He looks at me, trying to figure out where he knows me from. It's been a long time since I've seen him. I think the last time was ten years or so ago.

"Sydney?" he asks, grabbing my arm as I go by.

Twenty years ago

"We have to go, Sydney," my mother tells me as she wraps me in a hug. Tucking my wild curls behind my ears, I cross my arms, my mouth turned downward in an aggressive pout.

"I don't want to go over there."

"We all have to do things we don't want to do," she sighs.

"I don't like him," I sit on the floor, desperate to stay home.

My mom's eyes turn hard, and all I know is that I'm about to get in trouble. "Your dad is going to be mad."

"Dad is always mad."

My mom sits next to me, wrapping her arm around me as she pulls me close. "I didn't want this life for you, you know," she whispers.

I don't know what that means.

"Someday, this is going to be yours, and I want you to be stronger than I was. But right now, we have to do this."

I look up at her, watching as her green eyes shimmer. I want to be as beautiful as she is someday.

"I don't want to go, mommy." I feel panic set in, tears welling in my eyes.

"We have to be at Jeffrey's at five, my love. Come on."

Ronan whips around, his back stiff, fire in his eyes as he looks at Jeffrey's hand around my wrist. My breathing has quickened, my vision blurring as memories surface. Memories I've tried so hard to suppress my entire life.

Loosening his grip, Jeffrey's hand drops down to my hand, grabbing my fingers.

"Jeffrey?" I ask, plastering the biggest smile I can possibly muster onto my face. "What are you doing here? It's been forever!"

He doesn't smile. Instead, he looks to Ronan before I feel his finger brush against my ring. His eyes drop down to my hand in surprise, his eyebrows furrowing.

"It has been a long time," he says, refusing to meet my eyes.

"How's the company doing?" I ask him, making sure my voice sounds confident. Proud, even.

His eyes dart to mine, searching for something he's not going to find. "It's going well. We were so saddened by your parents' sudden departure. They've been missed."

Bullshit.

"I've been missing them lately, too," I tell him, taking my hand away from him and placing it on Ronan's chest as I sink into him. He wraps an arm around me, letting me do what I have to do.

Jeffrey's eyebrow shoots up as his wife looks at him. "I'm

sure you do," he says, not sounding too convinced. "And who is this?"

"This," I start, running my hand up Ronan's chest to his cheek, pulling his face down to meet mine, and planting a kiss on his lips. They're warm against mine. Firm and smooth. For a fraction of a second, I want to keep kissing him. I pull away, watching as he runs a finger over his lips, smiling. "This is Ronan, my husband."

"Husband, huh?"

"Yeah, we just got married two days ago, right, big guy?"

Ronan's eyes flicker to mine for a moment at the nickname before he nods. "Best day of my life,"

"I was so lucky to have him when they died. Really. The support was really appreciated." I nod, pulling him in tighter to me.

"I'm so glad you're doing great, sweetie," his wife tells me, and I smile at her. I don't know if she's an innocent party to any of this, and frankly, I don't really care much. No one can live with a monster and not be even a little suspicious. But she's always been nice to me.

"Thank you so much, Rebecca, you look so great." She looks at me appreciatively. I'm sure Jeffrey barely tells her good morning.

"How long have you two been together?" Jeffrey quizzes, biting his cheek. He's gone completely grey in his old age, his teeth yellowing, his beard patchy.

"About a year and a half, right, love?" I ask, looking up at Ronan.

"I think so. It feels like just yesterday, doesn't it? Time flies when you're with the right person."

"You're Emmerson's aid, aren't you, kid?" Jeffrey asks Ronan, his back straighter as he tucks his hands into his pockets.

"Yes, sir, I love working with him."

For a moment, I wonder if we're overdoing it. We may be.

But the point is we just need to get Jeffrey's wheels turning, that's about it. That's the goal. If we overdo it, what's he going to do? We're legally married; that much is true.

Jeffrey grunts, not saying a word as he grabs his wife and turns away from us, heading to the dining room.

"That was weird, right?" I whisper to Ronan.

"As weird as any of this. You may have overdone it a little bit there."

I scoff. "What do you mean I overdid it, Mr. *time flies when you're with the right person.*"

Ronan rolls his eyes, grabbing my hand with a smile and pulling me in the direction of the dining room as well. We find the table we're supposed to sit out, standing around it as we speak to other couples here.

"I feel like I've seen you around. Did you have black hair at some point?" a woman asks me as Ronan wraps his arm around me.

The question catches me off guard, and I sputter for a moment, trying to figure out the right answer. It should be simple, but as an over thinker my brain is muddled with questions. Did she see Ronan with her? If so, would she find my answer suspicious if I say no? What if I say yes and she's spoken to Jerry?

"She did!" Ronan tells her, pulling me into him.

"I love the natural color so much better, dear; you keep it that way." The woman smiles, turning to her husband and heading to their chair as the lights go down, and a tall man with a goatee wearing a three-piece suit makes his way to the microphone.

Ronan pushes me slightly, pulling out my chair for me.

"You doing okay?" he asks, catching my chin between his fingers as I sit down.

I look up at him, noticing the concern lacing his eyes. If we were just pretending, that wouldn't be there, would it? He wouldn't care how I was doing as long as I was doing a good job.

"Why? Am I doing something wrong?"

His face twists with confusion before the realization dawns on him. His lips thin as he runs his palm over my cheek. Bringing his lips to mine, he whispers, "you're doing perfect," against them.

The tension leaves my shoulders, and I sink into his touch. About to pull away, I open my eyes, catching Jeffery's eyes across the room. I quickly avert my attention, grabbing Ronan's neck as he stands back up, pulling him back down to me.

And I kiss him.

A real kiss.

A passionate, intense kiss that makes my thighs clench and my heart race. For a moment, I lose sight of where we are. Of who we are and what this is. All I can think about is this, right here.

It's dizzying. Exciting, warm. It feels like coming home after work and getting into bed. It feels like a promise.

And that's fucking terrifying.

But when everything comes rushing back, the low hum of voices around us growing louder once more, I break the kiss. He grabs the back of my neck, his eyes full of questions.

I tip my head back just slightly in the direction of Jeffrey across the room. "Have to play it up for the bit, right?" I ask him, biting my lip as I lower my gaze. This is for the mission. This isn't real.

Ronan keeps looking at me for a moment longer before clearing his throat, sitting in his seat next to me.

"That didn't feel like a bit," he says under his breath as he angles his chair slightly to see the speaker better.

"Are you admitting you liked it?"

"I may be."

"That sounds like I'm winning."

"That *feels* like you're trying to seduce me."

"Is it working?"

"And what if it does? Who wins then?"

I drop my eyes. "I think the obvious answer is me."

He smirks, his brown eyes searing into mine as the man in front of us taps his mic.

"Good evening, everyone! Thank you so much for being here tonight. We're just going to get sta—oh! No you're fine, come on in and sit down," he says, looking toward the entrance. Ronan watches him, his eyes drifting over to Jeffrey.

It's not until I hear someone at our table greet the newcomer that I look.

And I'm met with an extremely familiar face.

Fuck.

EIGHTEEN
RONAN

A SHARP PAIN in my shin has my head whipping toward Sydney, concern on my face.

Her eyes are wide, a tight smile on her face as her eyes dart across the table and back to me quickly.

And I can see why she's panicking.

Jeremy Reynolds.

He looks right at me, a smile on his face as he takes us in. He doesn't look surprised to see us here. Doesn't even look phased in the slightest.

I can feel her leg shaking against mine, a restless tick of hers. I grab her knee under the table, tapping it before running my hand up her thigh, capturing her hand in mine. It's been an unfortunate revelation tonight that we both calm at the other's touch. It's the last thing either of us need, and it's not something that's faked.

I squeeze it three times, and I feel her fingers tighten around mine.

After a moment, her shaking stops, and we turn our attention back to the speaker.

William Berner has been throwing these dinners for the last fifteen years, bringing some of the most powerful, influential people of DC together into one room so deals can be made, money being exchanged through the fake art that lines the walls. Rich people can support all sorts of horrible things under the guise of buying art.

He's also a member of the secret society we've been trying hard to track. Someone we have an interest in and will be continuing to watch after this mission is over. Usually, we're here to keep watch on the happenings here. Make sure that nothing too evil happens. There's a line that has to be crossed before we're personally allowed to step in, but that doesn't mean we don't gather all the intel we can and report it back to our handler, who lets the Agency know so they can get actual agents in on it, considering a lot of the money ends up going overseas.

He drones on and on about how he's so thankful that everyone is here and that they'll be opening up the bidding for the next thirty minutes. People can go around to each piece, putting a price down. They want it tracked, the Society. Information to hold over their heads in the future if need be. You'd be surprised how okay rich people are with having seedy information about them out there as long as they get something out of it first.

Finally, he lets everyone know that food will be served and that people can get up as they wish, and that after bidding is closed, everything will be taken to the back, and the winners announced. After that, there will be a ball.

The second he's done speaking, half the room gets up and files over to the different pieces, pretending to be interested. They're not stupid. They know there are people here watching.

People like Jeremy.

Sydney grabs her wine glass, taking a long sip as she looks down at the table. I watch as Jeremy's eyes zero in on her ring, his eyes flashing to mine before he chuckles, throwing his napkin down and following a guest over to the gallery wall.

"I don't know what to do; why is he here?" Sydney asks me.

I watch him as he walks, my hand still holding one of hers under the table. "I've never seen him here before, but there's usually a couple of FBI agents around."

"Why don't they just shut the whole thing down?" she asks innocently.

"You'd be surprised how many people and entities benefit from something like this, Princess."

She scowls for a second before her face evens out, and the white of her teeth peeks out, biting her lip.

"So what's our plan?"

"We act like we've been acting. Everything is normal. Nothing is out of place. We keep up the charade we have. It doesn't have to be complicated."

"But what if he wants to speak to me?"

"Then I trust that you would know what to do,"

She nods, her breathing uneven as she sucks in a lungful of air.

"Are you okay?"

She nods, looking away from me. "I think I just need to go to the bathroom quick. Splash some water on my face."

"Do you want me to take you?"

She shakes her head, standing up. Her legs shake slightly, and I steady her before she darts off in the direction of the bathrooms.

Not knowing what to do but seeing everyone chatting amongst each other at the gallery wall, I head over, my hands in my pocket as I pretend to be interested in the art.

"So I assume you know about the company," comes a voice behind me, a large hand landing on my shoulder. I look over, seeing Jeffrey next to me. He smells like cigars.

I nod. "I know enough."

"You know you guys can't take over, right?"

"Who said we want to take over?"

The man takes a sip of what smells like scotch, refusing to look at me. "Everyone wants a part of us, boy. It's better to be honest about it right now."

"Respectfully, I don't know what you're saying."

Casting me a sideways glance, Jeffrey chuckles, downing the rest of his drink before walking away. He's only a couple feet away before he turns to look at me from over his shoulder. "She's more trouble than she's worth, boy. Be careful where you tread."

Anger fills my body, threatening to explode. How someone could talk about anyone like that, I'm not sure.

Stewing, I chew on my lip as I head in Sydney's direction. Turning the corner toward the bathrooms, I practically run into her, placing my hands on her hips to steady her.

Her eyes are slightly red, wild, and sad. I'm not sure what's happening, but I just want to make it better.

I open my mouth to say something, but instead, she wraps her arms around my neck, bringing my lips to hers.

It's the second time she's kissed me tonight. Really kissed me. I'm starting to think this is something she wants.

Freezing in place, I glance to the side quickly, trying to see if she saw someone I didn't and wanted to make a show of it. But there's no one. Just us.

Bringing my hands up to cup both sides of her face, I angle it the way I want, taking the kiss deeper as my tongue explores hers, feeling her wild breathing against me. My head grows fuzzy as if I'm losing control, and I shake it off. But that only makes me all too aware of how she's affecting other places.

I break the kiss, tipping her head back to look in her large, green doe eyes.

"What was that for?"

She shakes her head, her hands finding their way around my wrists as I push her against the wall.

Biting my cheek, I look away before glancing back down at her, feeling emotions I've never felt before swell in my stomach.

"This is a lot," she whispers.

Rubbing her cheek with my thumb, I place a kiss on her forehead. "I know, baby, I know."

"Don't call me that," she snaps.

My trance is broken, my brows furrowing. "Why not?"

"Because you don't mean it. There's no one around. You don't have to put on a show."

"Sydney, you kissed me," I whisper, leveling her with a stare.

She looks away, not sure what to say to that.

"Syd, this doesn't feel like teasing."

Her face twists as she holds back tears. "It is,"

"You're a liar."

"Says the biggest liar of them all."

Stepping back, I drop my hands. I've dealt with this before. Her sister does the same fucking thing. "Cut the shit, Syd." Her eyes widen as her head snaps up. "Since we got to the compound, I haven't lied to you once. Not once. I've fucked with you, sure. But you've fucked with me. Where's that fire now, huh?" Anger flashes over her face, and she opens her mouth, but I'm too annoyed to let her speak. "No, shut the fuck up. You're so fucking strong. I've seen it with my own two eyes. Where's that girl tonight?"

"That girl takes time off from time to time."

"That girl is here. She's you. She's always been you. Not some separate entity. Do you know how much faith in life and love you have to have to go through the shit you've gone through in your life? A lot, Princess. Where's that woman who literally stole my keys and a three-million-dollar car? The one who accepted her fate the second day she

173

was at that compound? The one who went head-to-head with me after I admitted that I've had to *kill people* before, huh?" I say in a whisper over the loud music from the other room.

She doesn't say anything, just stares at me.

"You think that you're just some sheep. Just some plaything that we're going to throw out when we're done with her, and I don't know why. You're anything but. You're powerful. Beautiful. Capable." She looks away, but I force her eyes on mine again. "You got this, okay? I'm with you all the way. You can do whatever you want to me, Princess, and I'll accept it."

She takes a deep breath, looking at her shoes. "Jeffrey Wright abused me as a kid," she blurts quickly, and the second she notices the fury that runs through my body, my hands fisting at my sides, she quickly adds, "It's fine. I should have told you before we got here, but I thought I'd finally forgotten. I thought I'd be able to get through the night. I'm not sure why it took seeing Jeremy to lose my shit. It was just, I don't know. I think it was the last straw. The level of stress right now is too much."

I remain silent, fuming, and when I start to move toward the main room, she grabs my hand, pulling me back gently.

"Ronan, it's not worth it. We'll get him later. Don't do that now. Don't throw away everything we've been working toward."

I stare into her eyes for a whole minute, watching how they morph as she silently pleads with me.

"The second I can make it happen, he's a dead man," I tell her.

If there's one thing I hate, it's men who think they have the power to touch someone else. To make someone hurt. To mark them for the rest of their lives.

I don't let those kinds of men live.

Sydney grabs both of my hands, lifting them to her lips.

They feel cool against my hot skin. "I promise you, I won't stop you."

"And I'm with you every second he's around you."

"That's totally fine with me."

I nod, scratching my chin.

She bites her cheek, chuckling under her breath. "This feels almost real."

"*This* part is."

———

We're sitting at the table eating our steak dinners when Jeremy sits down, taking off his suit jacket and draping it over the back of his chair. Looking at the plate of chicken in front of him, his eyes flutter to me.

"So, Ronan, how was that case you were working on months ago?" he asks, cutting into the meat.

How does he know about that?

"I'm not sure what you mean; you may have someone else," I tell him despite the fact that he knows my name. It's not surprising, but I'm not sure how he knows about that case.

"Oh, I'm sure you do. You told your, uhh, *wife*, about it, right? Surely you did. Maybe she remembers."

I look at her, the questions in her eyes feeling like a stab.

"I mean, you were undercover, weren't you? With that woman? You'd tell your wife about that, I'm sure. So Sydney, how did it go?" he repeats, trying to get a rise out of us.

Her eyes narrow, and I hold my breath. He's trying to piss her off.

But instead of blowing up, she wipes her mouth with her napkin, placing it neatly folded on the table as her eyes meet his. "He said it went perfectly," she tells him, a smile on her face. Anyone who doesn't know her would think she's genuine.

"Well, you must be up to your own cases, right? God, I thought you were a programmer. Pretty cool that you guys both work undercover, though,"

I look around, thankful that everyone else is still occupied by the fake art on the walls.

"What do you mean?" Sydney's head tilts.

"I mean that that night I met with you at the bar. I asked you on a date. You were clearly trying to get information from me, right? I mean, you guys are married! He's out there hanging out with other women at clubs. You're accepting dates. Obviously, there's some… odd things going on."

Without missing a beat, Sydney rolls her eyes, taking a sip of wine. "Jesus Christ, man, just say you hate swingers and move on. You weren't interesting enough for me."

I choke on steak.

An actual choke. A whole piece of meat down the wrong pipe. My eyes tear up as I cough it up, only hearing Sydney say, "sorry, he hates when I tell people," before slapping me hard on the back.

When I can finally breathe again, I smile at Jeremy. "It's just a private thing, you know?"

He scowls at us, leaning back in his seat as the others file back to their tables. Bidding is done.

NINETEEN

SYDNEY

THE DINNER GOES by in a flash, no one feeling super chatty after their bids. I have to imagine that some of them are nervous, but it's also hard to imagine that the 80-year-old next to me is capable of possible war crimes.

Maybe that's something I should come to expect.

William finally appears back at the microphone a little after the tables are cleaned off, reading off everything people have bid on. Of course, we didn't bid on anything, and it seems like a lot of other people are in the same boat, which makes me feel slightly better about not having too much attention on us.

When people start getting up to dance, I look at Ronan, my brow arched. "Why is there a dance portion to this dinner?"

He shrugs. "A lot of older people just like an excuse to dance after they commit crimes."

I nod as if that's enough of an answer.

The scraping of chairs catches my attention, and I watch as Jeremy stands from his seat, his eyes meeting mine. "Do you mind if I ask your date to dance?" he asks Ronan.

I can feel him stiffen next to me, his fingers brushing against my leg. Calming me. Calming him.

"Sure," he says, surprising me.

That bastard! He was supposed to say no! I would have bet almost everything that he would have said no. Why in the world would he say yes?

Bringing his head to my temple, he places his lips on my skin, kissing me before whispering, "Try to find out what he knows, killer," before getting up and heading to the bar for another glass of wine. I gulp, looking back to Jeremy as he offers me his hand.

I take it, his skin warm against mine as he leads me to the dance floor.

Placing one hand on my waist and gripping my other in the opposite, Jeremy sways us to the beat, watching me.

"Are you going to cut the shit?" he asks finally, and my eyes snap to his, narrowing.

"I don't know what you're talking about," I reply innocently.

"I know you guys aren't really married." I open my mouth to offer a retort, "And you're not *swingers*, either. I don't know what Ronan does, but I know what you do, and you're not some kind of agent. So what's going on?"

"You were going to take me in for questioning the other night, weren't you?" I ask simply.

He shrugs. "And if I was?"

"Why would you? I hadn't seen my parents in years. There would have been no reason for it."

Jeremy nods, clicking his tongue. "See, I'm not sure I believe you. People with that much power? People making money, largely off the books, and funneling it to their daughter?"

My blood runs cold. "I never took any money from them."

"You may not have taken money, but it sure as hell was given to you. Don't play dumb."

And it's here that I realize that I have a couple of options. I can either keep playing dumb, playing up the role of a dumb redhead who doesn't know right from left, or I can wing it. But winging it means telling him a little more than I think Ronan would be comfortable with me saying.

But if there's one thing I've always been, it's a little bit impulsive.

"I didn't know you were going to take me in. I felt like something was off, and I didn't know what. But I wanted to get out of there, so I did."

Jeremy nods. "And if you haven't talked to your parents in years, why were you at the funeral?"

"They were my parents," I say. "It was their funeral. Of course, I'd be there."

"Because you're their only child."

Technically, legally speaking, I guess, I want to say, but I'd never admit it. "Yes."

"Do you know anything about their business practices?" he asks next.

"I recently found out, and I'm working hard to make sure that it doesn't continue."

He looks at me, shock written across his face. "And how are you going to do that?"

"How much do *you* know about their business practices?"

"Enough."

"Then you probably know that they were in deep and that there's some complicated rules in place."

"The cult," he nods.

"The cult," I confirm. "I can't say much, but I can say this. I didn't know about most of it until recently. Until after you and I met. I didn't run from the law that night; I just knew something was wrong. I think that's okay for me, as a woman, to feel and act on." He shrugs. "But I can tell you that I'm trying to bring them down. I have nothing to do with their company, but I have a plan to burn it to the ground, and I need you to stay out of my way while I do it. If you do, I'll tell you everything I know."

Jeremy studies me, his eyes seeming to peer into my soul. I hold my breath as he dips me, finally nodding.

"What do you know about Jeffrey Wright?"

"Not much," I say almost too fast.

"Are you sure?"

"Positive. I'm learning more. I know he was good friends with my parents, but I don't know if he had anything to do with them dying."

"Do you know who killed them?"

"So they were definitely killed?"

He casts me an annoyed glare. "Neither of us is stupid, Sydney."

"I don't know who killed them. Not any more than you do, at least. You probably have much more information about it than I do."

"How long do you need for this?" His eyes flicker behind me as his hands move down my waist just a touch.

"A couple days, I don't know. Maybe a week. Maybe two. I can figure out how to get ahold of you."

He nods, gripping me harder in his hands, pulling me into him.

Before I know it, I'm yanked from him, my back hitting a hard chest as his familiar scent fills my nose.

"Don't fucking touch my wife," Ronan hisses, moving to stand in front of me. I peek around him, watching as Jeremy smirks.

"Maybe I was wrong," he says, looking at me. "Maybe you two are together."

He walks away, and I look around, noticing a couple eyes on us, quiet whispers mumbled under the music.

"What was that for?" I ask him, my annoyance rising.

Ronan takes my hand, wrapping his other around my waist. "His hand was far too close to your ass."

"And?"

He gapes at me, annoyed. "You're my wife."

"And you can't fucking wait for the divorce, Ronan."

He spins me, pulling on my arm to bring me back to him. "What did he say to you?" he asks instead of responding to me.

"He told me that he knows that we were bullshitting, and he wanted in on what we were doing."

"And you refused to tell him, right?"

I look away. "I told him that I was taking care of it."

"Now, why would you do that?"

My back stiffens, kicking into defense. "Because it felt right."

"Do you do a lot of other things because they feel right?" he asks.

I tilt my head in question. "I'm not sure where you're going with this."

"Do you. Do other things. Because they feel right."

"If you're asking me if I'm impulsive, then of course. I feel like Jerry and I have that in common."

"I'm not asking about Jerry; I'm asking about you."

I'm not sure why him saying that makes me think about what life would have been like if I had Jerry in it when I was younger, but it does. Growing up as an only child with no one to protect me and no one to talk to about my problems and experiences was a lot.

I just want—

"Hey, where did you go?" Ronan interrupts my thoughts as we stop dancing, his finger gripping my chin. My eyes drift up to his.

"If you're asking me if I follow my heart, the answer is yes. Do you?"

He shakes his head. "I've never had a reason to."

"But you do now,"

"Yes."

I gulp, all too aware of his skin on mine. The way his fingers touch the naked skin on my back, drifting down to just above my ass.

"If you're worried that he's going to hurt me, I don't think you need to. I think he's a good dude; he's just doing his job."

I watch as his posture shifts, his shoulders rearing back as his entire energy shifts. "Whether I like it or not, you're my wife. No one is going to hurt you while you're mine."

He lets go of me, heading back to our seats. The table is empty except for his jacket.

I follow him, not saying a word.

Jacket in hand, Ronan silently moves toward the door, apparently deciding that we've had enough and that we can get going. I look around, not seeing anyone of importance anywhere.

"What are you doing?" I ask him, grabbing at his sleeve.

"This is work."

"That back there was *not* work, Ronan."

He stays silent, and I roll my eyes, letting go of him.

When the valet brings us his car, we both get in, not a word spoken.

And you see, that's just not fucking okay with me.

"Can you put on music?" I ask him, slumping down in my seat.

"No."

"Ronan,"

"Sydney,"

"Why."

"Because I can't even begin to process my thoughts even without music," he snaps, smacking my hand away gently as I reach for the dial.

"What is there to think about?"

We're on the road again, passing by houses and fields separated by patches of trees.

Ronan sighs, pulling off onto a side road. A small parking lot for a walking trail protected from view of the road by a thick patch of trees.

"What—" but I can't finish my question before his lips are on mine.

TWENTY

RONAN

"WHAT ARE YOU DOING?" Sydney asks, pushing me away. I sit back, running my hands through my hair.

"I want this," I tell her. "Selfishly, I want this. I can't stop thinking about it, and I have no idea why." My palm lands on her thigh, and I spread my digits out, feeling her leg break out in goosebumps as her breathing slows.

"Then why don't you take it?" she asks, moving her leg slightly so one side of the slit in her dress falls between her legs.

I swear the car gets ten times hotter as I consider her question. It's a good one. One I'm not completely sure I can answer. I palm my face, hitting the back of my head against the seat. "I don't know. I haven't had this. I get up in the morning, I do my job, I go home, I sleep. The next day is the same. I don't have time for relationships. I never have."

She looks down, studying her hands as her neck tips away from me. "You haven't had a relationship that you remember at all, have you?"

"Is this a relationship?" I ask, catching her off guard. I should have answered the question. I should have stopped myself from asking. But I want to know.

Kissing Sydney feels like freedom. A freedom I never really thought I needed.

Sydney doesn't say anything for a long time, the silence filling the car, settling on our shoulders with a heaviness neither of us are prepared to describe. The windows start fogging over as we sit, my hand back on her thigh, hers fisted in her lap.

"I've never had a single relationship that lasted," she says finally. "Not a single one. Everyone always left. No matter what I did for them, nothing was ever enough." She sighs, and I press my hand harder into her. "I tried to be the perfect girlfriend. The perfect little future housewife. I cooked for them, I cleaned for them, I offered them a place to stay, my bed to sleep in, my body whenever they wanted it. It was never enough." Her head turns to the side as she presses her forehead against the cool window, trying desperately to settle her nerves as his leg starts softly bouncing, her fingers wringing each other out. "Every single time, something came up that was more important than me. A job, usually."

My hand drifts higher up her leg, and she stills, looking back at me. "I know that this is fake, but I've never felt so comfortable around someone, even when you're mean to me."

And her words break me. I think about my reply carefully, running my tongue along my bottom lip before meeting her eyes, trying to convey every possible feeling that's running through my mind to her without words. But I find them anyway. "This is a job. And we can't screw it up. So much relies on this. But I can't help the feeling I get when I touch you."

She nods her head slightly, little tuffs of hair freeing themselves from her braids and falling into her face.

"When this is done, you're not going to want me, Syd. You're not. I'm not a good man, and you deserve so much better."

Her eyes squeeze shut, and I can see through the dark how white her palms are as she digs her nails into them.

"I just don't want to hurt you," I whisper. "But I also can't control how much I want you."

Her green eyes grow large as they meet mine, and I wonder if I've said the wrong thing. If she's going to yell, or scream, or get out of this car right now and get lost in the woods somewhere, never to be seen again. It's a thought that's crossed my mind from time to time two.

"I'm not a good person either, Ronan. I've run from my demons for far too long Ignored suffering. I was complacent. Happy with running. With ignoring the past. With moving past it. I should have stayed and fought."

"You were a kid, Sydney."

"And you were forced to do this, Ronan."

Her words sting. Something that I've never really thought about before. I've spent years and years of my life working for the Agency, doing whatever they wanted me to do. I've done things I'd rather forget over and over again. I turned my empathy off. I couldn't do it.

"Maybe we're more similar than either of us ever thought," I whisper.

"Maybe."

The only thing that moves between us is our chests, rising and falling with our breath as our eyes never once waver from the other.

"Where does that leave us?" she asks.

"Sydney Miller, do you want me to touch you?" I ask her, my voice dropping an octave as my hand moves up her thigh, higher and higher.

"I do, but not like this," she shakes her head, her eyes closing as she whimpers when I reach the top.

"What do you mean by that?"

Her eyes meet mine, only lit up by the moonlight above us. Her face seems younger here. Like she's seen less in this

189

life. Experienced less. There's something about that moonlight that invigorates us. That lets us live separate lives for just a few hours. Or maybe it's not a separate life. Maybe it's just simply a life we were promised by the sun but never got. Same, but different.

"I mean that I want you to take me home and have your way with me, Ronan Miller."

I don't waste a second. Putting the car in gear, I back up before peeling out onto the road, glad that we're not that far away. I can feel my pants growing tighter and tighter the more I think about stripping that dress off her slender shoulders and sliding it down her body.

"Spread your legs," I tell her suddenly, feeling impulsive for one of the first times in memory.

Her head swivels, a surprised look on her face. "What?"

"You heard me. Spread your legs."

Hesitantly, she does as she's told.

"Good girl," I tell her, my fingers tightening around the wheel as I try to desperately show at least a little bit of restraint. "Now touch yourself."

Sydney gasps, looking ahead. I'm speeding now, taking each turn recklessly. "Ronan, I don't think this is a goo—"

"Do what I said,"

She does.

Bringing her hand between her thighs, she extends her middle finger out, dragging it up her center over her lacy underwear. Her head drops back as her breathing becomes shallow. I can still see her eyes on the road.

"Move the underwear over and touch yourself. I want your eyes on me, Princess."

Casting one more nervous glance at the road as I turn a corner, her eyes land on me. I can feel them burning into my flesh as she looks up at me, her mouth open as she bites her lip.

"Does that feel good?" I ask her, feeling my restraint slipping away with every word.

"Yes," is all she can say through a moan.

I speed up. "Do you wish that was me?"

"*Fuck*, of course I do."

Without thinking, I take my right hand off the wheel, immediately placing it over her hand as I gently move it to her leg. Still keeping my eyes on the road, I run my fingers over her slick pussy, loving the way her back curves as she pushes into me.

"Patience," I tell her simply, biting back a smile as I see her eyes narrow out of the corner of mine.

Licking my lip, I cup her sex in my hand, carefully, slowly inserting one finger as I palm her clit. Her breath catches, her head landing on the back of the seat as she looks up at the ceiling, her lips parted.

I turn wildly, the car drifting as I go. Her eyes snap open, looking outside.

"Did I tell you to take your eyes off me?" I bark.

"No," she whispers, shifting her gaze back.

"Fucking look at you," I smile, biting my lip. "Spread for me in my car, dripping on my fingers. Are you close to coming, Sydney?"

Her eyes squeeze closed as I feel her contract around me, and I add another finger for good measure, pumping them in and out in a circular motion. Her body moves up, pressing down into them as her breathing becomes more and more ragged.

"Open them," I demand, and she does, irritation flashing through them before it's quickly replaced with lust.

"We're almost home," she says, and my brain is so focused on how she's about to come that I barely register that she called the compound home. I tell myself I'll ponder that later. That's not a question for right now.

Pulling my fingers from her, I place them on my tongue, running it over them one by one as I taste her for the first time. "Fucking perfect," I moan, gripping the wheel again. "When we get in there, get up to my room. Don't you dare take your dress off. I've been thinking about taking it off of you all day."

"Yes sir," she tells me with a smirk, her attitude making an appearance once more.

"I'm really glad I've learned I can fuck the attitude out of you," I respond, and her mouth clamps shut. "May have to take advantage of that."

She crosses her arms over her chest, pretending to look out the window when I can see her casting short sideways glances my way before her eyes move down over my chest and to my lap, my pants tight as my dick strains the fabric.

Pulling into the compound feels like a relief. But not for long.

Jerry sits on the couch, watching us pull in.

"Fuck," I say, looking at Sydney. "Get yourself straight and go up to the room. I'll be there in a minute.

She nods, not bothering to say anything. We both know that it's the best option.

I get out first, staying behind my car as I wait for Jerry to come over. Her hair is in a messy bun on top of her head, her sweats stained. She's been stressing today.

"How was it?" she asks as she stands next to Sydney's door, her arms over her chest as she shifts her weight to one leg.

"It was fine," I tell her simply. "We definitely got Jeffrey's attention. I think we'll be hearing from him in no time."

She nods, looking me over.

"You have lipstick on your mouth," she says simply. There's no malice there. No annoyance. Just stating a fact.

"We had to—"

"Ronan, I promise you I don't give a fuck. You guys can

fuck every single day if you want as long as this job gets done."

I clamp my mouth shut. Noted.

Jerry grabs the passenger-side door handle, opening it for Sydney. I'm really glad nothing else happened. She still looks fairly put together.

"Get upstairs," Jerry barks, not bothering to be nice to her.

"Do you want me to—"

"No. Go upstairs."

Sydney looks at me, and I nod once. Her lips thin as she heads for the stairs. I watch as she disappears.

"Listen," Jerry starts, leaning against the roof of my car. Her black hair falls out of her bun, and her eyes are sleepy. "I mean what I said. I don't care what you guys do. Truly. I don't want to hear about it, but I don't care. But you need to keep your head on your shoulders, got it? Don't let some girl mess you up."

"She's your—"

"She's some girl who's going to leave after this mission is over. You guys are going to get divorced, and she's going to go on her merry way. She's going to find someone who lives a normal life, can give her kids, and she's going to get married and have a family."

Her words hit hard. I know that that's what's going to happen. I know that I can't give her a family. I know that she's never going to be happy with me. Not really, anyway. But I want her to be. Desperately, for some reason I don't understand, I want her to be.

But this is Jerry. Jerry, the same woman who has nursed me back to health for years when I've been sick, just like she's done for the other three. She's the same one who makes sure that we come back home safe every single day. The same woman willing to walk in front of a bullet for each and every one of us.

She has a point, but that doesn't mean it doesn't hurt.

"I just don't understand this draw," I tell her, looking at my hands.

She places her chin on her arm, tilting her head as she looks at me. "All of us want to be loved, Ronan. All of us. We may not have been treated like humans, but we are. That's the one thing we've always missed. It's the reason Brandon and Elena have been hooking up. It's the reason Kim and Zach constantly fucking fight. Who have you had to turn to?"

I've had no one. Not a single soul.

"Who have you?" I ask.

Jerry chuckles. "I don't need anyone, Ronan. I can guarantee you that. What I'm trying to say is that it's natural to feel the pull. I've seen it so many times. But you just need to be careful not to lose your head, okay?"

I nod.

"If she wants you at the end of this, we can figure it out. I care about you enough to promise you that. But this isn't a life most people want, and you have to be okay with that."

She's right.

Digging my hands in my pockets, I look up towards my room, my heart twisting. I'm not sure what to do.

"You know I'm older than you, right? I feel like I should be giving you advice, not the other way around."

Jerry stands, tapping the roof of my car with her fingers. "It's never been like that, Ronan, and you know it." She smiles, and this time, it's a real one.

You can say what you want about Jerry, but she cares about us.

"Do you think that you could get along with her?" I ask.

She considers this, rubbing her eyes as she yawns. "I'm sure I could find it within me to be nicer to her one day if she chooses to stick around."

That's good enough for me.

It's later than I thought when I take two stairs at a time, reaching my room. Swinging the door open, I find Sydney sitting in the chair in the corner, her legs curled up under her, Shiloh in her lap.

Her eyes snap up to meet mine, and she looks sad.

"This has to stop," she says, and I nod. It should. "You're going to hurt me," she adds after a second.

"Why would I hurt you?" I ask her.

"The second this ends, you're going to wake up and realize that you're only feeling like this because we were forced together this way. You're going to realize that you don't want me. Not really. That this is just some fucked up type of mutual Stockholm syndrome. I don't want that for me, and I don't want it for you, either."

"I want you, Sydney."

She shakes her head. "No, you don't."

"I do."

She gets up, riffles through her clothes, and goes to head to the bathroom.

I catch her arm, spinning her into me. She makes a move to smack me, but I catch her wrist in my other hand, moving her backward as I push her aggressively onto the bed. Her eyes light with fire.

"I'm not going to do a single thing you don't want me to do, so tell me now if you want me to leave you alone. But all I'm going to tell you is that I've been picturing this for the last two days. I don't know why I feel this way, and I know it's wrong, but the thought of you not being mine kills me."

"It's this arrangement, I—"

"Can you shut up?" I ask her. "I'm not saying this is love, Sydney. But this is desire, and I know you feel it too. The way you react whenever I touch you," I run my fingers up her leg, and she trembles, her mouth falling open. "The way

195

you seek the feeling of my skin on yours whenever you're uncomfortable. Do you understand that I feel the same way?"

Her eyes open wide, her tongue peeking out as she licks her bottom lip. She props herself up on her forearms, watching me stand above her. My chest rises and falls heavily, my eyes piercing hers.

"What do you want me to do?" she asks.

"I want you to do what you're comfortable with."

"I want you to touch me."

She doesn't have to ask me twice.

"Stand up," I demand, and when her eyes narrow, I raise a threatening eyebrow. "If you don't listen to me, I'm going to fuck that attitude right out of you, Sydney. Choose wisely."

A shiver runs through her as I spread her legs, waiting for her to do as she's told. A small grin crosses her face as if she wants to piss me off.

I should have known.

I grab her waist, lifting her up so she's standing in front of me before putting pressure on her shoulders, moving her downward until she's kneeling in front of me.

"Fucking perfect," I tell her, palming her cheek as I move my thumb to her mouth, pulling the corner of it down. Her eyes close, and when they open, they're wicked.

With an evil smirk, Sydney's hands go to my belt, pulling it off. I watch her from above, my breathing labored as my cock strains my pants. She does it slowly. Deliberately. Carefully. It's so fucking annoying.

I take over for her, whipping my belt off before throwing it across the room. She looks at me innocently as she unbuttons my pants at the same speed.

"Keep doing that, I fucking dare you," I growl, lashing out to grip her chin in my palm, forcing her eyes on mine. "If you want to be punished, Princess, just say so."

"That's not as fun, though," she says as she pushes my

pants down, watching as my dick springs free of them, tenting my boxers. Her eyes grow large,

"You've had that in there, and you haven't blessed anyone with it?"

"Sydney," I say, losing control. "When you're with me, I don't want you mentioning other people. Not for me, not for you, got it? When you're with me, no other man's name leaves your lips, and no other woman exists in this world." I pry her mouth open, sticking my fingers into the back of her throat. "Now, be a good girl and close your mouth." She does. "Suck."

Doing as she's told, she keeps her eyes on mine until they roll back and she lets out a small moan. Reaching for my boxers, she pulls them down, watching my face as I spring free of them.

Her eyes don't even leave mine as she takes my fingers out of her mouth, moving her lips to the tip of my dick.

Licking the head once, she watches me from below as my breath hitches, watching her move to the base. Her tongue flickers out, running all the way up the length from the bottom. Her eyes are still on mine.

"Fuck, baby," I mutter, fisting her hair in my palm. I wrap it around my hand, pulling her head back. "Tongue out."

She does as she's told, kneeling before me, sweat beading on her forehead, her tongue out for me.

And I spit in it.

I watch her face carefully, calculating how she's going to react to anything else. She doesn't blink. Doesn't flinch. Instead, without closing her mouth, she pushes forward, wrapping her warm, wet lips around my throbbing dick as she takes it all the way in.

"Jesus Christ, look at you," I tell her as she pulls up, taking me in once more. She closes her eyes. "Eyes on me," I tell her, yanking on her hair.

Her eyes flutter open, darker than I've ever seen them.

Sultry. Intoxicating. I can get lost in them. "You're doing so fucking good, Princess," I encourage as she fills her throat with me.

She adds one hand, wrapping it around my cock tightly as she pumps in and out, keeping her eyes on me just like I told her to.

I toss my head back, a whimper escaping my lips. She grips it harder then, twisting her hand as she goes.

"I'm going to come, Sydney. I'm so close."

She hums onto me, gripping me harder and harder, feeling me pulse in her hand.

And I finally come undone.

She doesn't move away from me, instead licking every last drop that comes from me, making a show to swallow it, her eyes still locked on mine.

Is this what I've been missing?

Lifting her up, I move to take her dress off, wanting to pleasure her the way she pleasured me.

But she stops me.

Her hand on my wrist, she looks over her shoulder nervously. Gone is the confident woman on her knees before me. She looks scared again.

"Not tonight," she whispers, and my eyebrows furrow in confusion.

"Why not?" I ask, worrying that she's not enjoying herself.

She turns around, sitting on the bed in front of me. "I just want to take this slow," she says as she winces.

I kneel down in front of her now, grabbing her hips as I situate myself between her legs. "I'm good for whatever you're good for, Sydney. Are you okay?"

She nods, sending me a tight-lipped smile.

I don't know what's happening, but I'm not thrilled about it.

Standing up, I run my fingers through my hair, looking

around. Pulling my boxers on, I look back at her. "Why don't you go clean up, okay?" She looks away before back at me, and there's something in her eyes that looks an awful lot like shame, and I hate it.

But I can't force her to tell me what's wrong.

"I'm going to go downstairs and get some water and a snack. Do you want anything?"

She shakes her head.

I nod, heading out of the room, confusion clouding my brain.

TWENTY-ONE

SYDNEY

THE WARM WATER rains down on me, washing the sweat from my body.

I've never felt anything like I do with Ronan. I've never wanted to pleasure someone so badly. Never wanted someone to pleasure me so badly. But I'm terrified of scaring him away.

There are things about me he needs to know first.

Sighing, I think about what just transpired. I don't think I've ever given a hotter blowjob. I've always been into more aggressive sex. Always wanted to be pushed around a little bit. Him spitting in my mouth was one of the single most hottest things that anyone has ever done to me.

And I want him to do it again.

I squeeze some of his body wash onto my washcloth, moving it across my shoulders, imagining what it would feel like if it were him.

Sighing, I finish washing off, stepping out into the foggy bathroom as I grab the large towel from the hanger, drying myself off.

I brush my teeth slowly, taking my time before washing my face thoroughly with bar soap. I'm going to have to have someone go to the store with me at some point to grab proper face wash.

When I'm finally done, I look at the bathtub in the corner, promising myself that I'll take a bath tomorrow.

Opening the door, the bathroom clears, and I step out into his room to find him resting on his bed, his back against the headboard as he chugs a bottle of water. There's another one next to him, along with a small bowl of candy.

"I know you said you didn't want any, but I brought you water and something to eat," he tells me, his brown eyes searching mine. I know that he's confused about what just happened. I am, too, in a way. I'm just not ready to talk about it with him right now. I will at another time.

Right now, I just want to lay with him. To feel his hand on my back as we sleep, his breath on my neck.

"Thank you," I tell him as I move to the bed, looking to see what he brought. "Oh my god, yes!" I exclaim as my hand darts forward, grabbing an almond joy.

He raises a brow, the corner of his lips tilting up. "A favorite?"

"My absolute favorite," I confirm.

"I'll have to remember that,"

I nod, unwrapping the candy before taking a bite. Something about coconut and chocolate just goes so perfectly together.

"Do you want to talk to me about what happened earlier?" he asks, reaching for my hand. I grab it, climbing onto the bed. I sit on my knees beside him, grabbing another candy.

Ronan looks at me for a second before grabbing the towel from around me, pulling it off. I immediately cover myself, but he doesn't even look at me as he slides the large grey shirt he's wearing off of himself.

"Arms up," he says. I do as he says, curious, and he slides the shirt on me.

I'm stunned. "I," I start, not knowing what to say. "I don't have anything to say right now, no. It's not you, I promise. I loved everything about that," I assure him genuinely.

"I didn't go too far?"

I shake my head. "No, not at all. That was amazing."

He nods, pursing his lips.

In the dim light, his beard looks even thicker, and it makes me smile. He really doesn't need it, but I won't lie and say he doesn't look incredibly sexy with it.

I crumple up the wrappers in my hands, placing them back in the bowel. "Can we go to bed? I'm really tired."

He studies me for another moment before nodding, grabbing my hips, and pulling me toward him. Flipping me, he lifts the covers and lets me get under them before pulling me into him. I can feel him through his boxers against my bare ass.

Ronan wraps his arm around my waist, securing me at his side before he tucks his head into the crook of my neck, breathing deep.

"Did you use my body wash?" he mumbles into me.

"And what if I did?"

"Keep doing it."

───

When I wake in the morning, Ronan is nowhere to be found.

Shiloh is curled in my arms, his soft purrs waking me up gently as I blink away the sleep. Last night feels like a fever dream, but so has every single night since I first ran into Ronan Miller.

I wonder when it's going to stop feeling like one.

"Where did Ronan go?" I ask the grey cat next to me. He blinks at me lazily as if to say he doesn't care. He could go jump in a ditch somewhere, and he'd probably be happy.

"You're right. You're not the one to ask, are you?"

Sighing, I climb out of bed, heading to the closet to throw on some clothes.

Choosing a pair of fitted jeans and a ribbed tank top, I grab a cardigan, throwing it on over it all to keep warm. As the days get shorter and shorter, the compound gets more and more chilly, and I've only been here a few days. Ronan said that Jerry waits until the very last moment to turn on the heat, despite the fact that she doesn't have to personally pay the heating bill.

Throwing on some socks, I walk out of the room, closing the door quietly behind me so Shiloh can't get out. He's much too curious to have access to the entire compound, and I don't feel like having to find him in the sea of cars around us.

The low mumble of voices has me looking down into the kitchen, finding everyone there.

I stand there for a moment, watching them as they move around each other. Jerry stands at the kitchen island, watching as Elena once again makes a pan of eggs, checking the bacon she has cooking in the oven. When the toast pops up from the toaster, Elena shows Jerry the slice, to which Jerry shakes her head, asking her to put it in for longer. Elena takes all the other slices out, laying them on a plate before putting hers back in.

Brandon watches Elena as he gets the orange juice from the fridge. Zach retrieves cups from the cabinet.

Meanwhile, Ronan goes over paperwork at the counter, asking Jerry something I can't hear. She looks at him before spotting me from above. She doesn't glare at me, but she doesn't smile either. Instead, she just looks.

Ronan turns, finding my eyes. I can see even from up here that his face lights up, and Jerry notices.

Her lips press together as she turns around, watching Elena once more.

I'm sure this is weird for her. No matter what she says

about it being totally fine, it's odd to have your twin sister here. Especially since things have been so different for us.

Deciding it's time to make an appearance, I make my way down the metal stairs and into the kitchen, pulling my cardigan tighter around me.

"There she is!" Elena calls. "How did last night go? You looked absolutely stunning. I'm sure every man there was jealous of this idiot," she motions to Ronan.

I crack a smile, my eyes flickering to his as he continues watching me.

"It was good, I think," I tell her, sitting next to Ronan at the counter. Jerry doesn't turn, and when Elena turns back to face me, she flashes her a confused look.

Jerry sighs, finally turning to me. "Worked a little too well. Got word that Jeffrey wants you to call him."

I nod, curious. "Why is that a bad thing?"

"He's desperate right now, which means that this is a little more dangerous than I thought it was going to be." She studies my face to see what my reaction to that is, and when I don't give one, she continues on. "It's going to be fine. I just want to make sure that we do this the right way, and we didn't have much time to discuss everything going on."

Elena places a plate of breakfast in front of me, and Zach asks if I want orange juice as he hands a glass to Brandon. I nod, thankful.

"I don't have my phone," I tell her as I take a bite of toast.

Reaching into her pocket, she throws an object at me. It's cold and heavy in my hands. Pressing the power button, I watch it come to life. When it finally reaches the main lock screen, I scowl at her. "How long have you just been carrying my phone around with you?"

"Only a couple of hours," she tells me as she inspects her fingernails.

I roll my eyes.

"Okay, so what's the plan?" The four of them look at me,

but it's Ronan's eyes I feel the most.

"We're going to have you call Jeffrey, obviously," Jerry says, pointing to the phone in my hands.

"I don't have his number."

She takes a piece of paper from her other pocket, unfolding it and slides it in front of me. A ten-digit number is scrawled across in black ink.

"Thanks," I mumble as I unlock my phone.

Their eyes continue to be on me as I type the digits into my phone, and it occurs to me that Ronan hasn't spoken a single word to me since I came down here. I look at him, finding his brown eyes on mine, watching me intently.

I tip my head down the smallest amount, and when he does the same, butterflies erupt in my stomach at the silent confirmation that we're in this together.

Taking a deep breath, I press the call button, putting the phone on speaker.

It only takes a couple of rings.

"Sydney," he says curtly, and it makes me want to scrub my skin raw. I only wonder where he got my number for a moment before I realize that it's a stupid question. It's just off-putting that he had it readily in his phone.

"Jeffrey, nice to hear your voice," I say as the others hold their breath.

He grunts, and I can hear the riffling of papers on the other end.

"Well, let's get to it. I'd like to meet with the board." There's a pause on the other end as he processes my words. He had to know that was why I was calling,

"I don't think that would be wise," is what he settles with, his voice low.

"It's my parents' company, Jeffrey; I'd like to at least meet with them."

He clears his throat. "Speaking with the board would be an absolute waste of time for you, Sydney. There is no reason to. They're never going to approve you, and all you'll do is make a fool of yourself."

"Why?" I ask, feeling emboldened.

A pause.

"You've proven throughout your life that you're unfit to run this. Being married for two days proves nothing. The board will see right through it."

"Jeffrey, schedule me a meeting with them, or I'm going to go above you and schedule it myself."

There are several moments of silence as he decides what to say next. "I'll schedule a meeting. Ronan must be there with you." There's a pregnant pause. "And Ronan? Reign in your whore. She was mine first."

The line goes dead.

And my heart stops.

I stare at the phone as the others look at each other, the realization of what he means dawning on their faces.

But I don't hear what they're saying. I don't see what their next moves are. All I see is my phone. After a moment, the screen darkens before turning off completely.

There's nothing around me but memories.

My heart lurches, my blood running cold as sweat dots my forehead. Stars line my vision, and I'm stuck.

I'm stuck sitting here, unable to move, desperately wanting to be swallowed whole by the ground beneath me.

I don't know how long this goes on for. It could have been minutes. Hours. Days. But it's more likely it was only a few.

It takes me a couple moments to realize someone is grabbing me, and I flinch away as everything comes back to me. Their voices, their faces, their words.

"What the *fuck* does he mean by that?" Jerry seethes, her eyes narrowed.

"Don't fucking talk to her like that," Ronan barks, seething as he watches me, not wanting to touch me and scare me more.

"I'm not trying to be an asshole, Ronan. I'm trying to find a reason not to kill this man right this second."

"Jerry, she needs space; wait a minute," Elena says, grabbing her arm and pulling her back. She shakes her off, holding her hand up.

"Let's give them space," Brandon tells Zach as they step out of the kitchen.

"Are you okay?" Ronan stands in front of me, offering his hand. Like I'm some fucking kicked puppy. Like I'm injured and weak.

"I'm fine," I tell him. "Completely."

"Ronan, go cool off and give her some time," Jerry demands, stepping between us.

Pissed, Ronan throws his hands up. "That's rich coming from you," he says angrily, looking me in the eye. I nod, giving him permission to go.

Jerry grabs my arm, but it's not angry like usual. This time, she's soft with it as she leads me to the side. Sitting me down at a small table with a chess set in the center, she takes a seat on the other end, staring at me.

After a moment of silence, she piles her hair on top of her head before she moves a pawn two spaces, sitting back in her seat once more.

I look at the pawn for a long time. Studying it. Thinking about what her next move will be.

But her move depends on mine.

So I move one of mine two spaces, situating it right in front of hers.

She moves another pawn to c4, right next to her other.

I move my next to c6.

"I assume this happened before you ran away," she says, keeping her eyes on the chessboard. I nod, and her eyes flash to mine before going right back to the chess pieces in front of us.

Her knight to c3.

"How old were you, Syd?"

I move my knight to f16, silently sitting back. I don't take my eyes off her hands as they hover above the board, planning her next move.

"Six."

Her hand freezes as she places her second knight on f3. She stays there, hovering, as her eyes lock on me.

I don't dare look at her.

Without waiting for her to back off the board, I move a pawn to e6.

"Did our parents know?"

I think about it for a second. "I don't know. Sometimes I felt like they did."

She lets out a deep, labored breath. The kind you take when you're considering doing something horrible and you're trying to force yourself to calm down. The kind that you learn about in therapy but don't really work in real life.

Her pawn to e3.

"How long?" she asks, her anger barely restrained.

"Ten years," I whisper.

My knight to d7.

Her fingers turn white as she grips her bishop, moving it to d3.

"Why didn't you tell me?" she asks softly. The softest I've ever heard her speak.

"Would you have listened?" I look at her.

I really look at her.

We have the same face, but hers is unarguably more aged than mine. Whether it be the stress of the job, the cigarettes, or something else, worry lines line her forehead as she frowns, her eyes sad.

I move my pawn to c4, taking hers.

"I don't know why I took the job here," she says suddenly, sighing. "I didn't think I was cut out for it. Didn't think it would be good for me, you know? I don't know. I don't trust the government. I don't trust the systems that are supposed to work."

She clicks her tongue, moving her bishop to c4, taking my pawn.

"I don't either," I tell her, thinking about how small I truly feel around her for the first time since I was brought here.

Maverick walks over to us, placing his pointed face in my lap, his brown eyes looking up at me. I look back at him for a moment before placing my palm on his head, petting him.

"The first time mom visited me was when I was moved to a new foster home," she begins as I move my pawn to b5. She immediately moves her bishop back to d3, so I can't take it. "Dad didn't know. She did it in secret. She was away for something. I'm not sure what. I remember I was eight, though."

I move my bishop to b7.

"I remember being surprised. I hadn't heard much about my parents. All I knew was that the foster home I went to was terrible. All I knew was that I was being abused. I brought it up to a case worker and was ignored for quite some time until finally, one day, they believed me."

Her pawn to e4, mine to b4.

"Anyways, the guy was a piece of shit. In his fifties, he only ate canned meat and fish, and definitely took advantage of the foster care system the same way he took advantage of little girls placed in his care."

My neck bristles, my eyes snapping to hers.

"You got out of there?" I ask.

Her head bobbles back and forth as she moves her knight to a4. "I got out of *there,* only to be placed in another."

My heart hurts.

My pawn to c5, hers to e5. My knight to d5, and after a moment of hesitation, Jerry switches her king and rook.

My pawn moves to d4, taking one of hers.

"That happened a lot, actually," she says. "But when I met

mom for the first time, she was apologetic. She wanted to help. She made me feel loved. She said she'd bring me home one day. She told me I had a little sister that looked exactly like me."

"You were born first?"

"I was born first."

A small smile creeps up the corner of my lips, disappearing as she moves her knight to d4, capturing my pawn.

"For the first time in my short life, I felt like things could look up. I mean, how many people are able to be reunited with their real family?"

My pawn to g6, hers to f4. Mine to a6, hers to f5.

"Did you tell her what was happening?"

Jerry nods her head as I move my queen across the board to h4.

"What did she say?"

Her pawn takes mine at e6. My queen slides over after, taking her pawn. Her king moves to h1.

"She said that sometimes things in this life aren't fair," she tells me as she studies the board. "She said that sometimes it's important to just close your eyes and go to a happier place. That you can't help what happens to you in this world."

My stomach drops.

It's the same thing she told me.

I move my rook to d8, moving my king to c8 at the same time.

"I assume she told you the same?"

I nod.

Her pawn to d7, taking my knight. My king to b8, getting out of its way.

"It's interesting how it all works, isn't it?"

"What's that?"

"The system."

"Mom and dad belonged to a cult for a long time."

She nods. "I know. But it's more than that, isn't it."

"What do you mean?"

Her bishop to a6, taking my pawn. My queen to e5, taking her pawn. Her rook to e1. I quickly move my queen out of the way, back to d6.

"I mean that the system benefits men. That much is true." I nod. "But how does it brainwash women into believing that their desires are more important, even if they're evil."

"Not everyone is evil."

"A lot of them are, though," she tells me, and it occurs to me that although we're bonding over our shared trauma, she's still been through more than I have at more hands. That doesn't make her trauma any more or less important, but it's still something to be sensitive about.

Her rook to e8. My queen to d7. Her bishop to f4. My king is in danger.

My queen moves between them, blocking the way at d6. Her rook takes mine at h8.

"You know, I worked for years and years to forget."

We both look at the board, trying to figure out our next moves. I could easily take her rook, eliminating it from the board and getting rid of the danger to my king. Her bishop could take mine, and I'd be forced to move my king. But my queen would take it, and it would be off the board.

"Every year after things happened, I told myself that I would just forget it. Like it was some sort of affirmation. One day, if I said it enough times, I would." I pause, my head tilting as I keep studying the board. "And I did. I did forget it eventually. I found that, eventually, I wouldn't think about it every day. The time between thinking about it would grow. I'd go, "It's been longer since the last time. I'm making progress.""

Jerry moves her hand to hover over her queen but realizes there's no good place to move her.

"After years and years of little goals, I was finally able to stop thinking about it. Stop feeling his breath on me. Stop seeing his face when I went to sleep. I stopped hearing my mom make excuses for not listening to me. Something would always come up. Something would always be more important to deal with at the time. There was always a reason that I needed to go over to his house with them, no matter what." I think I see a move, but I realize it wouldn't do me any good, either.

Jerry leans back in her seat, her eyes on me as I keep looking for ways to win this. But she looks done.

"Mom was raised in the cult. One where she wasn't respected. One where she had to be silent. And I'm willing to bet anything that the same things happened to her."

I look up, meeting her eyes. The same green as mine. The same green as mom's.

"It's a stalemate," Jerry says simply, her arms crossed, not bothering to look at the board.

"It's a stalemate," I agree.

She blinks once. Blinks twice. Her nose twitches.

And then she reaches across the table, extending me her hand. I look at it for a long moment, trying to figure out her move. Trying to figure out her angle.

But I don't think there is one.

I take it.

"We're going to make that man regret the day he met you," she tells me, her eyes hardening, her voice predatory.

My lips tip up just a touch. "I hope so,"

There's a heavy silence between us, and we let it hang there for a long time. "Hey, how did you learn how to play chess?"

She smirks. "Mom gave me my first set that time she visited me. Told me to channel my frustration and hurt into chess. It would make the bad things hurt less."

I nod. She did the same thing for me.

TWENTY-TWO

RONAN

THREE DAYS HAVE GONE by since the call.

To say seeing Sydney and Jerry getting along is weird is an understatement, but it's a pleasant surprise.

After their talk, Sydney came to find me. To apologize. I was befuddled, angry that she ever thought she had to apologize to me.

I knew that something happened. She had told me as much. But I didn't know just how much I wanted to kill him. To feel his neck snap in my hands. To see him dead on the ground.

There are just some people who are too evil to walk this earth.

Jeffrey Wright is one of them.

I've given her three days to relax. To figure out what she wants to do next. We haven't heard from Jeffrey yet about a date for the meeting, and I'm growing impatient.

But I'm also growing impatient with myself. I want her. I want more than just cuddling in bed, my head in her hair. I want more than just candy as we watch a movie.

Because that's what's been happening.

Today was a long day at work, and I'm exhausted. There

have been some issues in my office, and I'm going to have to report it to the Agency. Good news, I may have to call it quits on the job in dramatic fashion. Bad news, I'll have to get reassigned to something else, which may be a lot more work.

I was liking the stability of just being an aid. I'd get all the information I needed from gossip and my boss, not even having to pry too hard.

Maybe I'd quit and work for someone else as one.

Maybe the Agency would redirect my path, and I'd work as something else entirely.

I won't know until it happens.

Running my hands through my hair, I head upstairs to my room, looking for Sydney. Except she's not there. Shiloh sits in the middle of the bed, his eyes wide as I close the door, looking innocent like he didn't keep me up until one in the morning, sneezing.

But I hear the shower running.

I decide I'm going to try today. I don't need to go very far. I don't need her to prove anything to me. But I want to make an effort. Show her that I'm still interested. That it's not just the job.

Taking a deep breath, I open the door, stepping into the steamy room.

Sydney stands in my shower, the glass hiding nothing from me. She doesn't see me as I walk in, peeling my clothes off, but she notices when I open the door, her head swiveling toward me, her eyes wide as her mouth sits open.

"May I?" I ask.

She nods, and I step in, closing the door behind me.

"What are you doing?" she asks, standing under the scorching hot water. Her skin is practically red from the heat, and I wonder, not for the first time, how she does that.

I turn the knob all the way to the coldest setting. Her eyes widen.

"I wanted to touch my wife," I tell her, carefully grabbing her hips.

She flinches a little as the water finally turns cold, but she doesn't move. Instead, she looks up at me as my hands creep up her sides slowly. My hot touch on her suddenly cold skin until I reach her nipples. They're hard from the temperature.

Kneeling in front of her, I bring her in closer, kissing up her stomach as I look up, watching as her head tips back, her eyes closed.

"I want you to look at me," I tell her, and when she does, I lick from her sternum to her nipple, capturing it in my mouth.

She gasps, her hands going to my hair, pulling at the strands as she arches her back, a moan escaping her.

I nip at it, pulling it in my teeth, watching her whimper above me.

And then I make my way back down again, kissing the sensitive skin between her hips before sliding my tongue down, flicking her clit with my tongue.

Leaning back against the glass, I angle her hips for better access.

When she looks away, I stop, only starting again when her eyes meet mine once more.

"Ronan," she whimpers, and I've had enough.

Opening the door to the shower, I grab our towels, drying her off quickly before lifting her up and bringing her out into the bedroom.

Checking to make sure Shiloh moved, I toss her on the bed, crawling on top of her, devouring her lips.

"Ronan, I can't," she says, pushing me a little.

I pull back, confused. "Are you okay?"

"I want to, god do I want to," she tells me, dropping back to the pillow and squeezing her eyes shut.

"It's going to hurt."

I roll over next to her, pulling her hip so she's facing me. "What do you mean it's going to hurt, Princess?"

She doesn't open her eyes.

"I'm cramping."

I don't say anything. I've always heard orgasms help cramps, but maybe that's just something men say to make themselves feel better about it. I wouldn't know.

"Are you okay? Is it your period?" I ask finally. I feel like I would have noticed.

She sighs, opening her eyes. "There's nothing I want more than for you to have me right here, I swear. But I have a chronic disease. The stress of the last couple of days, everything happening, I've been cramping since I got here, and today it's really bad."

I tip her chin up, my lips landing on hers as my hand grips the back of her neck. Pulling away, I cup her face in my palm again. "You never have to apologize to me, Sydney."

Her eyes widen, and her throat works in a rough swallow, her lips parting as she looks at mine.

"I'm sorry if I ruined something," she looks down again.

I force her to look at me once more. "Stop apologizing. You don't owe me a single thing." I shake my head, kissing her lips.

"What is it? What can I do to help?"

She sits up, pulling the blanket around her. She's still cold from the water. "I have endometriosis. I have for a long time. It's not always an issue, but I flair up when I'm stressed."

"And you cramp when that happens?"

She nods. "And more."

"Is it just the cramps that hurt right now?"

"Yes, but sex makes it worse," she says quietly, looking away. I hate the amount of shame she has.

"Why didn't you say anything about your pain before?"

She shrugs. "I don't want to be a burden, and I don't want you to be afraid of touching me."

I pull her down again, hugging her into me. "I may be concerned about you, but I'm not going to treat you like glass unless you want me to. I don't want you to ever worry about me when it comes to this, do you hear me?" I pull away, looking into her eyes, our noses practically touching. "What else happens?"

She thinks for a minute, worrying her lip as she debates what to tell me. I want her to tell me everything.

"There's these electric shocks that sometimes run down my legs. My stomach gets really bloated, and I feel sick," she tells me as she looks at her hands.

I hug her to me. "I'm so sorry."

"It is what it is, but," she pauses, sighing. "It's expensive to take care of. That's," she squeezes her eyes shut, her shoulders slumping. "That's part of the reason I took the money given to me. Medical bills are expensive."

I let our a breath, my eyes drifting closed as I kiss her head. She couldn't hold a job because they would ruin it for her. Which means she had to get her own insurance. I'm positive stress doesn't help this condition. We should have known. Should have looked further into her documents.

"Now, what can I do for you?"

She studies my face, her eyes searching mine, but I don't know what for.

She winces, her hand shooting down to her lower stomach, and I let her sit up.

She looks around the room, sighing. "Can I just take a bath?" she asks, getting up.

"Of course," I say as I follow her. Except while she goes to find clothes for afterward, I head to the bathroom.

Turning on the tub, I test the water for the perfect temperature. Just too hot for me, yet not so scorching that it'll hurt her.

Exiting the bathroom, Sydney looks at me curiously as I

grab sweatpants, pulling them on before leaving the room. I walk down three doors, knocking a couple times.

Elena answers, her face rosy as I watch Brandon duck into the bathroom. I pretend not to notice. "Hey, do you have some kind of bubble bath?" Out of the two other women here, Elena would be the one to have it. The thought of Jerry in a bath full of bubbles is enough to send me into a fit of hysterics. It would never happen in a million years.

"Yeah!" she says before her brows furrow. "Why?"

I point back to my room. "Sydney."

She nods, shooting me a knowing look. Her lips tip up as she heads to her bathroom, coming back with a large container of bubble bath.

I take it from her, thanking her as I walk back to my room. Opening the door, I find Sydney in the same spot I left her. She watches me as I head back into the bathroom, dumping what's probably way too much bubble bath into the water. I watch as the soapy water starts to bubble, and when the water is finally high enough, I head back into the room.

Sydney still hasn't moved.

Walking to her with purpose, I scoop her into my arms, ignoring the adorable squeak she lets out when her feet leave the ground, and I bring her into the bathroom. Feet first, I ask her if the temperature is okay before sitting her in the large bathtub.

Grabbing a towel, I spread it out next to the tub, kneeling next to her.

Grabbing the hand shower, I turn the knob, watching as water flows from it.

Sydney's eyes don't leave me the entire time. But she understands what I'm trying to do, tipping her head back.

I silently rinse her already wet hair, massaging her scalp before putting a dollop of shampoo in my palm, rubbing them together before massaging it into her roots, careful not to go too low.

She looks at me suspiciously.

"Where did you learn this?" she asks.

I look at her innocently. "Learn what?"

"To only wash the roots."

"The internet."

"Why were you looking it up on the internet?"

I shrug. "Why not? It sounded like something I should look up if I was married."

She studies my face as I continue massaging her scalp, my fingers rubbing in circular motions down the back of her head. Her eyes flutter closed with pleasure, and finally, her muscles relax, her head tilting back even more.

I bring my fingers up to her temples, massaging there too, before rinsing her hair out and repeating the process with the conditioner I bought her two days ago after she complained about our hard water making her hair feel stiff.

"Can I ask you a question?" she asks.

"Anything you'd like."

She bites her fingernail, wincing as she looks at me. "So you don't remember anything at all about your childhood?"

I shake my head. "I don't, no."

"Nothing at all until they took your memories? How do they even do that?"

There's not much I even know about it other than it happens. But I try to answer her question to the best of my abilities. "It's a shot they give us," I tell her honestly. "I'm not sure what is in it or what it does to the body, but I know we wake up with no memories. Maybe they do something to us while we're out. I'm not sure. They keep that close."

She nods, thinking. "So it's not like the neuralyzer."

It's my turn to be confused.

"What is that?"

She gasps, twisting around to face me, water splashing to the floor. Her hair, filled with what's likely entirely too much conditioner—an amount I did *not* look up—piled on top of her head, falls slowly. "You don't know Men in Black?"

"Should I?"

She rolls her eyes. "It's a *classic*, Ronan. Oh my god, how many movies do you not remember? Because you've definitely seen them. I don't care who you are; you've seen Men in Black at least once."

I try not to smile at her newfound energy.

"I don't remember ever seeing that one, no. Who's in it?"

She stares at me, her eyes wide. "You really haven't seen it, have you? It's Will Smith? Tommy Lee Jones? There's a weird talking pug in one of them?"

I shake my head.

"We're watching it," she says, turning back around. "After we're out of here, we're curling up and watching Men in Black. I'll look up where we can find it online."

I chuckle, giving in.

But we don't leave for a long time. Instead, I massage her shoulders as we talk about the good parts of growing up for her. There weren't many, but there were some.

Her aunt's house, where she only went a couple times. The dollhouse her mom got her for her birthday one year, only to go missing the next. I asked her about her favorite movies growing up—a funny romcom about a girl playing on a boy's soccer team—and she asks me about things I had to rediscover I loved, like sci-fi movies. When I told her that, her mouth dropped open, incredibly confused as to how I still hadn't seen Men in Black.

She wanted to get out soon after that, asking me to pull it up on my TV.

I leave her in the bathroom to dry off, set up the movie, and then ask her what I can do to help her cramps. She holds her stomach, a frown on her lips.

"Back at home, I had a rice sock," she says, and I stand

there, a deep v between my brows, trying to understand what she's getting at.

"A rice sock?"

She nods.

"A sock. That's full of rice."

"Okay…"

"You warm it up for thirty seconds or so in the microwave and put it over your uterus. Well, not *your* uterus. You get what I mean," she smiles.

I think I do.

"It's heavy, so the weight feels nice, but the warmth feels great, too."

"I'm on it," I assure her, heading to my sock drawer. I think about choosing an older one, but I feel like she deserves one that isn't practically threadbare, so I choose one of my newer, thicker ones instead.

"You don't have to—" she starts.

I go back to her, sock in hand, and kiss her lips, shutting her up. "I'll be right back. Get in bed and get comfy."

Leaving the room, I take the steps two at a time, heading for the kitchen. Grabbing our giant bag of rice, I find a funnel and pour two cups into the sock, tying the end off before placing it in our microwave. Thirty seconds later, I have a hot sock full of rice and a bag of almond joys in my hand, heading back to her.

We fall asleep to Tommy Lee Jones' voice.

TWENTY-THREE

SYDNEY

I DON'T KNOW what to think.

On one hand, I don't think Ronan is capable of faking his feelings. The kindness he showed me the night before was someone I've never really experienced. Not with friends, not with family, not with ex-boyfriends.

It warmed me, and I don't ever want to let it go.

But I also can't lie and say that part of me isn't suspicious. No matter how many times I tell myself I should just let my guard down now, that it's safe. I can't help but have flashbacks to the moment I realized that I was being taken away from my home and that there was someone who looked exactly like me in the car with us.

It hurt. It still hurts in a way.

After my chess game with Jerry, she's been treating me differently. Like she actually likes me. Not even that she just tolerates me. No. Like she actually wants me around, even. Offering me snacks and asking me to play another round of chess. We keep ending games in draws, neither of us winning.

It's fascinating, really.

The more time I spend here, the more time I feel like these

people are family. Even Brandon and Zach, who are often in a world of their own. Whether they be out and about on day-long missions or holed up in their rooms playing video games, the two of them are always together. Well, that is, when Brandon isn't with Elena, which they're still horribly trying to hide from everyone.

I don't even know them that well, and I can see it clear as day.

"Sydney!" Jerry calls from across the room. She has papers in her hands, her hair bouncing behind her as she strides toward me.

"Yeah?"

"We finally got a date."

"When is it?"

She flips through a couple of the pages before finding what she's looking for. "In three days in Texas. You and Ronan are going to fly out tomorrow morning and then stay at the Texas compound until the meeting.

"Are you sure we're going to be safe there?" I ask her, hesitant. I've come to trust these people here, but I know nothing about the people in Texas.

"They're a top-secret CIA compound in the middle of Texas. It's on a ranch. They literally have more guns than half the compounds in the country in that one building. You're going to be fine."

Okay.

I think for a minute, realizing that I've completely lost track of the calendar. "What's the date of the meeting?" I ask her.

She looks down again before smiling. "October 11th."

I count back in my head. "that means that today is—"

"Our birthday."

We look at each other. Her eyes are bright as she looks at me, her lips tilting in a smile. Something I thought I'd never see if I'm honest.

"Are we celebrating?"

"As soon as the boys get home, we're going out."

I smile, looking down at the ground.

I slept in today, and when I woke up, Ronan was gone. He had to go to work, and I tried not to let the disappointment ruin my day. He left me a note on his pillow telling me where the secret stash of candy is.

I pause, not sure what to say. "Do you want to get ready together?" I ask her.

And we do.

She tells me a little bit more about growing up as she goes through all of the clothes I got with Ronan, choosing something she thought would make Ronan combust, and I was pleasantly surprised to find out that it wasn't all bad. She had some good things happen to her, too.

"How did you meet the guys?" I ask her.

"Like I said, I was initiated kind of out of pity, if I'm honest. I went through everything other than the memory stuff. I didn't want to fuck with that, and because I wasn't here because of some bigger circumstance, they didn't have to bring me back from the dead basically. They let me get away with not doing it. There are still people who come out of that sleep remembering things. Even if it's just bits and pieces. People like Ronan don't want to remember at all, but there are some people who do.

"What other process do you have to go through?" I ask. I hadn't thought to ask Ronan.

"Oh, they cut your uterus cut," Jerry tells me, chuckling as she sees my horrified face. "snip the men, too. I'm sure you and Ronan have already done the deed, and he told you, right?"

I shake my head.

"Wait, he didn't tell you, or you haven't had sex?"

"The latter. Well, and the first. Both."

She shoots me a look, going back to riffling through my skirts. "That's surprising."

I'm not going to tell her about the things we *have* done, so I just ask her why.

"Because that man is a puppy dog for you. I've never seen him react to anyone the way he reacts to you when you just simply step in the room. It's insane," she tells me, rolling her eyes.

"Really?"

"Really."

She throws a dress at me, and I don't manage to catch it before it's on my face. Pulling it off, I ask, "What is, um, what is the policy for relationships?"

She casts me a sideways glance before smirking. "Well, you'd have to join us. That's about it."

"And how do you do that?"

"You prove to the CIA that they can use you. And they're picky. If a Fallen Angel chooses you, you have to understand that at some point, you have to either prove yourself useful or they'll take you out."

My head whips up. "Wait, does that mean I was always going to have a target on my back?"

Jerry shakes her head with a chuckle. "No. If you're here for a mission, they'll usually let it slide. We could have lied and said you didn't know anything, too. I'm not sure. They can be idiots over there if I'm being completely frank."

I laugh at that, lifting the dress. I don't remember trying this one on. Or seeing it at all, actually.

"Will this even cover my ass?" I ask, standing up and holding it against me.

"You didn't try it on?"

I shake my head.

She smiles up at me mischievously. "Ronan definitely threw that in there when you weren't looking."

I look down at it, deciding that if I was going to go all out, I might really go all out.

———

"What are you wearing?" comes a voice from behind me.

I turn around, watching as Ronan walks into his bedroom, his mouth agape as he looks me up and down.

"Don't you like it? It somehow ended up in my closet," I respond, smiling as I spin.

The tight black dress barely covers my ass, and there's a wide slit that goes up until my hip.

I almost expected him to appreciate it for a moment and then tell me to take it off. To tell me that it's too much. That he doesn't want anyone to even look in my direction. I almost wanted him to say it.

But he doesn't.

Instead, he comes over to me, scoops me into his arms, kisses me, and tells me that I look beautiful.

"Going out and having you on my arm?" he says with a smile, kissing my neck. "that's a win enough for me, Princess."

I smile, patting his cheek before squirming to get out of his hold. He lets me go, heading to the bathroom to freshen up for the night.

"How are you feeling?" he asks after a moment. I can tell that he doesn't want me to think that he's treating me any differently while also curious. It's clear that we have something, and it's clear that both of us want each other, but neither of us has made a move yet, and it's hard.

I smirk at him, shrugging. "I think I'll be okay."

"You were hurting just last night, though, I just don't want to do something that'll make things worse. I was looking it up at work and—"

Ronan goes on to tell me about everything he learned

about endometriosis when he was at work, hanging out at his desk. He looked at everything. Ways that it could be made better, what it actually is, and things he could help me with. He thought of everything, and he looked it all up.

My mind goes numb halfway through, trying to process the fact that someone likes me enough to make a significant effort to help.

"If you don't want to keep using the sock, there's these portable heating pads you can get," he tells me as he sits on the bed. He hasn't shut up for the last ten minutes, and it sends butterflies through my stomach.

"I don't know about that. I really like the sock."

"You have to go downstairs to warm up the sock, though. And then what if someone else comes down and asks why you're microwaving a sock."

I shrug. "It's a sock full of rice. I feel like it's pretty self-explanatory."

He stares at me for a moment before shrugging.

"What?" I ask as I laugh, the sound ringing through the room. "They use those socks for migraines, too!"

Ronan's face doesn't really look like he believes me.

"It's true!"

We bicker for a little longer until we hear a sharp knock on the door. "You guys ready?" Elena calls from the other side.

Gathering our things, Ronan pulls me into him, kissing the top of my head before patting my butt as we head out.

"Jerry was banned from one of the last clubs we went to, so this is a totally new one for us," Brandon tells me, annoyed.

I'm in the backseat of his car as Ronan rides in the passenger seat. Elena is next to me, smiling at me. "She got in a fight with one of the bouncers. It was a night we had guests there with us, too. I'm really glad they left early."

If there's one thing I can see Jerry doing, it's getting in a fight with enforcement of any kind. Whether it be a club bouncer, a cop, or another agent, she's a little argumentative.

"I loved that place," Brandon says.

"I'm sure if we wait it out just a little bit, we can go back," Elena tells him, patting his shoulder from behind.

When we pull up at the new club, Smitten's, I look around, excited to be back in the city.

It's always been home to me. The place where I feel safest. Until now, I think.

Ronan opens my door for me, grabbing my hand and helping me out. Holding me to him, he leads me up to the front of the line with the others. A female bouncer sits at the entrance, and all Jerry has to do is bat her eyelashes, and she's let in.

Following her into the club, I'm overwhelmed by the lights. I've never been here. Never even heard of it, actually.

And for a moment, I wonder if Adam would come here. Would I see him? I need to call him at some point.

I wonder how much of this I could tell him or if I'd put him in danger.

Sadness washes over me for only a moment as I worry about how much he would be able to be in my life if I chose this other path, but it's short-lived before Elena is pulling me to the bar.

"What do you drink?" she asks me over the music as she holds her card out to the bartender.

"A honey whiskey, please," I reply loudly, looking around.

The place is dark, illuminated by lights and lasers as the bass thrums through my bones. Girls are in every corner, filling the dance floor wearing the smallest skirts I've ever seen. I find Ronan across the room, and when I realize his eyes are on me, I blush, turning as Elena taps me on the shoulder, drink in hand.

"What do you want, Jerry?" she asks her as Jerry stares at someone in the distance. She doesn't answer, so I snap my fingers in her face, finally gaining her attention.

"An Everclear," she says, her face completely straight. We stare at her for a moment, trying to figure out if she's joking.

"Like, as a shot?" Elena asks, confused.

"No, like on the rocks. Like you have."

We look at the bartender, who's busy with someone else at the end of the bar. He's steadily making his way back to us.

"Okay," Elena says, her eyes wide as she turns to order.

When Jerry finally has her drink, I'm dragged to the center of the dance floor by the women, dancing between them. The beat takes over, and the more alcohol is consumed, the more I forget about everything happening in my life.

And it dawns on me that this is what it's like having friends. Having family. This is the very first time I've had this other than Adam.

I have my sister beside me, getting fucked up on Everclear and seemingly feelings for someone she sees across the bar but won't talk to, and a new friend who's been nothing but kind to me since the moment I met her, even when everyone else hated me.

And I have Ronan.

The man who sits next to Brandon and Zach, his eyes never leaving my body as he watches me dance.

I run my hands up torso, holding them up above my head as I dance to the heavy beat, my eyelids growing heavy as I realize more and more that I want him.

But not tonight.

It wouldn't be a good idea.

I'd rather not make this worse and suffer for the next couple of days. It should be better tomorrow.

"Ronan hasn't looked anywhere else," Elena whispers to me. "Go get him."

At this point, I've had more than enough alcohol. I'll do anything anyone tells me to do within reason. So I do.

Marching my way over to him, I grab his hands, leading him to the bar. Getting in line, I press myself into him, bringing his hands to my hips.

"Is there something you want?" Ronan asks in my ear, his voice deep. Sultry even.

"I want what I can't have tonight, but that doesn't mean we can't have fun."

"Are you feeling better?"

I nod. "I am. I'm not feeling it right now, but I know that it's going to hurt. One more day "

He nods, his eyes lighting up. "One more day, and you're mine," he says.

I smile at him, and he smiles back, all teeth and dazzling eyes. He looks beautiful.

Ronan doesn't order a drink, instead taking mine for me as I bring him to the dance floor.

Grabbing his neck, I sway with him to the music, refusing to look away from his handsome face. His dazzling dark eyes, his beautiful pouty lips. His mouthwatering jawline.

He hasn't shaved since we got married. Not once. Maybe a trim, actually. But he has a nice beard coming in, and the way it tickles my neck when he kisses it sends a thrill to places I'd rather not feel anything right now.

Who am I kidding? I'd rather feel it for sure. I just can't.

But another drink in, and I'm ready to have some fun with him.

Standing on my tiptoes, his hands on my ass, I bite his ear. "You know what I can't stop thinking about?" I ask.

He tilts his head instead of answering.

"That first night together,"

"When you had my dick in your mouth?" he whispers into my ear, and the only thing that exists around me is him.

I nod.

"That's good to know."

I nod, not quite knowing what I expected him to do.

Kissing up my neck, Ronan reaches my lips, capturing them between his. Devouring them. And then, when I think he's done, he takes my whiskey, taking a sip but not swallowing before kissing me again.

The whiskey mingles with our tongues, drowning everything else out.

If someone had mentioned doing this to me in any other circumstance, I would have thought they were absolutely insane. Maybe even gross. But here, right now, experiencing this with Ronan... this is one of the single hottest things I've ever experienced in my whole life.

He clutches my hips like I'm his lifeline. Like I'm his oxygen, and he can't get enough. Like the second he lets go, he'll die of thirst.

And it occurs to me that I feel free. I'm not. Not quite. But I feel like I am, and that has to count for something.

"Did you know that people are more creative in the shower?" I mumble, looking up at him as I take another sip.

The corner of his lips tilt up in a smile. "Yeah?"

I nod, batting my eyelashes.

"I think we need to take more showers," he tells me.

I can feel the alcohol hitting me harder and harder the more I look at him, studying his face like I could forget it at any second.

TWENTY-FOUR

RONAN

SYDNEY IS drunk out of her mind and we have a plane to catch in 9 hours.

The second Sydney started doing her little doe-eyed drunk performance, I knew she was gone. It was cute, that's for sure.

I leave the girls on the dance floor, heading back to where Brandon and Zach lounge in a booth. Brandon has always let Elena do what she wants. If she wants him to dance with her, she'll let him know. Right now she's having too much fun with Jerry and Sydney.

"You're fucked, you know that right?" Zach tells me as I sit down, a shit-eating grin on his face.

"I don't know what you're talking about," I lie. I know exactly what he's talking about.

"Yes, you do. You know exactly what. That girl has you around her little finger, and you're eating it up."

I nod. "I think you're right."

"What are you going to do?"

I shrug. "I do whatever she wants after this. Either we go our separate ways, or she wants to stay. It's totally up to her."

"You're not going to try to convince her one way or another?" Brandon asks.

I shake my head from side to side. "Nope."

Brandon took us home early so that I could get Sydney at least a little bit sober before our trip tomorrow.

"I think I'm feeling okay," she tells me, a wicked grin across her shiny lips.

I give her a kiss, quickly pulling away before she can get her hands latched into my hair to keep me there.

She pouts, looking up at me from under her lashes.

"What?" I chuckle.

"I just really want you,"

"I know, Princess, but not tonight."

I hand her a water bottle, instructing her to drink it. To drink it all. Every single last drop.

She salutes me, twisting the top off before guzzling it in one go. I give her another one.

"I'm going to be peeing for half the morning," she mumbles.

"It's a private plane. You can spend as much time as you want in the bathroom."

Her eyes snap to mine, a grin spreading across her lips slowly.

"We're not having sex on the plane," I sigh, letting her down easy.

She rolls her eyes, slumping in her chair.

"Do you want food? Coffee?"

She tells me she's just fine, laying her head on the counter.

"Hey," I say to get her attention. Her eyes flash to mine, and I sit down next to her, laying my head down next to hers. "You know I want you. I just don't want the first time together to be when you're shitfaced, and I'm stone-cold sober, okay?"

Her eyes are glassy as she nods, letting out a big sigh.

"Everything alright?"

She shakes her head, worry lines appearing across her forehead. "I'm worried about this trip," she says.

"What about it?"

"I don't know. It doesn't feel good. I feel like something bad is going to happen, but I'm not sure what." She wipes her face with her hands, letting out a big yawn as she stretches.

I'm not sure what, either. It should be fairly cut and dry. We'll also have the Texas compound to hide out in. The guys there are lethal.

Running my fingers through her hair, I kiss her forehead. "It's going to be okay."

"What are we going to do after the meeting?"

I think about it for a second. "We're going to take over the company and burn it to the ground," I tell her honestly.

"No, I mean with us. What's going to happen with us."

I bite my lip. "That's entirely up to you, Syd. This world is yours. All I want to do is kneel before you and watch you burn it to the ground."

She nods, her eyes fluttering shut for a couple moments.

And I've seen enough. Scooping her up in my arms, I carry her up to my room, laying her in bed as I pull out my suitcase, packing half of it with her things and half with mine.

What I don't tell her is that I'm also worried about this trip. This is a big mission, and a lot relies on how this goes. We both need to impress the board while also somehow convincing them that we'd be a better fit than Jeffrey.

And then we have to take care of Jeffrey.

Although her parents wanted her to take over if she was married, there are rules in place to make that as hard as possible. Naturally.

When everything is finally packed, I peel off my clothes, climb into bed next to her, and pass out.

TWENTY-FIVE

SYDNEY

I WAKE up to an alarm going off for the first time in days, and I'm already irritated.

The more I wake up, the more irritated I get as the sun streaming in the window has my head spinning.

"Fuck, close the freaking blinds," I mutter to Ronan.

"We gotta go, Syd."

I roll over, pulling the comforter over me.

"Syd."

I don't respond.

And suddenly, I'm suspended in the air, my face at his back. My head quakes, and I just want to be knocked out.

I'm wishing for death.

Praying for it.

Setting me down on the floor, I put my arms out to steady myself, looking around. Black spots dot my vision as I close my eyes, opening them again. I try to shake it off.

"Go get washed up beautiful; we're leaving in about thirty minutes. I put out some clothes for you," he points to the seat in the corner of his room. I flash him a look, trudging into the bathroom. I wonder if I can leck the door and just sleep on one of the bathmats.

Bending over the sink, I look at myself in the mirror. I'm still wearing my makeup from the night before. My eyeliner is completely smudged, and I feel like I resemble more of a raccoon than a human being.

I grab for my face wash, but it's gone. Looking around, I don't find it anywhere, and I'm confused.

Walking back into the room, I ask Ronan where it is.

"I packed it," he tells me, pointing to our suitcase.

My heart melts a little bit. "I left your toothbrush out, but I should have thought about that; I'm sorry."

It's been over a week since I arrived, and in the span of a week, Ronan and I have become something so much different. I'm not sure how it happened; I'm not sure why it was so fast. I'm not sure I'll ever understand it. I'm sure it has to do with trauma and the forced proximity. It may even have to do with the ginormous rock on my ring finger. All I know is that I probably can't unpack all of it with my therapist. There's too much I wouldn't be able to tell her.

But then I started thinking. Do these guys have therapists? They have to, right? I'm sure of it.

Maybe if I stay, I can talk to her. I'd be able to open up about my life a little more. Give them the full picture of why I am the way I am.

Maybe they could help me more.

"It's okay," I assure him as I turn back into the bathroom. I can do it the old-fashioned way.

Finding a washcloth, I run it under warm water and rub a bar of soap into it before massaging my face gently, careful not to get the soap in my eyeball, which, of course, I was unsuccessful at.

I quickly brush my teeth before throwing the brush and toothpaste into a bag and packing it in Ronan's oversized backpack.

And before I know it, we're on our way to the airport.

"The Texas compound is really cool," Jerry says as she drives us. "Super southern looking."

"It's a ranch, Jerry. I'm not sure how else you expect it to look."

She shrugs. "It's just really pretty for a ranch, is all."

Twelve years ago

"Can we go back to the cottage?" I ask my mom, my shoulders slumping.

"We have things to do, sweetie. Why don't you go get your homework done?"

"I just want to go."

The house is cold tonight. Frigid. I'm exhausted from all the training my father has made me do over the last couple of days. Over the last couple of years. I'm tired of having guns held to my head. Of being tied up and asked for information. Of being screamed at.

I just want that moment of peace. I just want to be alone for even a couple minutes.

Mom puts her pen down, exhaustion clear in her eyes. "I can see if someone can bring you honey, but I'm not going to go with you."

My shoulders slump as exhaustion envelopes my body. If someone brings me, I know that training is going to continue. If someone brings me, I know that that person is more than likely my father's friend, Jeffrey Wright. There's nothing I want less than to be alone with that man.

"Never mind," I tell her, heading back out of the room.

My footsteps echo through the hallway as I get to my room, settling on my bed. I throw myself back, staring at the ceiling as I settle in.

A knock on the door sends my spine stilling, a chill drifting over me.

But when my mom's face peeks in, I settle.

"I'm sorry honey," she tells me as she enters, closing the door quietly. "There's just not much I can control here, you know that."

"It's fine," I tell her simply as I turn away.

Heading to the bookshelf, my mom grabs the chess set from the second shelf, bringing it over to my bed.

"We'll get through this, okay honey?"

I eye her, trying to figure out where she's going with this."

"What do you mean?" I sit up in my bed.

"I just want you to know that you're loved, is all."

We stay up for most of the night playing chess.

TWENTY-SIX

RONAN

SYDNEY PASSES out on the plane, which is to be expected. I would have, too if I had had that much to drink the night before. But I don't fault her for it. I'm glad she was having fun.

The fact that she and her sister are getting along now warms my heart, but mostly, it gives me hope that she may want to stick around after this is all over.

I've found that I like my wife a lot more than I thought I would.

When we finally arrive in Texas, we're picked up by a van.

"Why is it so hot here?" Sydney asks as she fans herself. "I mean, we're in Texas."

She grunts. "I think I'd rather be anywhere else,"

I agree with her. At least when we climb into the van, the AC hits us.

The drive isn't long, but it is scenic. If it wasn't so hot I think I'd like it here.

We drive past field after field, and although there doesn't seem to be much in the way of grass here, there's a whole lot of trees. It's a lot more green than I expected it to be.

I don't come here much. I visited with Jerry when we had some business around here, but it was only for a night, and we didn't actually go anywhere.

I look over at Sydney next to me as she places her forehead against the window. "Are you doing better?" I ask. I gave her a pill for her motion sickness when we took off, and she's been a little sleepy ever since.

"Doing fantastic," she mutters. "I'm mostly not hungover anymore. So at least there's that."

At least there's that.

"We'll get situated at the house, and then we can explore the ranch if you'd like."

"It's a whole ranch?" she asks, perking up.

I nod, watching as she puts her hair up. It really is hot here.

About ten minutes later, we pull into the long road that leads to the Texas Fallen Angel compound. A field sits on either side of the dirt road, and I look out, watching the birds fly through the sky as the sun sits high in the noon sky. Dust kicks up all around us.

But when the van comes to a halt outside of the ginormous fortress, I feel a deep sense of longing.

I love the DC compound. I really do. But sometimes, it doesn't feel like a home more than a place to hang out. A lair of sorts.

This is a home.

A beautiful white home set against the blue sky, the Texas compound is something to be admired, that's for sure. Several fields sit behind it, and I can see cows and a couple horses in the distance. A large garden sits to the left, overflowing with some of the largest vegetables I've ever seen. So large I can see them from here.

"This place is gorgeous," Sydney tells me as she looks around, her mouth hung open in wonder as she takes the place in.

I nod. It is gorgeous.

Getting out, Sydney looks around, her red hair whipping around in the wind as she shields her eyes, looking into the distance. "I think I see cows," she says excitedly.

I smile watching her be excited about something. I feel like I haven't seen that in a long time.

"They have them over there. Lots of them." She looks at me, her eyes shiny.

The front door opens, and the one and only Matthew Ellis walks out, his cowboy hat tipped to the side, his light wash jeans maybe a size too small. He wears a white t-shirt under a long-sleeve flannel, and I'm sure the idea is to protect his skin from the sun, but I cannot for the life of me imagine wearing that in the sweltering Texas heat for hours at a time.

"Hey man!" Matthew calls, jogging up to us. He offers me his hand, bringing me in for a short hug before reaching for Sydney. "And who's this?"

"This happens to be Sydney, Jerry's sister," I tell him.

He rears back. "God dammit, man, for a second there, I thought Jerry got a new look, 'an I was gonna look like an asshole. They sure do look alike."

"We're twins," Sydney says with a smile, shaking his hand.

Matthew shakes his head. He knows Jerry. He's gotten an earful from her before. He knows how difficult she can be.

"Anyways, I heard you guys won't be here too long. Let me show you the guest wing. We don't have anyone else here for a bit, so you can wander around with no problem. Just watch out for Ted."

"Who's Ted?" Sydney mouths.

"I'll tell you later," I mouth back at her.

"Oh, and don't go into the basement, got it?"

We look at each other, but we both nod. There's been rumors, but none of them have been confirmed.

"Are you guys gonna have dinner here?" Matthew asks,

turning around to cast a quick glance my way. His tan skin is covered in a glistening layer of sweat, his blue eyes still bright and happy despite everything that happens here.

There's not many people like him.

"I was going to take Sydney out," I tell him.

Matthew spins, walking backward up the stairs to the compound. He points in the direction of the garage.

"There's a couple cars over there for you to use if you want. It can take a long time for one of our vans to get here, and if you ask me, the drivers aren't very friendly."

"They don't talk much, do they?" I ask.

"No sir, they don't."

He opens the door for us, allowing Sydney to enter first before me. He follows us, making sure the door is tightly closed before showing us down the hall and into the beautiful main room of the guest wing.

The room is open with a beautiful kitchen and family room that has floor-to-ceiling windows opening up into the back of the property, giving the best view of everything the ranch has to offer.

"This place is so pretty," Sydney says, her eyes wide with wonder.

"Thank you, ma'am. Worked on it myself." Matthew says, taking his hat off and wiping his filthy hands through his sandy hair.

"You did this yourself?"

He nods, smiling. "Anyhow, I'll leave you two to it. If you need me, you have my number, Ronan." He smacks my shoulder on the way out.

"He's nice," Sydney says, flopping down on one of the couches.

"Yeah, he's a good guy. He puts a lot of work into this place."

"Is that his only job around here?"

"Kind of?" I'm not sure how to explain it to her. Crossing

the room, I sit in the chair opposite her, slouching as I let the AC hit my face. "He's kind of like the Jerry of Texas, except he can't leave."

Her face twists, her head tilting slightly.

I shake my head. "I don't know the full story; I think Jerry knows more about it, to be honest." I rake my fingers through my hair and scratch at my beard. "But from what I've heard, he tried to turn his back on the Angels at one point."

Surprise clouds her eyes as she only looks more confused. "Wouldn't someone get killed for that?"

I tap my fingers on the leather of the seat. "Most of the time, yes. But sometimes, someone gets lucky. He's stuck here, but he didn't get off scot-free. There are things he has to do here that I'd rather not say."

Sydney's nose wrinkles, and I notice a few more freckles dot her face. Maybe the Texas sun is good for something.

"He seems too nice to do anything bad," she tells me, looking out the large windows to the fields.

"Some people are just like that."

We settle into a peaceful silence as we take a moment to just be. Sydney has been cooped up in the compound for almost 2 weeks, barely making it out, and I've been to work and back in order to spend time with her.

I'm not sure when I turned to mush.

The feelings I have for Sydney are still foreign, and I still don't want to put a name to them just yet. We've done this backward: getting married and then almost… dating? If you could call it that.

But it feels too soon. To society's standards, it really does. But we live in a pressure cooker, and feelings of any kind develop so much faster within it.

Sydney is the first woman who's ever caught my attention, and I promised myself that I would keep it professional.

Yet here we are.

The giant rock on her finger, the one that's glistening in

the sunlight right now, means something so much more than it did that first night I gave it to her.

And it makes me want to get her a new one. One from me. One to actually slip on her finger myself.

"I've been thinking," Sydney says, interrupting our quiet.

"Yeah? That's almost never good," I joke, and her eyes sparkle when they look at me, almost as green as the trees outside, lit by the sun high in the sky.

"I talked to Jerry about what happens if, well, if I want to stay."

"Stay?" I ask, pretending to not understand what she's saying. My heart races a little faster. I've thought about this, too. I've thought about it a lot.

Stay with me.

"What would need to happen?"

I take a deep breath, not sure if this is going to chase her off. "You'd need to talk to our handler, Veronica. She's been great. Works with a couple of other compounds around the country, too. From there, she'd put you in touch with someone at the Agency, who would come by and do a thorough interview. They want to make sure that you're sane, pretty much," I chuckle because I'm not sure any of us are really sane.

"Then you'd just have to go through the different testing stages they have for everyone. To make sure you're healthy, to see if you need anything. That one is fairly simple. I don't think they'd require your memory to be wiped if they didn't require Jerry's to be. They usually use that for those whom they've saved to be in the Project. After that," I pause, looking at her across from me. She looks serious about this, but this is the part that I'm not sure about. "They'd probably require you to get a hysterectomy."

She pauses. "Jerry told me about that," she says, shrugging. "I don't think I want to have kids anyway,"

Now, it's my turn to be curious. Not that I wanted them either. "Why not?"

Sydney crosses her left leg over her right, leaning against the right side of the chair. "I don't know. I've just seen too much ugly in the world. I haven't gotten proper help to process everything that's happened in my life, and I don't want to pass my instability to my kids, you know?"

I swallow roughly. It's starting to sound like she's really considering this.

"We can talk about it later if you'd like. Further down the line. When all of this is done."

She smiles at me, and the sight of it takes my breath away.

There's nothing I want more.

Sitting up, I slap my thighs. "Alright, you ready to get dinner?"

Sydney and I climb into one of the new Challengers the Texas compound provides. They're slick and black, looking almost exactly like the cop cars around the city. It's honestly a really good idea.

"Do you think you're going to get the car back?" Sydney says suddenly.

"The one that you stole?"

She nods.

"Eventually, I think. I'm pretty sure Zach has made it his personal mission."

"I still think it was stupid to hide keys to a car like that under your bed."

I rear back, pulling out onto the road.

"You do realize that every single one of those cars have keys inside of them, right? All of them. You could have gone down and chosen any of them other than that car."

She looks at me in shock, her mouth hanging open. "That's not true!"

I laugh, a deep, throaty laugh I haven't heard from myself in a long time. "It's true! Look when you get back home!"

It's only about fifteen minutes back into the city when we park. I round the car to open her door for her. I watch as she slides out, her mess of wavy red hair looking perfect here in the South.

I wonder when I became downright obsessed.

"You know, you don't have to get my door for me all the time."

"I'll remember that," I tell her with a smile.

I also wonder when I started giving people genuine smiles. I don't remember the last time I gave out so many.

The restaurant was recommended by Matthew. A fancy steakhouse that serves something called a blooming onion. I'm not quite sure what that is, but Matthew said Stella brought them home for him all the time, and they were always great.

We sit at our table, and the waitress brings us waters, asking for our drink orders. After last night, Sydney doesn't want anything, and I don't either. She leaves to grab us the onion dish for an appetizer while we look over everything else.

We both settle on steak and after the orders are in, we settle into another silence.

But this time it's almost awkward.

I don't think either of us knows how to talk about things that don't have to do with the Angels or her crappy childhood.

"What did you study in college?" I ask, figuring this is a great time to get to know more about her. Things that I haven't gotten the chance to ask.

"I studied programming. Specifically in data science. I

love gathering data, and I also love doing things that people tell me I can't do."

"People told you you can't do that?"

She takes a sip of her water, tucking her hair behind her ear as she nods. "I mean, yeah. It's a male-dominated field. Of course I was going to get people saying that I couldn't do it. That's only natural. But once I have my mind set on something, I make it happen no matter what. Programming was a passion of mine, and I was going to make it work for a career."

And because I'm me and this girl has me wrapped around my finger, I start thinking about the ways that the Agency could use that. Ways that would make it easier for her to plead her case for staying.

Not that I really think she has anything to worry about. Especially after all of this is over. If she manages to help us, I think they'd let her in, no questions asked.

When our meals are placed in front of us, Sydney grows quiet.

"You doing okay?" I ask her.

She nods. "I was going to ask at some point. If I join, I probably can't speak to Adam at all anymore, right?"

"That's not true," I shake my head, cutting into the steak in front of me. "You're allowed to have friends outside of the compound. You just have to be careful about it."

She purses her lips, picking up her fork. "We've been friends for a really long time, and I just miss him a lot. I hope you're okay with—"

I put my hand up, stopping her.

"Don't even finish that sentence, Syd. I'm a man. I don't get jealous of friends. I'm not that kind of person. Now, if I see someone you don't know trying to touch you, I can't promise I won't break his arm. But Adam is okay."

She looks down, her hands twisting her shirt in her lap. "What's wrong?"

"You're just too nice to me."

"You deserve it. Don't let anyone else tell you otherwise, Syd."

"Thank you for bringing me out," Sydney tells me as we step out into the hot Texas heat. The sun has started going down by now, disappearing behind the buildings in front of us. It casts a beautiful orange hue across the sky, complete with pink clouds, the blue sky peeking through here and there.

We both stop to admire it. We don't get these kinds of skies in DC much.

Grabbing her hand, I pull her toward the parking garage. The second we round the corner, bullets fly.

Sydney screams, ducking. I quickly remember her distaste for guns as I pull mine out of the back of my jeans. "Get behind that dumpster," I yell to her, gesturing wildly to it. She does what I say, crouching behind it as I stand in the open, my gun pointed and ready. A man dressed in all black peeks out from behind a concrete pole in the garage, and it only takes one shot to take him out, blood spraying on the car behind him, the alarm going off as he lands on the hood.

Two more men appear to the right, and I'm quick with the trigger, taking them down within seconds of them appearing. After two more, I turn to Sydney, offering her my hand.

She looks scared, her eyes open wide as she looks at the bodies around us. "Do we have to clean them up?" she asks, looking around for anyone who may have seen us.

I shake my head. "Not if we go now." I whip my phone out, dialing Stella.

"Hey! I heard you're in town," she answers, chipper as ever, on the second ring.

"We are, and we were just attacked downtown. Can you

erase all video footage?" I ask her quickly, wanting to get off the phone as quickly as possible.

"Of course! On Trent Street, right? I hope you tried those onions. I told Matthew to tell you about them. So good."

Stella has always been a talker, regardless of the time and place.

"Thank you, Stella, I owe you one," I say simply as I hang up on her, stuffing my phone back into my pocket.

I keep my gun drawn as we approach one of the men. His gun lies beside him, and I pick it up carefully, handing it to Sydney. She takes it between her thumb and pointer finger, her face a mask of disgust.

"I know you hate them, Princess, but this is life or death right now. If you have to use it, you have to use it."

She stares at it longer, lost in thought. I grab her chin, forcing her to look into my eyes. "Did you hear me?"

She nods, looking absolutely petrified.

Carefully maneuvering around the corner, we come to our car. Knowing Texas, the whole thing is bulletproof, which only grants me a speck of solace

We're about to get in when three more men appear, raining bullets down on us. I take out one as a bullet flies past my head, and I feel blood dripping down my cheek. Putting my hand up, I find just a graze. I'll be fine.

Turning, I find one of the men cornering Sydney, watching as she struggles with the gun.

I shoot him quickly, and he goes down right in front of her. He groans as I stride over to him.

Grabbing the front of his uniform, I take him in.

Tactical gear. A military-grade weapon. His face is half covered. "Who sent you?" I ask, but I already know the answer.

"Fuck you, man," he says in response, and I drop him to the ground, point my gun at his chest, and fire. Once, twice, three times for good measure before I cast an incredulous look at Sydney.

She holds her hands up, looking panicked. "I got it now! I know how to do it. I'm just rusty, I swear."

I shouldn't be smiling right now.

Unlocking the car, I throw her door open, blocking her from view as she climbs in. It's not until she's completely inside and buckled that I close the door and head to the driver's seat.

"Keep your head down, okay?" I tell her, backing up out of our spot quickly and pulling out onto the street.

I speed down the strip of road, not bothering to abide by traffic laws. There aren't that many people out right now. Enough to be mildly stressful but not enough to get caught in traffic.

"Who were those people?" she asks, and I grind my molars, just trying to get out of the city.

"Jeffrey sent them. They were mercenaries. Killers for hire. He must have put a price on your head."

"Why didn't that man just kill me then when he had a chance?" Sydney's head whips around as she looks out all sides of the car, looking for anyone following us.

"Because some men like to play with their victims, Syd. These people aren't good." I'm getting mildly irritated at her questions and have to remind myself that she hasn't been around this for a very long time. I know that she was subjected to a lot of horrible things, but I'm not sure her parents brought her around mercenaries or talked about the hits in front of her.

She continues staring out the back window, and I check the rearview mirror, watching as a giant black hummer revs its engine behind us. It taps the back of my car, surging us forward. Sydney whips around, grabbing her chest.

When the truck does it once more, I switch into gear, taking a wide left turn, dodging oncoming traffic. Sydney grabs the safety handle above her, her other hand on the dash to stabilize herself.

For a moment, I think that we got rid of them, but it doesn't last long as another truck pops up. There's one more behind it, and I'm hoping and praying it's just the first one.

A shot rings out, ricocheting off of the back window.

Usually, this wouldn't stress me out so much. But the stakes are high, and Sydney is precious cargo in more ways than one.

I hand her my gun, making sure hers is still in her lap. "I need you to start shooting. Aim for their tires."

"What?" she asks, her jaw on the floor.

"Sydney, please, I need you to do this for me, okay? You either need to shoot at them, or you need to drive. Which one would you rather do?"

Gripping the gun in her hand, she takes her seatbelt off, instead wrapping it around her arm to steady her as she peeks out the back.

She shoots twice, the bullets flying ten feet to the right of the trucks. I look back, making sure she didn't hit anyone before pulling the back of her shirt back into the car. She looks at me, surprised.

"You're driving," I tell her, grabbing both of the guns from her lap.

"I was going to get it!" she grunts in frustration but ultimately doesn't argue anymore.

I look behind us, planning the switch accordingly. "In a couple seconds, we're going to turn this corner and take an immediate right," I tell her, looking ahead of us on the navigation system. "It's only going to give us a couple of seconds, so we're not stopping. You need to slip your foot in under mine as we trade spots, do you hear me? It looks like that road is straight, though, so it should be pretty easy."

She only nods, looking like a deer in the headlights.

"Are you sure you understand what I just said?" I ask, keeping my cool.

Her eyes meet mine, sparkling with nerves. She nods once, placing the guns on the dash.

I turn the wheel sharply, drifting around the turn and narrowly avoiding two cars hitting me. I immediately take the right, lifting myself off the seat as I keep my foot on the pedal.

Sydney slides over the center consul, shoving her foot under mine to take over as she grabs the wheel from me. I fall into the passenger seat, reminding myself to never do that ever again. I'm way too tall to fold up like that.

Grabbing the guns from the other side of the dash where they slid while we turned, lean out the window, aiming to shoot out their tires.

I can see the bullets bouncing off the rubber.

"Fuck!" I yell, slamming myself back into the seat.

Sydney swerves in front of a car at an intersection, accelerating down the street, a look of pure determination on her face.

"You're not actually that bad at this," I tell her, impressed.

"I mean I *was* able to steal your three-million-dollar stolen car."

True.

Bullets spray the back of our car, one finally getting stuck in the glass. It could shatter at any moment.

"Keep looking back at them through the mirror. The second you see them pop up and start shooting, start swerving, got it?"

She salutes me.

I move to lean out the window again, aiming once again at the tires.

They're much bigger than us. They can squish us like bugs, and easily. The manpower they have means that they're just trying to full-out kill us, not just slow us down.

But all I want to do is slow them down so we can get away.

Emptying my rounds, I lift off of the seat, digging in my back pocket for my backup cartridge. Whipping it out, I eject the old one, clicking the new one in place.

It takes ten more bullets to finally get one to stick in the wheel.

"Syd, I need you to trust me, okay?" I say, my heart racing.

She nods, not taking her eyes off the road.

"I need you to slow down a little. I need to be closer to them."

Without a word, Sydney takes her foot off the gas, letting the car naturally slow down a little. The hummer gets closer… and closer…

I hold the gun out, ducking as bullets are shot at me before peeking back out once more.

I watch the wheels turn.

"A little closer, Syd. Yeah, that's good. I can see it."

I take aim, waiting for the right moment… and pull the trigger.

My bullet hits the bullet lodged in the rubber tire, pushing it all the way through. The tire explodes, and the Hummer rolls. The other truck behind him can't stop in time and is sent backward with the hit.

The crunch of metal is loud, echoing through the streets as we continue speeding away.

"How do cops not know this is happening?" Sydney asks.

"They're paid off," I tell her flatly, the entire situation leaving me on edge.

She looks at me, lips pressing together as her knuckles turn white.

"Let's drive around a little longer before we go back, okay?" I ask her, sinking into the seat and breathing deep.

"Of course," she replies stiffly

Hitting my head against the back of the seat, I watch as she drives around the city. She doesn't seem scared right now. She isn't looking out the back constantly. She looks out the window at the large building with a tall sign or points out a pedestrian breaking the law.

It seems oddly, well, normal for something that's happening right after a high-speed chase.

Eventually, after an hour of making sure no one is on our tail, we head back to the compound.

TWENTY-SEVEN

SYDNEY

THE SECOND I pull into the Texas compound, Ronan is out the door. He's been fuming for the past hour, on his phone almost the whole time.

I follow behind him as he enters the house and goes to the guest wing, immediately getting back on the phone. It's a call this time.

"I don't think anyone was injured during it, no. At least not by us." He listens for a moment. "No, I don't think that's necessary. We're fine right now; I just wanted to know what you would personally suggest." After another couple of moments of silence, he rolls his eyes, turning away from me as his head tips back.

This conversation is not going how he wants it to, apparently.

"Fine," he snaps as he ends the call, still stewing.

"You doing okay?" I ask, standing in front of him. I look up at him, studying his face in the warm light of the room. He looks tired. Extremely tired. And he looks scared.

He looks at me for a long moment before grabbing me, pulling me in for a long hug. "I just don't want to lose you," he says, kissing the top of my head.

"I'm nothing special, Ronan."

He shakes his head. "You're the one person who's been able to love me the way I think I deserve to be loved. One of the very few people who would ever consider being with me. I appreciate you more than you could know."

I give him a tight-lipped smile, casting a downward glance at the floor.

"I have to go talk to Stella about erasing that footage. Are you okay to wait here?"

"Why wouldn't I be?" I challenge.

One of his shoulders tips up as he offers me a tense, closed-mouth smile. "I just don't know how you would have taken what just happened."

"I took it okay, I promise."

And I did. That's not really a lie. I think I took it fantastically. I may not have been a great shot, but I was a fantastic driver, and that's what mattered.

"Okay," he says, his hand slipping off my shoulder. "I'll be right back, I promise."

But the longer he leaves me alone, the worse my nerves get.

It occurs to me that I shouldn't be left in a room alone when preparing for such a huge day because all I can think about is all the different ways I can screw it up.

After about thirty minutes of stewing alone, I head to our room, turning the light on before digging into our suitcase.

This place really is beautiful. The rooms are all a nice light green color, the beds high with fluffy white blankets. There has to be at least five rooms here. It makes me wonder how many visitors they usually get.

But there's no one other than Ronan and I tonight.

Tired of looking for a comfy shirt, I yank one of Ronan's large t-shirts from the pile. Stripping off all my other clothes, I pull it over my head, loving how free I feel in it. Nothing restricting me.

And then there's the other elephant in the room. Our whole relationship. What is it? Do we have a name for it? Is it going to go anywhere? Should I even spend energy thinking about a possible future together?

This seems like way too much to deal with.

I sit on the bed for another ten minutes, hoping Ronan will be back. But he's not. Of course.

Since no one else is staying here tonight, I feel emboldened to make my way into the main room despite my lack of pants. I just want to be comfy as I lounge.

I curl up on the couch as I wait for him to get back, trying not to look outside for too long. The view is so nice during the day but spooky at night.

Finally, about an hour later, Ronan walks through the door, fury following him. I stay where I am, watching him carefully as he scowls at the ground.

"Are you okay?" I ask, my voice bolder than I feel.

"Yeah," he starts, biting his cheek as he scratches the back of his neck. "Just had a little bit of a fight with our handler, is all. I keep telling her that we need some way of being able to erase security footage ourselves. There are ways out there. Stella doesn't have to be responsible for it every single time."

"I'm sorry," I tell him because I'm not sure what else there is to say.

He sighs, closing his eyes. He stands like that for a long moment, and I take the time to check him out. Like always.

His hands are on top of his head as he stretches his shoulders, his biceps popping through his shirt. He has the thighs of a defensive end, his jeans looking almost too tight at times. It's mouthwatering.

"Do you want to come sit over here and listen to my problems, cowboy?" I joke. A small smile slips onto his soft lips, and I can't help but grin back at him.

"You have problems?" he asks, feigning shock.

"Lots of them," I waggle my eyebrows.

He puts his arms down and walks over to the couch, flopping onto it as he watches me carefully. Noticing I'm wearing his shirt, his eyes narrow as he runs his tongue along his lower lip, propping his head against his fist.

"I'm worried about tomorrow. I don't know what to expect."

"They're going to be assholes to you. They're going to ask us a ton of questions, but if I'm honest, it's probably going to be mostly directed at me. They're only interested in a man taking over. I highly doubt they're going to have much interest in what you have to say."

"How do you think they would feel if they knew that the head of the company hired mercenaries to kill his late friend's daughter?" I chuckle darkly, flicking a fuzzy off my knee.

"If I'm honest, I don't think they'd care that much. A paycheck is a paycheck to most of them. As long as they're still making money, they likely don't care much."

I nod, resting my head on the back of the chair. "Sometimes I just wish I had the guts that Jerry has," I whisper. Ronan sits up, asking me to repeat what I said, and when I do, he shakes his head vigorously, his black hair falling into his face.

"I, for one, am glad you're not your sister. Let's just get that out of the way right now," he says. "And as for wanting to have guts like hers, I think you do. You've proven you do it over and over and over again. I'm not sure what more you can do.

"But—"

He cuts me off. "Jerry may be the glue that keeps us all together, sure. But you're the only one who can bring this empire down. If she's the lightning, you're the goddamn thunder."

A pang of unease goes off in my chest as I realize that he truly is one of the few people who's ever been genuinely nice to me. Which is why I pause, thinking something over carefully.

"I think we should stop this," I tell him, cracking every single finger over and over again in my lap as I speak.

"Stop what?"

"Stop this," I motion between us "I know that this is a means to an end. I don't; I don't understand why you want to be with me. It's only been two weeks."

"Two weeks that we've spent every waking moment with each other? Every single night? That we've dealt with things that even married couples who have been together for over fifty years don't have to face? Sydney, stop pushing people away when they show they care."

I shake my head vigorously, annoyed.

"I tell myself every single day that I'm not a naïve woman. That I'm smart. And yet, every day I make decisions that would prove that wrong. Every single damn day. My entire body screamed when you brought me back to my place that night. My entire body. Telling me not to. But I did because my heart said it was okay.

"I'd like, at some point, to just be able to live my life. I don't want to get my heart broken, Ronan. I can't do that."

"Why the hell would I break your heart?" He runs his palms over his face before leveling me with a stare, sucking in his bottom lip.

"Because I'm this naïve girl excited about this man who's showing her even the smallest bit of decency, caught up in him. I can't think of anything else. And you're here, huge and hulking, so established in his career and life. Why would you want me?"

"I feel like I don't have to say it, Sydney. Why are you determined not to look at this as something real?"

I hold up my hand, flashing him my ring. "What do you mean, why are you determined not to look at this as something real? Ronan, we're married to take down a company. That's it. You told me multiple times in the beginning that this was fake."

"And that changed," he barks, his hands fists on his lap. He moves to the edge of the couch, spreading his legs as he leans against them. "That teasing was me trying to convince myself to stay professional, Princess."

I stay quiet, listening to him. "That teasing was me trying to keep my distance because something about you pulled me in from the very moment I saw you at that funeral. A girl hanging out at her parents' funeral, looking like she'd rather be anywhere else. Like any person in that room would bite her at any point. I was intrigued.

"Then I convinced myself that you were too much of a rich girl. That you had too many expensive things for me. But turns out that's a lie, too. And you know what? It makes me feel good. It makes me feel great, even."

My breath catches, and I watch him, wide-eyed, as he goes on and on about how he's seen me. Really saw me and how much he wants to be there for me.

And I realize that someone is fighting for me. Sure, it's a small fight, but it's a fight nonetheless.

And someone is fighting. For me.

"I need water," I grumble as I get up, heading to the kitchen. Grabbing a glass, I fill it with tap water, throwing it back with a gulp.

Large hands grab at my waist, pulling me into him as he hugs me from behind. His mouth finds the crook of my neck, and I breathe him in. He smells like whiskey, as always. Despite me never seeing him drink.

I turn around in his arms, getting lost in his deep brown eyes. He stays like that for a couple of minutes, just us, looking into each other's eyes.

And I feel at home.

My nerves go away.

This is where I want to be.

He captures my lips in his, holding my face between his hands. I turn to putty.

Reaching out to grab the back of his head, I weave my fingers in his hair, pulling on it as he does the same, fisting mine, forcing my head back as he kisses up my neck and back to my lips.

Ronan picks me up, placing me carefully on top of the kitchen island, running his hands along my body. I grab his face in mine, kissing him with every last bit of energy I have today, our tongues dancing as I wrap my legs around his body, pulling him in tighter.

His hands go down to my thighs, pressing into them as his fingers make their way higher and higher.

"Are you completely naked under this?" he murmurs into my lips, and I smile as he explores further.

Stepping back, Ronan lifts my arms, peeling off the shirt.

"There could be people outside," I tell him, only slightly worried.

He flips off the lights. "Is that better?" he asks.

I nod nervously.

Ronan stands there in front of me, biting his lip as his eyes trace every single curve of my body. Every single dip. Every single flaw. He sees all of it, yet he would never consider any of them flaws.

Maybe I should be nicer to myself.

He starts with my neck. Licking it once, he sucks at my skin, taking his time to do the job right. His short beard scratches my skin, and I feel like I'm on fire.

Trailing his tongue back up my neck, Ronan's tongue slides against mine as he wraps my long hair around his wrist, pulling me back.

He leans me back, but not far enough to lay down, no.

Instead, I prop myself up on my forearms, watching as his mouth makes its way back down my body, capturing my nipping between his teeth. He pinches the opposite, rolling it between his fingers as I feel all of my blood run south.

I moan, and he uses the opportunity to kiss me again. Sloppy. Possessive. Animalistic. We don't worry about how it looks, instead getting lost in the moment, our kisses becoming more and more desperate as I palm his shirt, desperate for him to take it off.

When he does, all I can do is appreciate the view. I've seen it so many times in the last two weeks, but it's nothing compared to when I have my legs wrapped around him.

Sliding closer to the edge of the counter, I press him into me harder, feeling him through his jeans.

"Nope, not yet," he rasps, his chest rising and falling quicker than I've ever seen it. He's not out of breath. This isn't exercise. He's just gotten lost in himself. In me.

And I have too.

"Please," I beg, looking up at him, my eyes wide. This powerful man that has saved me more than once. This kind man who has made me feel safe and at home for the first time in my miserable life. The man who gave me another chance to live.

He shakes his head, pushing me down even lower on the cool stone.

"We never actually had dessert," he mumbles as he stands over me. Dropping down to his knees, I feel his tongue at my center, exploring every inch of me. The cold countertop bites my skin, but he holds me firm, his hand pressed to my stomach, holding me down.

Before I know it, fire rips through me, and I feel as if I've burst into flames. My body shakes, goosebumps breaking out all over my body. As I sit up, I find him watching me with unrestrained curiosity.

"Are you feeling better today?" he asks, his voice low as he licks his bottom lip.

All I can do is nod in response, still coming down.

"Good."

Standing, Ronan grabs me, carrying me in his arms bridal-style into our bedroom, kicking the door shut, clearly not caring who hears by how hard.

I'm thrown onto the bed as he tears his clothes off, back on me in a second.

"Are you okay with me not having a—"

I shut him up with a kiss. "I know you can't have kids. You're good," I confirm desperately. All I want is to feel him inside of me, filling me up.

Looking into my eyes, he takes it slow. Shows restraint.

And it feels amazing.

I let my eyes flutter shut as I moan, tipping my head back as I arch my back into him. Ronan takes the opportunity to capture my nipping between his teeth, flicking it with his tongue, and when I moan into his ear, pulling his black hair, he lets out a whimper.

And I shatter.

I shatter like a mirror.

Pieces of me lay around the room. I can be put back together again, but I'll never look quite the same.

And right now? That's a good thing.

"For fucks sake, Princess, just let me love you," Ronan whispers as he continues filling me, pumping into me harder and harder. The desperation is insurmountable.

"Can you come for me again, Sydney?" Ronan all but moans, slamming into me as I wrap my legs around him, tilting my hips so he can reach deeper.

"Yes," I whisper.

"Speak up, Princess; I want to hear you say you're mine. I want to hear you say my name as you come. Can you do that for me?"

I can only nod, feeling it building inside of me. I'm panting, unable to catch my breath as my body shudders, my muscles tensing as my insides explode.

"Who do you belong to?" Ronan asks, his voice shaking like he's using the very last of his restraint.

"I'm yours. I'm yours, Ronan."

TWENTY-EIGHT

RONAN

I'VE SPENT years of my life looking for a real purpose. Yet somehow, I found it in the woman next to me. This woman, the same one who stole my car and almost blew my cover, is the one thing I'm scared to lose.

And I've never felt anything like it. Never shared anything like it with someone. The desire to give them everything.

We use our day off to explore the ranch, and when we're not outside looking at cows, each other. Every single moment with her is more special than the last.

But the real fun comes when she gets mouthy. I almost regret threatening her. Almost. Fucking the attitude out of her is my new favorite pastime.

"What's that?" Sydney asks me as I take the thin bullet-proof vest out from my suitcase.

"I'm fitting it to you. You're not going in there tomorrow without it."

She gulps, those big green eyes blinking up at me as I fit it over her head, adjusting it so it conforms to her curves.

It's a new technology that we're being allowed to test out. Practically as thin as paper, these bulletproof vests have been proven to absorb the impact of even small bombs, leaving whoever is wearing it safe.

Well, relatively. But if something happened, I'd rather be hospitalized than dead.

"Do you have one too?" she asks, looking around me and into the suitcase.

"Yeah, it's in there."

Her lips thin as she stands, her arms out at her sides as I adjust everything.

I kiss both of her cheeks before placing one on her soft lips, brushing her hair out of her face. "I don't trust a single man in that room, beautiful, and I'm going to make sure you're protected."

Our eyes meet as she lets out a shallow sigh. She's nervous. I can tell.

When she first came to the DC compound, she was a bundle of nerves. I watched her as she would wring her fingers together, cracking each finger slowly before doing them all over again. Her knees were jumpy, her shoulders tight.

After a couple of days, that slowed down. She became more confident in herself. More sure.

But now, getting ready for this meeting, she's anything but calm.

"I would just rather not be in a room with him," she whispers, pouting.

I close my eyes, wishing I could take her hurt away. I wish I could change things about her past for her. I'd do anything to do that for her. Anything to make things better.

But I know I can't.

"Let's get you dressed in everything else," I say finally, tapping her shoulders.

She shakes, and I try to calm her by rubbing her shoulders. "Hey, you're the key to this whole operation. You walk into that room, and they'll be on their knees, shaking, knowing their end is near. Do you hear me? Do you understand how much power you have?"

She shakes her head, not meeting my eyes as I come around her, grabbing her face in my hands.

"You're one of the most powerful people in this world right now. I need you to know that. To feel it. To understand it. You're unstoppable, and that's why you're so scared. That's what they have to lose. Understand that."

A knock on the door alerts us to a visitor, and we both turn, finding a small blonde woman with a computer. She smiles at us, holding up a wire.

"I'm Stella, it's so nice to meet you!" she greets Sydney, grabbing her hand and shaking it. "I've heard so many great things about you," she says, and I wonder who from. Sydney and Jerry have been getting along great, but I don't think I believe that Jerry is singing her praises to anyone who will listen. That's just not her.

Stella fits Sydney with a wire, being careful to hide it well as she places a small recording device the size of a grain of rice in her ear.

"Just don't scratch it off," she tells Sydney, and knowing her, that's going to be all she'll think about for the next two hours.

Thirty minutes later, we're out the door, wishing Matthew farewell. We'll be going directly from the meeting to the plane and back home.

The idea of that feels so bittersweet. We never get vacations, but that one day alone with Sydney yesterday? It almost felt like one. Like we could forget the world, and it could just be us for just one day. Like nothing else in the whole world matters except for the other.

I wish we could have stayed here forever, but we have to get back to reality.

And hopefully, if the board makes their decision quickly, we'll have a decision soon, and Sydney can decide whether she wants to stay or leave.

I hope it's the first option.

More than anything.

TWENTY-NINE

SYDNEY

THE ROOM IS cold and dim, the brown curtains drawn over the windows, the dark tables lined with papers.

In front of me sits eight men, each and every single one of them singing my father's praises as I get myself ready for questioning.

"We miss him so much," one of them said.

"He was such a good man. Really cared about his friends," another mentioned.

But there's one particular friend who happens to be missing from the meeting, and that's Jeffrey Wright.

I don't say a word back to them, instead just sitting where I was told to take a seat, holding Ronan's hand in a way that makes the large diamond on my finger stand out the most.

The door bursts open, and Jeffrey walks in, a deep grimace on his face as his eyes flash to mine. Smacking the files on the table, he sits, watching me from the platform they sit on.

Although the other men were nice about my father, they all look equally as mean as Jeffrey Wright. Equally as criminal. Anyone involved in this company is, surely. But these men look like they take pleasure in hurting people. It gets them off. And I'm never going to be okay with that.

"I think we're ready to get started," one of the men says, clearing his throat.

I sit up tall in my chair, my chest puffed out. I belong here, I tell myself. I belong with these men.

The problem is, I don't. Not at all. And I think they know that. I don't want to belong with them.

"The first line of questioning is going to be about your parents. Do you, Sydney, know how your parents died?"

I shake my head, acting innocent. They were burned to a crisp, but technically, I'm not sure how it happened.

The man nods, writing something in his notes.

The next one goes.

"When was the last time you spoke to your parents?"

I answer honestly. It was a couple of years ago for only a couple of minutes.

"And what, to your understanding, does this company do?"

I tell them exactly what they do. They kill people. A lot of people. But obviously, I phrase it like it's one of the best ideas I've ever heard.

"Why are you choosing now to come forward?" Jeffrey asks.

"Because it's what my mom and dad wanted."

"I don't think you've ever cared about what they've wanted before," he drawls, tapping his glasses on his lips. His eyes are small and beady, his nose lumpy.

"I cared a lot about what they wanted, which is why I left," I tell him, keeping steady.

Jeffrey looks unsure of himself, like he knows he may corner himself into something he doesn't want revealed.

Because I would do it. I would do it in a heartbeat.

"When did you find out about what this company really does?"

"One of the last times I spoke to my parents."

I'm questioned for about an hour just about my parents, and by the end, I feel as though I may scream. I'm so over it.

But Jeffrey takes an interest in Ronan.

"Did you know what company her parents were a part of before you married her?" Jeffrey asks him dully, his voice lacking emotion.

Ronan shakes his head. "No, actually, I didn't. I had no idea until they died, sir."

I risk a look over at him, spotting that wild twinkle in his eyes that tells me he's up to no good.

"Is that because Sydney hasn't associated with them in years?"

"No sir, it's because they were so busy. Their company is well known in circles like ours for being important. They had a lot on their plates."

Jeffrey nods, his eyes thinning.

"Are you aware of how this company works?" Jeffrey seems to ask both of us.

We look at each other, and I can tell that he, too is trying to decide what to say.

"That in order to run the company, you have to be married to a man, yes," I say a little too curtly.

"You don't seem to like that?"

"I think it's old-fashioned," I retort.

They look at each other, then back down at their papers. What's on those papers, I have no idea.

"We really appreciate your interest in this, Mrs…"

"Miller," I tell him, extending my hand. He takes it, shaking it once before letting it drop like it was coated in something gross.

Incredibly rude.

The men file into a room next door, their quiet whispers a low hum I can't make out. Ronan grabs my hand, holding it tight as he leans into me, pressing his lips against my forehead.

"I'm with you," he says, wrapping me in a hug.

No matter what happens here, I have him, and that's all that matters.

The men file back into the room as if they rule the world. Each and every one of them wears a grim frown, and I'm almost certain the answer is going to be no.

"Thank you for coming in here today, Sydney. Let's cut to the chase, shall we?" one of the older, scrawnier men says as he sits down. "There have been concerns brought up by specific individuals who believe this isn't real. That being said, we do try to do our due diligence and get as much information as we can on you before the meeting, and we can confirm that you are legally married, and when it comes to this company and your parents' wishes, that's what ultimately mattered to them.

I nod, my hands crossed in my lap as I keep my chin up. I don't spare a glance at Jeffrey, but I can feel his eyes burning a hole in my head.

"Because of this and what your parents meant to this company, we are deeming you fit to take over."

"This is bullshit, and you know it," Jeffrey hisses across the desk at him. The man disregards him with a side eye, instead focusing back on me.

"Ronan, if you can just give me your phone number so we can be in touch to hand it over," the man says, and while the fact that they regard women as property and cash is problematic, I'm glad I don't have to have this man's number in my phone.

Ronan walks back to the table, a grin plastered across his face, his eyes sparkling.

We did it.

"They're going to bring this company down, so help me

God," Jeffrey complains, his arm outstretched toward us as he tries to get his peers to listen to him. He's desperate, and there's honestly something so musical about it. So beautiful.

No one is going to believe him.

He's right, of course. We *are* going to burn it down. But they won't listen to him. Why would they?

When the men are done with us, or, well, Ronan, he takes my hand in his, the feeling of his warm skin on mine more relaxing than ever, and leads me out the doors into the hot Texas sun.

"You know, I really don't like it here," I tell him with a chuckle, shielding my eyes as I attempt to see where we're headed.

"It's definitely a lot to get used to," he says with a smile.

We silently walk to our parked car, reveling in our win. It's not every day that everything goes right and the good guys win.

And, well, it was easy. I won't lie. Much easier than I thought. But there's also no possible way I could have done it myself.

Ronan opens the door for me, and I climb in, fanning myself. A moment later, he climbs in as well, starting the car. He looks at me, beaming, and I feel like I'm on top of the world.

"You did that," he reminds me, and I can't help but grin. We both did it.

Despite what those men back there said at the end, they were looking for any reason to not give it to me. One misstep, and they would have said I was unfit.

We pull out onto the road and head for the airport, ready to be home.

It's an incredibly welcoming thought.

I lean back in my seat, closing my eyes and thinking about everything that's going to come next. How satisfying it's going to be. They get lawyers to write up the deal, we read it and sign it, and I'm officially the head of a billion-dollar criminal enterprise. I take the information I have available to me and distribute it to journalists around the world.

And a woman is doing it to them.

Ronan looks over at me, sending me a dazzling smile that warms my insides. I reach for his hand and—

The crunch of metal is all I hear as my seatbelt works overtime to keep me situated as the car rolls over and over across the road. Shattered glass fragments fly into my hair, cutting my scalp and face, and when I reach up to protect my eyes, a large shard gets jammed into the back of my hand.

I scream, but I don't hear anything but metal on metal.

My heart races, and the second I can, I brave a look at Ronan, watching as his head lolls to the side as if he has no control over it.

Screaming his name, I claw at my seatbelt, desperate to get out. I don't look at who's around us. At what happened. All I care about is if he's breathing.

Which was the wrong move.

A man in all black runs up, weapon at the ready, his gun trained on Ronan in his seat. He falls forward, and I use the opportunity to grab his gun from his back pocket. Without thinking, I remove the safety, aim it, and fire it at the man's neck, the one place untouched by armor.

I think I'm going to be sick.

Watching the blood spray behind him as he falls over is horrifying, and all I want to do is throw the gun away from me. But I need to make sure we're safe, and it's the only way.

Fists aren't winning me this fight.

I get out of the car, running over to the driver's side, yanking open the mangled door and pulling him out onto the ground. My eyes are hot with tears, my mouth is filled with blood flowing from my head. Next to me, the man twitches.

I jump, not even thinking when I shoot him three more times for good measure.

Bullets rain down on us, and then as another truck arrives, two men leaping out, guns raised. I drag Ronan behind the back of the car, the only part that isn't completely destroyed, and slap his face.

"Please get up. Please wake up, Ronan I swear to god if you fucking die on me and leave me here with a gun, I'm going to be so pissed at you." I peek over the car, aiming the gun as I close one eye, trying to keep on target. Squeezing the trigger, I hit the man square in the chest, but he keeps walking, bullets firing from his riffle.

"I will fucking haunt you, Ronan. I swear to god if you die, I die and I will make sure you know *no* peace in the afterlife. Your ghost ass is getting haunted."

The men are closer now, and I think I can aim a little better. Peeking up over the car once more, I squeeze the trigger, hoping for the best.

It hits one man square in the throat the other in the head and they fall. I'm not positive the second man is dead. Probably just knocked out. But I have hope that he is.

I smack Ronan hard across the face, shaking him. We only have a couple minutes before we're both dead, and I can feel him breathing.

"Ronan, I love you please don't do this to me," I whimper, clutching his chest.

His eyes slowly open, a smile on his lips. "You love me, Sydney Miller?"

I roll my eyes. "Ronan, we're about to be murdered get the hell up. I've been trying wake you for two minutes."

His brown eyes widen as he looks around us before they land on me. Like he wasn't quite sure what was going on before. Like he was dreaming. Letting out a sigh of relief, he grabs my head and kisses me. Hard.

"We have to go," I interrupt him, my words muffled by his lips.

He tries to get up but flinches, clearly in a lot of pain. We don't have time for that. I grab his arm, hauling him up. He takes a couple of steps, getting his feet under him, and we take off back toward the city as fast as we can.

Which isn't the quickest.

My hair is still a mess, glass shards still sticking out of it. My hand bleeds, the chunk of glass cutting it who knows how deep. My clothes are ripped and so are Ronan's. There's nowhere we can go.

"What are we going to do?" I ask him, barely able to breathe from panic and exhaustion. Electric shocks zing the back of my thighs, and I can feel the cramping start.

"We have to find a car to steal. I think that's our only option right now," he says as he looks over our clothes.

We stay in the shadows, watching as men in black uniforms walk through the streets. It's not a busy part of the city, that's for sure. But it's still strange that no one has a problem with it.

We're about to turn a corner when one of the men turns right into us. Ronan, already holding his gun, grabs the man, places the gun between his vest and pants, and shoots twice. It's quiet, and the man goes down without a sound.

"You remind me of John Wick right now," I whisper as we rush through the city.

"I don't know who that is," Ronan hisses back.

"Are you fucking kidding me right now? It's not even an old movie!" I throw my hands in the air, rolling my eyes. "We're watching it when we get home."

He casts me a sideways glance, looking done with me.

Ronan takes out his broken phone and manages to call Jerry.

"We were attacked on the road. We're fine. Banged up. We're getting a car now, and we'll be at the airport in five minutes." Silence. "I know it's ten minutes away from us right now, but we're getting there in five. Please tell the pilot to be ready." Silence. "Yes, as in, the second we get on that plane, it's taking off."

Ronan thumbs the keypad, trying to hang up the phone. When it doesn't work, he throws the phone in the trash. "I have extras at home," he explains when I gape at him.

Finding a car fast enough to get away from these men doesn't come easy, but when we finally find a corvette, we climb in. Ronan pulls wires out, hot-wiring it. "The only people who drive corvettes are middle-aged white men who are going through a mid-life crisis," I tell him, judging him just a smidge.

"Well we're not going to live until we're middle-aged white people if we don't get this going," he hisses, sliding into the seat.

The engine roars to life, and he hits the gas, lurching forward.

We fly through the streets quickly, mostly avoiding roads where men are stationed. It isn't until we're almost to the airport that a car pulls out behind us, speeding up so they're on our tail.

Ronan grinds his molars, hitting the steering wheel with his fist.

Up ahead, we see our plane. and I've never seen a more welcoming sight.

"We just have to go for it," Ronan tells me. "We don't have any other choice. The second we stop, run. And don't stop running, got it? If I fall behind, you get on that plane."

"I'm not doing that," I tell him, grabbing his shoulders. "I'm not leaving you here no matter what."

"You have to."

"You have to, too."

He grabs my hand as we burst through the security gate to the tarmac, coming to a screeching halt outside of the plane. The large car follows us, a man shooting out the side window.

"Now!" Ronan yells, and we fling our doors open, staying low as we make a run for it. The door to the plane is open, and the stairs are rolled out. I can feel bullets flying by my head, but we stay low enough, weaving back and forth, that we make it.

As the plane closes the door, I watch as the men fire bullet after bullet at the plane. All they do is ricochet off.

I can't help but think that's cool.

The pilot takes off without question the second the door is shut, and we're on our way back home.

THIRTY

RONAN

SYDNEY and I are antsy the entire way home.

We have five hours to clean up, and thankfully, there's a case full of medical supplies sitting in the bathroom of the plane.

"Hold still," I tell her, carefully pulling the shard of glass out of her hand. It went deep, and she definitely may have nerve damage. "Princess, you're not sitting still."

"I have glass in my fucking hand, and you're yanking it out. Of course I'm not sitting still."

I roll my eyes, attempting to be gentler.

Although I couldn't find rubbing alcohol in the back, I did find vodka. Pouring it on a rag, I place it on her cuts, and she yells. It's not a pleasant sound, and I hate doing something that hurts her.

But we need to clean the wounds.

I strip of my shirt and vest, thankful I really did decide to wear it, and tend to a gash on my lower stomach, pouring vodka over it before grabbing medical tape to try to hold the skin together until we get home. Zach is fantastic with stitches.

"Do you think it was just Jeffrey or all of them?" Sydney asks, and if I'm honest, I don't know. It could be either.

I shrug, wincing in pain. "I'm not sure, but it was at least Jeffrey. And there's a hit out on us."

"What does that mean?" She sits in her seat, her legs curled up underneath her as she watches my every move like a hawk, ready to jump up at any moment and help me.

"I mean that in a second we're going to have problems."

"Fuck."

"Yeah."

"What are we going to do?"

"The only thing we can do is fight back."

Right before we land in DC, I take Sydney to the back of the plane, opening our big storage compartment. The thing is totally filled to the brim with different kinds of weapons.

"If you want any chance of getting out of here, you're going to have to use one of them," I tell her. She looks through them all, asking me a couple of questions about them.

I can tell that she regrets not remembering much about her training with them, but that's okay. I can always train her again. Make happier memories.

Grabbing a handgun that packs a punch, she tucks it into the front of her pants, giving me the thumbs up. I smile at her, but I can tell she can see right through it. I'm exhausted, still covered in spots of blood, and I just want to be home, safe and sound where we can sleep. I've been on plenty of hard missions, but this has been unrelenting.

We just have to try to get home alive.

If we can even go home. We can't just lead people directly to the building.

I'm not sure what my plan is going to be. I don't have a phone, and I don't have a car to get there.

"Get ready when we get off, okay?"

She nods.

The plane lands, and I watch her cradle the gun closer to her chest, making sure she knows where everything she may need is on it.

I count down from ten as the door opens, and when it's done, we rush out.

And we're immediately met with bullets raining down on us.

There are men all around, hiding in small crevices, and Sydney and I stand back-to-back, taking them out as fast as we possibly can.

"I got one!" she yells, excited.

"We need to get more than just one, keep going," I cry out above the shots.

The men start coming out of hiding, circling us. I grab her hip as we watch them close in on us. She grabs my hand, interlocking our fingers, holding on for dear life.

She's my lifeline.

But suddenly, bullets are flying from another direction, taking out the men surrounding us one by one.

I look around, trying to figure out where it's coming from.

But there, at the top of the roof, sits Jeremy.

He nods once to me, aiming his large sniper rifle before taking out another. And another. Sydney and I get back to work, taking out more and more as we go. They keep coming, and I have to wonder how much money they put on our heads that people all over the country would be looking. This many people is insane.

When it doesn't seem like there's any more, I yank on her hand, leading her in the direction of the airport. We burst through the doors, panic swelling in our chests as we keep moving.

Passing by a kiosk, I swipe a burner phone, stuffing it quietly into my jacket as we leave. When we're finally far enough away, I take it out, ripping the box open to get to it. Opening the back, I cut two small wires, switching them. Sydney watches me, her brows furrowed.

"What are you doing?"

"I'm getting us out of here."

Plugging in Jerry's number, I hit call, holding it up to my ear.

"Where the fuck are you?" Jerry's voice comes from the other end of the phone, and I almost want to chuckle at the fact she knew it was me despite the blocked caller.

"We're in DC. At the airport. Where are you?"

"You can't come home."

My blood runs cold, despite the fact that I was assuming this would happen.

"There's a nationwide hit out on you two. Millions of dollars. There's no way you can come home right now."

I throw my hands up in the air, looking around the airport. Sydney stands only a couple feet from me, her blood starting to seep through her bandaged hand.

"You need to take him out. Find him, kill him, and make sure that the hit is cleared. I don't know what to tell you, Ronan, there's nothing we can do here. I've tried."

"Can you please try harder?" I grit through my teeth, grinding my molars.

"We can keep trying, but you need to find Jeffrey."

"He was just in fucking Texas, Jerry do you expect us to go all the way back there?"

"I'll ask the others to see if we can find him. Get the Texas Angels on it."

"Matthew can't leave."

She pauses. "I know that."

"Okay."

"Find someplace to hide and lay low for a minute; I'll let

you know what I find. Stella can probably find his face on a camera somewhere."

I hang up without saying goodbye, pissed and annoyed. I'm not sure why we didn't think about this happening, but I think I assumed that the other men at that table would keep him in check.

But Jeffrey Wright is as bad as they come, and giving him even an ounce of power was one of the worst things they could have done.

Maybe they were willing to give Sydney the company because of how awful he was. They just wanted to get rid of him, too.

Sighing, I grab Sydney's hand and drag her along with me toward the entrance. Taking a right, we end up in a parking garage.

We walk through it, trying to find a car to take, when a white van pulls in front of us, the back sliding open.

"Get in."

I whip around, yanking my gun from the back of my pants, and find Jeremy leaning against the side of the van, his arms crossed, a cocky look on his face.

"Are you going to get in or not?"

I look at Sydney, searching for whether this is a good idea or not. After a moment, I run my hand through my hair. "Screw it," I mumble as I help her into the van before climbing in myself.

"You guys are in a bit of trouble," Jeremy says, whistling.

"Thank you for informing us; we really needed that," Sydney says, and it puts a little smirk on my face.

"I'm just saying. Do you have any information for me?" Jeremy asks her.

Her eyes flash to mine before going back to his. "I have unfinished business. After it's done, I can give you everything."

But the thing is, she's not going to be able to do that. But I can't tell her that right now.

"Stay here until you figure out what the hell you guys are doing," he barks, opening the back door and hopping out.

Whipping out the burner phone, I call Jerry back. "Have anything for me?"

"Stella isn't seeing him anywhere but the airport. I think he went back home, too."

"That would be convenient," I say, hitting my head on the side of the van.

"Where are you guys right now?"

"Don't worry about it."

There's silence.

"Hey Sydney, do you have any idea where he may go?"

She thinks about it for a moment, her arms flung over her knees. Her lips rub together as does, her fingers playing with a loose strand of fabric from her pants.

"I have one idea."

"Okay, that's a start," I say, perking up.

"I think he may be at my parents' old place. The vacation home in the country."

"Why would he be there?"

"It was peaceful for me because they left me alone," she explains, "but they only left me alone because they had so much business to conduct there. That entire property is completely stacked with bodies under that soil. The whole thing. I used to watch them bring construction workers in to bury them.

"Whole fields of bodies, and they'd just put dirt over them, turning it into one of the fields I played in as a kid."

"Jesus Christ, how many people did your parents kill?" Jerry asks, going back to *your* parents.

"Mom killed my second nanny because she gave her a regular soda instead of a diet one time. I'm not joking."

The more I hear about these parents, the more grossly

concerned I am. I'm not sure how they birthed either of these women. I wouldn't tell a soul, but Jerry got emotional about Zach killing a moth the other week.

People, on the other hand, are a little bit of a different story to her.

"Go there. I'll meet you,"

She hangs up.

THIRTY-ONE

SYDNEY

THE KILLING FIELDS.

It's what I started calling that place after I left. After I ran away. It was my one place of peace growing up. How screwed up is that.

Thirty minutes out of the way, Ronan and I *borrowed* someone's car, an inconspicuous little piece of shit that'll get us there. We don't need speed for this. No one is going to be looking for us around there.

Ronan grabs my hand to stop my shaking, and I instantly feel a tranquility wash over me.

"Are you doing okay?" he asks, but he knows the answer to that.

"I want him dead."

Ronan nods. "I do, too."

Running his thumb over my fingers, he squeezes my hand three times before lacing his fingers through mine.

"After this is all over, I want you to move in with me. Get rid of that apartment. Come live at the complex."

At first the thought didn't sound great to me. Why would you want to live with a bunch of other people? But it's a bunch of people who have no family of their own. Who are on their own. Who have made a family for themselves.

And I like that.

I've lived in a house of horrors for most of my life, hiding from parents who wouldn't hesitate to shoot someone dead for simply looking at them wrong. I was careful. I tried to do everything right.

Most of all, I was never protected. I was a kid, and I wasn't protected by the people who were supposed to protect me.

But at the compound, I hear that door open, and Elena is home, laughing about something she saw on social media. And a little later, Brandon is trying to sneak into her room, pretending to ask for a book. I've never once seen that man read in the time I've been there. I have, however, heard him ask to borrow a book numerous times, only to disappear into her room.

Or Zach cooking up something random in the kitchen to eat when he's high.

And then Jerry would come inside from her walk with Maverick, talking to him about her day. "I didn't do too much today, but I'm glad everyone here is doing well," she said one time.

Despite having a heart of steel, Jerry cares a lot. She's just selective.

And finally, Ronan.

The thought of leaving him makes my heart skip. All I want to do is curl up in his arms, safe and sound.

I want to be at his side no matter what. Whether it be a mission, at the grocery store, or even picking out our burial plots. I can't imagine a single other person next to me.

"I think I'd like that," I tell him finally, folding my shaking hands in my lap as I look out the window.

"Hey, eyes on me," he says, reaching for my chin.

I smile, rolling my eyes. But it helps.

I stay calm for the rest of the ride.

Jerry pulls in the second we do, leaping out of her car, guns blazing. She didn't bring the others, but honestly, it makes sense. This is a family matter.

The second I get out of the car, she throws me a small handgun, and Ronan takes his out, positioning it in front of him, ready. We're not sure what we're getting into.

But the place is silent.

And it's just like I remember.

The fields sit over a couple dozen acres. I used to think they went to the end of the earth as a kid. Everything at the end seems so far away.

The large cabin sits before us, smoke coming from the chimney. The chilly October air is nipping at my skin, and the wound on my hand hurts.

Jerry puts a finger to her lips, directing us to follow her.

Trying the front door, Jerry finds it unlocked, pulling it open. She leads, checking the corners before we follow her.

We silently scope the place out, but it's empty. Not a thing.

My father's old study, where he kept all of his company paperwork, has been completely emptied. Not a single thing in sight. The house stands, but there is no sign of life other than the fireplace raging, the smoke rising from the chimney like the dead.

But it's when we exit to the back porch that we find it.

Or him.

Jeffrey Wright sits on the porch swing he'd often torment me on as a kid, using his foot to swing himself slightly. He barely glances our way as we step out.

"I knew I was going to die here," he says, a small smile creeping onto his lips. "And I knew you would probably be the one to do it. Well, unless you died a martyr. You were always one for theatrics, weren't you." Jeffrey lets out a bone-chilling chuckle.

He sighs as we stay silent.

"I knew since the time you were a little girl that you weren't going to take over this company. I knew it with every fiber of my being. You were always too good for it. Even as a kid. They couldn't train you. Couldn't mold you into something you refused to be. But you could have been powerful. You could have controlled the world."

"No single person is supposed to control the world," I tell him. "And you don't. You get paid by people who want to watch the world burn."

He shrugs.

"You know, I think you should thank me for Ronan," he smiles, looking out across the fields.

"Why would I do that?" My heart starts beating faster and faster as I realize we're on the edge of something I can't possibly come back from.

"Who do you think sent all your boyfriends away? I knew that when the day came that your parents passed, you couldn't be married. Do you know how easy it was to pay them off?" he looks me in the eyes, chuckling. "They took the money and ran far away from you, child."

A shiver of disgust runs down my back. I don't think I'm strong enough to ask him about what he did to me. I don't think I have to be.

"You talk like you wanted them out of the way," I say, my head tilting. "Who killed them, Jeffrey?"

He shrugs, his shoulders dropping dramatically.

"I did," comes the voice to my left.

My head whips to the left, my eyes wide as I watch her shrug.

"I lit their car on fire. I don't have a single regret about it."

Jeffrey's eyes find Jerry's, as if he's just realizing she's here. As if there are two other people with me.

"She really did give you up, didn't she? We were taking bets on whether she brought you out back and drowned you."

Jerry doesn't move a muscle.

My mother was an awful person, and the world is better without her, but she was also a victim too. I think it's important to recognize that.

Ronan shifts uncomfortably next to me. "Did you know?" I ask him, his gaze intense on mine.

He shakes his head. "I didn't know."

I look back to Jerry. "He didn't," she confirms. "I got word they were going to take out a little girl. Their operation was growing, and we had just had to deal with a girl from fucking Seattle being targeted. We were all put in danger because of it. What better way to get the plan moving along than to kill them." She shrugs as if nothing she's saying is problematic.

"That's very sweet of you," Jeffrey quips up from his seat. "But—"

Before he can finish, there's a bullet hole between his eyes.

Ronan and I turn to Jerry, jaws hanging open.

"What the hell was that."

"We got all we needed to know. No use hearing him drone one and say something else fucked up, right?" she shrugs.

"I kind of pictured killing him."

She rolls her eyes. "You wouldn't have. And I wouldn't have let you. You're too good for that."

Ronan holds up his hand. "She killed a man in Texas."

Jerry's eyes widen. She looks impressed. Maybe even proud.

"Well, he was about to shoot Ronan, so…" I trail off. She's right. The thought of it makes me feel a little sick.

We look back at the body in front of us.

"Should we move him?" I ask.

Jerry thinks about it for a second. "Nope," she says quickly as she reaches for his coat, pulling out his phone.

"Sydney, come hold his eyes open for me."

I rear back, not believing what I'm hearing right now.

"Do you want to cancel this hit or not?" she snaps, and I do as she asks.

"Wait, you really killed your parents?" Zach asks at the dinner table.

"Why is everyone surprised?"

"We're surprised that you hid it from all of us mostly," Brandon says through a mouthful of food.

"Was I supposed to meet Sydney for the first time and go, "hey, I'm your secret twin sister, and by the way, I killed our parents. Just saying. Now, please work with me on this mission."

Elena looks at me, her eyes flashing with sympathy. "Would that have worked on you?"

I shake my head, leaning back in my seat and crossing my arms.

"Okay, that's enough," Ronan says, setting down a plate of salad. Jerry looks at it, her nose turning up as she passes it to Zach next to her.

"I understand it bu—" My words are interrupted by Ronan's phone ringing next to me. There's no caller ID.

He picks it up without a second thought, pressing it to his ear. "Yes, sir, this is Ronan Miller."

Getting up, Ronan walks to the couch to finish the call. While the others bicker back and forth, I try with all my might to listen to what they're talking about behind me.

"Yes, and I can sign that here? Is there anything else I have to do after that?"

There's a pause.

"Fantastic, thank you so much, sir."

Hanging up the phone, Ronan joins us once more.

"Well, that was the call." Taking my hand, he kisses the top of it. "You're officially the owner of a criminal enterprise.

Go me.

"You've been quiet for the last couple of days," Ronan teases me as he brushes my hair, placing it over my shoulder. I sigh as his lips meet the tender skin beneath my ear, kissing down my jawline.

"A lot has changed in a short amount of time."

He nods, pushing me back on the bed.

"Are we allowed to talk about the future now?" he asks, hovering over me.

"We still have work to do," I murmur, running my fingers through his hair.

Shiloh jumps onto the bed, and I reach out to pet him. He's almost never here when Ronan is. But when I do, I feel something hard around his neck. Confused, I look up.

"When did you get him a collar? And more importantly, how did you get it on him?"

Ronan shrugs. "He just let me."

I look at him. He smirks at me, confident and playful as he looks at Shiloh again.

I do the same.

"What is that?" I ask, propping myself up to get a closer look. I grab him, pulling him into my lap.

It's a ring.

A sparkly, large emerald cut ring.

Ronan clears his throat.

"I didn't pick that ring out, and even when this was fake, I thought I should have. It was only right."

I rip the old one off, handing the new one to him as I hold my hand out.

Grinning like an idiot, he slides the ring onto my finger before placing it in his mouth.

My nose crinkles as I smile. "You see, I don't think that women find that as hot as men do."

"It was worth a try."

Grabbing my ass, Ronan pulls me to him, wrapping me in a bear hug before placing kisses down my body.

His hands roam, marking my body as his with each kiss and each pinch.

He knows what he's doing.

"Kiss me," I demand, dragging his face to my lips.

"Yes, ma'am," he murmurs, licking his lips. He softly drags them over mine, and I close my eyes.

"What did I tell you about closing your eyes?" He growls.

"Hmm," is all I give him, not daring to open them.

He stops touching me, pulling away.

Opening my eyes, I pout, my arms stretched above my head.

Although he pushed my shirt up, he never took it completely off. Pushing it up only a little further, Ronan ties it around my wrists, bringing it back down around my face.

"What—"

Ronan places a kiss on my naval before continuing his trek down.

Suddenly, not being able to see what he's about to do isn't so fun anymore.

His tongue darts out, lightly hitting my clit before he blows on it and repeats the process.

And I love it.

"Tell me you love me," Ronan says, kissing back up my body.

"I've been telling you that."

"I want to hear it again."

"I love you, Ronan Miller. And I think a very very small part of me, like a microscopic part of me loved you since the moment I saw you."

I can feel him smiling despite my face being covered.

"And I love you, Sydney Miller. Till death do we part."

THIRTY-TWO

RONAN

"DID YOU DISTRIBUTE THOSE?" Sydney asks me, pointing at the computer screen.

I roll my eyes. "Yes, I distributed them. Everything is good."

She nods, going back to the couch.

Sydney is officially the head of Atlee Enterprises, and we've officially started to tear the company down piece by piece.

With a little help from Jeremy.

Although Sydney really wanted to go to the press about everything, the CIA was, let's say, not a fan. Something about mass hysteria within the country was not exactly something they were into.

"They'd have to start talking about aliens again," Jerry says.

Sydney's brows furrow. "What do you mean?"

"Whenever there's shady shit going on with us, they always start talking about aliens. Gets the attention off of it.

She stares at me for several beats before going back to her work.

Instead, we attacked the company from the outside.

Anyone involved with it was given to Fallen Angels across the country on strict orders to take them out.

After that happened, Sydney would go dark on all the *employees* they had. No more contact. No more money spent.

Finally, they would dissolve the company, getting rid of any and all information about it. Documents were shredded, and buildings burned.

The Killing Field was dug up and dealt with. Shockingly, it didn't make much news at all because of a large UFO sighting that spawned a press conference.

Sydney and I have thought about changing our names because of what happened with Atlee Enterprises, but we haven't decided yet. I'm not sure how much of a real threat mercenaries who aren't getting paid are.

But one thing I am serious about is her protection.

"I just want to go to Target, Ronan. That's all. Just Target."

"I could go with you. I'll carry all of your things."

She signs, spinning on her heel to look me square in the eye.

"I am not taking you to Target with me. That's a woman's paradise, and I'm not going to let you ruin it by following me around and telling me I don't need things."

I scoff. "Sydney, I literally buy you everything you want at all times. You can get whatever you want there."

"I just—" I don't let her finish, instead pulling her into a long kiss. When she pulls away, I pull her into another one.

I want to keep her close.

And I know I'm never letting go.

I'm not sure I can make up for all the years of pain, but I'll die trying.

EPILOGUE

ONE YEAR *later*

"Why are you doing this to me?" I ask him as he leads me out the back of the compound.

"You're going to ruin the surprise for yourself if you keep insisting on knowing. You're about to find out."

I sigh, crossing my arms over my chest.

It's a chilly fall day, and although I love the summer, there's something about the fall that just feels like freedom. Like letting go of expectations. Like book clubs and lattes and slippers.

There's something about fall that feels like home.

Just like Ronan.

"Is this a good surprise? I ask him.

"Why would it be a bad one?"

I scoff. "You've had bad surprises before."

I can feel the eyeball from here.

"Jesus Christ, what's taking them so long?" I hear Jerry say. She doesn't sound too far away. Interesting.

"What's Jerry doing here?" I ask.

"She's just being a grouch like always. Ignore her."

Reasonable.

317

"Okay, are you ready?" he asks, already unfastening the blindfold.

"I think so?"

The afternoon sun blinds me, and I have to shield my face in order for my eyes to adjust. But when they do, I can't help but feel teary.

"What is this?"

"It's our wedding," Ronan says, reaching for my hand.

He wears a nice black suit. The one I complimented him the most on when we go to dinners and galas as part of his cover.

His hair is messy, tousled in that *I just got out of bed* way that only a man can pull off.

His facial hair is grown out, but it's shaved pretty close to his face. I told him he was treading on thin ice with that one.

Which isn't really true. I love his face no matter what it looks like, whether it be naked or hairy.

His eyes are sparkling as he takes my hand, spinning me.

He dressed me upstairs after blindfolding me, telling me to promise not to feel the fabric or cheat and try to spot it in a mirror somewhere. Which, to be fair, is a reasonable request, considering I always tip my head back all the way, trying to get a peek.

There are a couple chairs lining a little makeshift aisle. It's surrounded by flowers leading to a beautiful arch covered in hydrangeas.

Standing under it is Jerry, who holds several pieces of paper in her hands.

She beams at me, her eyes misty.

Elena, Kim, Brandon, and Zach all sit around, smiling up at me as they watch us.

My dress is a long white silk number with little flowy sleeves and lace detailing.

My hair, now a shade darker than it was, is half up and

half down, braided into a bun at the top of my head by Elena, who told me that Ronan was bringing me on a date.

I didn't think a date meant a date to the backyard to get remarried.

"You didn't invite Paul?" I chuckle, watching as Jerry winks at me.

Jerry, who has been very secretive about her very own love life. Disappearing most nights and only coming home when the sun is about to come back out.

She's been tired lately, but she deserves it. She works hard.

As for me, I was approved to become a Fallen Angel. I think it was a mix of Jerry pulling for me, Ronan admitting that we were already, indeed, married, and the fact that I have no family left other than Jerry.

But I'm just glad it happened.

Ronan takes my hand, leading me through the flowers. We stop in front of Jerry, who hugs me.

"You deserve this, you dickhead," she pauses as we smile at each other, crinkling the paper in her hands before clearing her throat.

"Ronan, do you take my beautiful twin sister to be your wedded wife, to have and to hold, so that every time I piss you off, you can't stop thinking about it?"

"I don't think this is what they really say at weddings," Zach whispers loudly.

Jerry doesn't let him answer.

"And Sydney, do you take this man I forced you to marry against your will to be your husband?"

"Wow, no handsome husband? No—"

"Ronan shut up," Brandon hisses. "This is so romantic."

"I do," I say.

Ronan smiles. "Till death do us part."

"I don't think that's the phrase, either," Zach smiles.

"What are you up to?"

"I think I'm going to go out tonight. I'm not sure though, have to figure out what's going on with work," Adam sighs into the phone.

It's been a year and I still haven't been able to tell Adam exactly what happened with me, but Ronan has set up times for me to get together with him. We've hung out a couple of times, and it's been like I never left.

Of course he's been suspicious of my new life, but that's just something I have to accept.

"You need to settle down at some point," I tell him with an eye roll. "Get a girlfriend. Stop going out all the time."

"No can do Syd. I have some living to do before that,"

Despite all of my attempts, Adam has refused to settle down even now, but I'm positive it'll happen eventually. Maybe when he least expects it.

"Adam there's so much living to do after, too."

SNEEK PEAK

PENANCE

PROJECT FALLEN ANGEL BOOK 3

MATTHEW

A man in the basement screams as I load the cart up with feed for the pigs. It's what I do every single day here. Wake up, get a cup of coffee, look at the weather, and feed the pigs leftovers of whoever was kept here at the ranch last week.

Pigs really will eat anything

Sighing, I put my hat on my head before marching out the back door to the pig pen.

I don't like watching them eat much. My stomach is a little squirmy that way. I'm fine dealing with the guys, getting them ready to be breakfast, but when it comes to watching the pigs eatin' 'em? Nah.

So I turn around, instead admiring how beautiful this ranch is. How perfect the house looks when the sun is risin'.

It's beautiful, for sure, but it's the only thing I've known for the last eight years.

As much as I love this ranch, I yearn to see something different. An ocean, a cabin in the woods somewhere, a mountain or two. Maybe a lake.

But I paid my price, and now I owe my whole life to the Fallen Angels. Only while they all come and go, I never leave.

Every week, I work with animals.

Cime lords.

Rapists.

Serial Killers.

They get tied up in the basement and tortured for information, and yet all I can think about is if they pity me.

No one knows what really goes on here.

And I've never really thought about leaving.

A cowboy only ever has one true home, and this is mine.

Project Fallen Angel Book 3: Penance is a western dark thriller between a cowboy spy and his ex-girlfriend, a now notorious serial killer.

Out February 2024

ACKNOWLEDGMENTS

I feel like acknowledgments are sometimes always the hardest part. I'm not sure why. There's so many people I'd like to thank, as always.

A special thank you to my boyfriend Alex for always supporting me no matter what. The super late nights when I'm up writing after working all day, the Masterchef episodes missed… It never goes unappreciated. I love you.

To Ariana and Darlene, than you guys for brightening up my days. Thank you for always being there to talk to me and encourage me no matter what, and to run plot ideas by.

A huge thank you to Bea, who is CONSTANTLY hyping me up and one of the most wonderful people on this floating rock. I adore you and I can't wait to see what you put into this world yourself!

To Jen, who I've had the pleasure of knowing for a couple of years now. You're a joy and I'm so thankful for you and your constant unwavering support and book recommendations.

To Jules, I ADORE you and hope you know that I'm absolutely in your corner. You're an amazing woman.

To Lilly, who is genuinely one of the sweetest, kindest human beings on this planet. I'm SO incredibly thankful to have found you, and I hope you know that you are so loved and so appreciated.

To Dotty, who I'm SO happy to have met. I'm proud of everything you've done this year and I literally can't stop watching your stories for your cats. I'm so in love with their little faces.

A huge thank you to Nicki for being a source of constant support and someone who has quickly become a great friend. You're amazing and I really appreciate you!

Next I want to thank all my street team members and ARC readers for making releasing a book a possibility. I adore you all.

Thank you to my brother Cameron for helping me with a few car related questions, including answering a text at 11:50 pm asking "Tomorrow if you have time can you please explain how a 7-speed dual clutch PDK transmission works, and what would happen if someone randomly got in a car trying to panic steal it but doesn't know how to drive stick shift, and possibly what the shift lever looks like?" and immediately responding with "Are you writing about a specific car it sound like?" Instead of thinking I'm insane.

Thank you to friends and family, and to all of you future readers.

TERMS

Agent: A person unofficially employed by an intelligence service. They are usually used as a source of information.

Agent-in-place: A government employee who is influenced by a spy to cooperate with a foreign government instead of defecting. These agents work for two employers rather than one.

Agent-of-influence: Someone who works within the government or media of a target country to influence policy.

Asset: A clandestine source or method, usually an agent.

Babysitter: Bodyguard

Bang and Burn: Demolition and sabotage operations.

Black Bag Job: Secret entry into a home of office with the intention of stealing or copying materials.

Black Operations: Covert operations that are not attributable to the organization permitting them.

Black Propaganda: Disinformation that is deniable by its source, and cannot be traced back to them.

Blown: The discovery of an agent's true identity or a clandestine activity's real purpose.

Brush Pass: A brief encounter where something is passed between case officer and agent.

Burned: When a case officer or agent is compromised.

CIA: Central Intelligence Agency; The United States's foreign intelligence gathering service.

Cipher: A system for disguising messages by replacing letters with other letters or numbers. They can also be shuffled.

Clandestine Operation: An intelligence operation designed to remain secret

Cobbler: A spy who creates false passports, visas, diplomas, and other documents.

Code: A system for disguising a message by replacing its words with groups of letters or numbers.

Codebook: A list of plain language words opposite their codeword or number.

Compromised: An operation, asset, or agent uncovered that cannot remain secret.

Controller: Officer in charge of agents (a handler).

Dead Drop: A secret location where materials can be left for another party to retrieve.

Discard: An agent whom a service will permit to be detected and arrested so as to protect more valuable agents

Dry Clean: Actions agents take to determine if they are under surveillance.

Escort: An operations officer assigned to lead a defector along an escape route.

Espionage: The practice of spying or using spies to obtain secret or confidential information about the plans and activities or a foreign government or competing company.

Exfiltration Operation: A clandestine rescue operation designed to bring defector, refugee, or an operative and his or her families out of harm's way.

FBI: Federal Bureau of Investigation; U.S.'s domestic counterintelligence service and federal law enforcement agency.

Ghoul: An agent who searches obituaries and graveyards for names of the deceased for use by agents.

Handler: A case officer who is responsible for handling agents in operations.

Honey Trap: Men or women using sexual situations to intimidate or snare others.

Infiltration: The secret movement of an operative into a target area with the intent that his or her presence will go undetected.

Intelligence Officer: Professionals trained by governments. Most often called case officers, operational officers, or handlers, they run operations and recruit and manage spies.

Legend: A spy's claimed background or biography, usually supported by documents and memorized details.

NSA: National Security Agency; branch of the U.S. Department of Defense responsible for ensuring the security of American communications and for breaking into the communications of other countries.

Pattern: The behavior and daily routine of an operative that makes his or her identity unique

Playback: To provide false information to the enemy while gaining accurate information from him or her.

Spy: In the intelligence world, a spy is strictly defined as someone used to steal secrets for an intelligence organization. Also called an agent or asset, a spy is not a professional intelligence officer, and doesn't usually receive formal training (though may be taught basic tradecraft).

Spymaster: The leader of espionage activities, and an agent handler

Station: Post from where espionage is conducted.

Throwaway: An agent considered expendable

Wet Job: An operation in which blood is shed.

ABOUT THE AUTHOR

Anna Noel is an action romance writer based in Upstate New York. Getting her start writing when she was only 11 years old, Anna made it her life's mission to build a career around books.

Anna has been writing and selling plots to authors for over 7 years, and went full-time with her freelance writing career in 2020. Since then, she's worked as a copywriter, plot writer, eulogy writer, and ghostwriter.

Anna has been working on her Project Fallen Angel series for years and is looking forward to finally publishing them!

When she's not writing, Anna can be found watching Star Wars, cheering on the Baltimore Orioles and Ravens, cooking, and hanging out with her two cats and boyfriend.

Her website: https://www.goodreads.com/author/show/29903584.Anna_Noel

Connect with Anna to stay up to date.

ALSO BY ANNA NOEL

Reprisal (Project Fallen Angel Book One)

Read for free on KU

Enemies to lovers, forced-proximity, action romance novel

Penance (Project Fallen Angel Book Three)

Pre-order now. Out February 2024

Second chance western romance novel, lovers to enemies to lovers, forced-proximity, DARK action romance

Love on the Waiver Wire (A Baltimore Cobras Novel)

Pre-order now. Out December 2023

Fantasy football themed sports romance romcom. Brother's best friend, secret lovers

Milton Keynes UK
Ingram Content Group UK Ltd.
UKHW010624291123
433416UK00005B/383

"THIS WORLD IS YOURS. ALL I WANT TO DO IS KNEEL BEFORE YOU AND WATCH YOU BURN IT TO THE GROUND."

SYDNEY

WHEN I HEARD MY PARENTS HAD DIED IN A TRAGIC ACCIDENT, ALL I COULD FEE
WAS RELIEF. I WAS FINALLY FREE. FINALLY ABLE TO GO ABOUT MY LIFE WITHOU
THE WEIGHT OF ALL THE LIVES THEY'VE TAKEN ON MY SHOULDERS.
THAT IS UNTIL I MET RONAN MILLER.
TRICKED INTO A FALSE SENSE OF SAFETY, RONAN USES MY TRUST TO DELIVE
ME TO THE LAST PERSON I EVER EXPECTED. MY TWIN SISTER I NEVER KNEW
EXISTED.
AS FAMILY SECRETS UNRAVEL BEFORE ME, I LEARN ONE THING: I'M THE
HARBINGER OF RUINATION.

RONAN

I'VE DEDICATED MY LIFE TO HELPING JERRY LEAD THE DC FALLEN ANGELS.
WORKING AS AN AGENT OF INFLUENCE IN POLITICS, MY LIFE IS CONSTANTLY
TEETERING ON THE BRINK OF COLLAPSE, AND I LIKE IT THAT WAY.
BUT THEN MY MISSION CHANGED.
FIRST, IT WAS BRINGING SYDNEY, THE KEY TO BRINGING DOWN ONE OF THE
WORLD'S LARGEST CRIME SYNDICATES, TO THE FALLEN ANGELS. THEN, IT'S TO
MARRY HER.
A FORCED MARRIAGE THAT BENEFITS US BOTH, WE MUST WORK TOGETHER
DESPITE OUR DISDAIN FOR EACH OTHER.
SHE'S THE KEY TO BRINGING THE ENTIRE OPERATION DOWN, IF ONLY WE DON'
KILL EACH OTHER ON THE WAY.

"YOU'RE THE KEY TO THIS WHOLE OPERATION.
YOU WALK INTO THAT ROOM, AND THEY'LL BE ON THEIR KNEES
SHAKING, KNOWING THEIR END IS NEAR."

ISBN 979-8-8689-2072-1

WWW.ANNANOELBOOKS.COM

9 798868 920721